MW01026476

INSPE
DEATH ON THE

Freeman Wills Crofts (1879–1957), the son of an army doctor who died before he was born, was raised in Northern Ireland and became a civil engineer on the railways. His first book, *The Cask*, written in 1919 during a long illness, was published in the summer of 1920, immediately establishing him as a new master of detective fiction. Regularly outselling Agatha Christie, it was with his fifth book that Crofts introduced his iconic Scotland Yard detective, Inspector Joseph French, who would feature in no less than thirty books over the next three decades. He was a founder member of the Detection Club and was elected a Fellow of the Royal Society of Arts in 1939. Continually praised for his ingenious plotting and meticulous attention to detail—including the intricacies of railway timetables—Crofts was once dubbed 'The King of Detective Story Writers' and described by Raymond Chandler as 'the soundest builder of them all'.

Also in this series

Inspector French's Greatest Case
Inspector French and the Cheyne Mystery
Inspector French and the Starvel Hollow Tragedy
Inspector French and the Sea Mystery
Inspector French and the Box Office Murders
Inspector French and Sir John Magill's Last Journey
Inspector French: Sudden Death
Inspector French: Death on the Way
Inspector French and the Mystery on Southampton Water
Inspector French and the Crime at Guildford
Inspector French and the Loss of the 'Jane Vosper'
Inspector French: Man Overboard!

By the same author

The Cask
The Ponson Case
The Pit-Prop Syndicate
The Groote Park Murder
*Six Against the Yard**
*The Anatomy of Murder**

*with other Detection Club authors

FREEMAN WILLS CROFTS

Inspector French: Death on the Way

COLLINS
CRIME
CLUB

COLLINS CRIME CLUB
An imprint of HarperCollins*Publishers*
1 London Bridge Street
London SE1 9GF
www.harpercollins.co.uk

This paperback edition 2020

First published in Great Britain for the Crime Club
by Wm Collins Sons & Co. Ltd 1932

Copyright © Estate of Freeman Wills Crofts 1932

Freeman Wills Crofts asserts the moral right
to be identified as the author of this work

This novel is entirely a work of fiction. It is presented in
its original form and may depict ethnic, racial and sexual prejudices
that were commonplace at the time it was written.

A catalogue record for this book is
available from the British Library

ISBN 978-0-00-839318-2

Set in Sabon Lt Std by Palimpsest Book Production Ltd, Falkirk, Stirlingshire

Printed and bound in Great Britain
by CPI Group (UK) Ltd, Croydon CR0 4YY

All rights reserved. No part of this publication may be reproduced,
stored in a retrieval system, or transmitted, in any form or by any means,
electronic, mechanical, photocopying, recording or otherwise, without
the prior written permission of the publishers.

FSC www.fsc.org
MIX
Paper from
responsible sources
FSC C007454

This book is produced from independently certified FSC™ paper
to ensure responsible forest management.

Find out more about HarperCollins and the environment at
www.harpercollins.co.uk/green

Contents

1

Prelude to Tragedy

Clifford Parry sat in the corner of a first-class compartment of the 8.20 a.m. train from Lydmouth to Whitness and beyond, gazing gloomily out on the series of views which passed successively before his eyes. A more depressing series it would not have been easy to find. It was late October, a dull and sombre morning. The railway ran along by the sea and the receding tide had laid bare a vast area of mud flats, broken here and there by slimy stones, patches of dank seaweed and the twisting beds of tiny streams. A chill drifting rain fell hopelessly, adding a colder gray to the drab colours of the shore. In the distance, half blotted out by the mist, was a sea of the colour of tarnished lead.

Parry, though travelling thus luxuriously, was a son of toil on his way to his daily round. He was junior assistant engineer in the divisional engineer's office of the Southern Railway at Lydmouth, in Dorset, and he was going down to Whitness to calculate earthwork quantities on the new Redchurch-Whitness Widening, or doubling of a single line, which the Railway Company was carrying out between those places. An uninteresting job, calculating earthwork, some might have said. Not so Parry. Before it had come his way he had passed through several extremely unhappy years. Since his release from the army after the War he had until now been able to obtain only precarious employment, and indeed had had spells of total idleness which left him face to face with actual want. Work, to him, was an inestimable boon. Dull, wearing, monotonous work would have been an inestimable boon, and his present job certainly could not be so described. As work, he enjoyed almost all of it.

Presently the train began to slacken speed, for Redchurch. At Redchurch he would be joined by his colleague, Ackerley. Ackerley was superior in rank to Parry, being the resident engineer in charge of the Widening. Ackerley was a general favourite, a hard worker, and very keen on his job.

As the train drew up at the platform Parry looked out. Yes, there was Ronnie Ackerley, a tall, well-built young fellow made up in mackintosh and huge boots and with a knapsack over his arm. He approached Parry's compartment.

'Hullo, Ack!' Parry greeted him. 'Beastly morning.'

'Rotten,' Ackerley agreed concisely, and the weather had been duly weighed in the balances, found wanting, and dismissed.

'Where's Bragg?' Ackerley went on presently.

'Coming down later. He had to meet some of those Westinghouse people about the Lydmouth signalling.'

Bragg was the third in command in the technical staff of the office. He was responsible for such design as was carried out in the divisional office and was Ackerley's senior in charge of the widening operations.

Ackerley nodded. 'Wonderful how quickly you get out of things,' he remarked. 'I was quite keen on that signalling job when we were getting out the plans, and now since I've come down here I've lost all interest in it.'

'You can't do everything,' Parry pointed out.

Ackerley grunted. 'I say, that darned pump gave up again last night,' he went on.

'Is the water rising?'

'No, Lowell got the pulsometer working. But it meant keeping the boiler going all night.'

'They've never got those Pier IV foundations dry?'

'No, nor never will. Not with those pumps at all events.'

Though no longer young enough to enjoy the continuous talking of shop merely for its own sake, Parry was naturally anxious to be as well up as he could in everything concerning the Widening. Now, however, he did not reply to Ackerley's last observation, but sat gazing moodily out of the window. They were once again running along the shore, but here the mud flats had given place to deep water. The railway embankment, in fact, formed the actual battery. The wind was sou'-west and the sea choppy. The water looked cold and gray and uninviting.

Ackerley glanced curiously at his companion. 'What's up?' he demanded.

Parry roused himself. 'Nothing. Only a bad tooth. Are you expecting many people tonight, Ack?'

That evening the Ackerleys were giving a dance at their house in Redchurch and Parry had been invited. Ronnie Ackerley, indeed, had asked him home to change and dine. Parry had accepted, and his suitcase containing his evening things was on the rack above his head. Ronnie had felt a certain amusement when giving the invitation. It was popularly believed that Parry had become deeply enamoured of Pearl, Ronnie's sister, and that anyone should fall in love with Pearl struck Ronnie as a good joke.

Presently they plunged into a tunnel which pierced a bluff chalk headland, the White Ness, from which the adjoining little town got its name, then emerging on to a viaduct crossing a deep chine, they ran half a mile or more along level ground through the outskirts of a watering place and finally drew up in Whitness station.

'I'm going out on the ballast train to Cannan's Cutting,' said Ackerley as they got out. 'I'll be back in the afternoon, if not for lunch. You're dining with us?'

Parry pointed to the suitcase he was carrying. 'Thanks awfully. I've got my things here.'

Parry crossed the platform and left the suitcase in the stationmaster's office, wishing that official an absent-minded good-morning. Then he set off to walk back along the line over which they had just passed. His objective was the contractors' headquarters. On level ground near the edge of Whit Chine Messrs John Spence & Co. had rented a field beside the line, which they were using as a 'yard'. Into it they had run a siding and had located their offices, stores, carpenters' and smiths' shops and general plant. In a corner the Railway Company had erected a two-roomed hut for their own engineers. Here Parry was to calculate his earthwork quantities.

He reached the barbed-wire enclosure and passed in through the railway gate. Near the carpenters' shop a number of men were loading timber framing on to a wagon. Talking to their foreman was a big-built, heavy-visaged young man in oilskins and a sou'-wester. He turned, and seeing Parry, walked across.

'Hullo, Parry! Seen Ackerley?'

This was Lowell, Messrs Spence's second-in-command, Ackerley's opposite number on the contractors' side.

'He's gone out on the ballast train to Cannan's Cutting. He said he'd be in this afternoon.'

'That's that slip at Peg 124, I expect. He's fairly got the wind up about it.'

'This rain won't do it much good.'

'It's not heavy enough to do it any harm,' Lowell declared with the wisdom of five-and-twenty. 'I wanted to see Ackerley,' and he descended into technicalities.

Parry replied in kind, then letting himself into the railway hut, absently took off his coat and hat, stoked up the fires in the two stoves and began to get out his papers. For a moment he stood looking vacantly out of the window, then with a sigh he sat down at his desk and began to work.

Clifford Parry had just reached his thirty-second birthday. He had been educated at Lydmouth, where his people lived and where there was an excellent school. Instead of going on to college, as his parents had intended, he joined up in 1916. He served till within a month of the end of the War, being then invalided out, shell-shocked and quite broken in health. During his period of service his father had died, and he found his mother in poor health and circumstances. With a struggle they managed to exist; Parry, as he grew stronger, continuing the engineering course he had begun. He would, however, have had to give this up and get a job, had it not been that a relative died and left Mrs Parry some £500. After long discussion it was decided that the money should be spent in letting Parry continue his studies. At length he qualified by passing the examination for Associate Membership of the Institution of Civil Engineers.

But before the news came that he had got through, his mother contracted a chill and died.

Left alone and practically penniless, for his mother's pittance had died with her, Parry turned to look for a job. Then the real bitterness of life entered into his soul. First there were debts, which he himself had contracted before he realised how limited were their resources. Next, no one wanted an ex-service man of poor health and with just his qualifications. Absolute want began to stare him in the face. He took a job as a junior clerk; and was glad to get it. That kept him from starvation. He lost that job owing to a reduction of hands, then got another of the same kind. In one way or another he had worked along, till one day, finding himself back in Lydmouth, he had taken his courage in both hands and gone once again to see Mr Marlowe, the divisional engineer of the railway. Marlowe had known his father and on that account saw him at once. Luckily for Parry, work on the Widening was just about to begin, and Marlowe, with some misgivings, offered him a job as junior assistant engineer. It was made clear to him that though he was four years older than Ackerley, he was to be his junior in rank. Parry took the job with thankfulness, and though he was embittered from his experiences, he loyally accepted the conditions and did his very best to make good. The debts, however, still hung over him, and for a time after starting on the railway he remained badly crippled. Then once again he had come into some money. That money had just made the difference. It had enabled him to pay off what he owed. That and the outdoor life, which suited his health, was bringing him back competence and vigour. Two qualities also stood him in good stead. One was an extraordinary gift of inventive ingenuity. If confronted with a puzzling situation he could always cover want of knowledge by devising some original means of meeting the difficulty. The other was a great natural charm of manner which tended to smooth his relations with his fellows.

Ronald Ackerley's history was very dissimilar. He had obtained his degree in engineering in the University of London and had started work in the Southern Railway's head office. Then a vacancy had occurred at Lydmouth, and as his people lived at Redchurch, he had applied for and obtained it. This had enabled him to live at home, and each day he had travelled the fifteen miles in and out of Lydmouth. When work on the Widening had started and he had been appointed junior resident engineer, he had continued to live at home. He was at this time twenty-eight years of age and a thoroughly good man at his job. His manner occasionally left a little to be desired, but he was liked and respected by everyone.

For a couple of hours Parry worked steadily. His aim was that important figure, the amount of earthwork completed during the previous four-weekly period. It was a figure which had been widely discussed, guessed, and betted on by all concerned. It was a figure which showed the progress of the job, as a patient's temperature shows his health. It was, moreover, an important item in the make up of the 'certificate', the four-weekly statement of the total work done on the job, upon which the contractors were paid.

Suddenly the door opened and a tall burly man of about five-and-forty entered. He had a dark skin and almost black hair and eyes, as if southern blood coursed in his veins. His air was leisurely but competent.

'Hullo, young Parry,' he drawled as he took off his wet coat. 'Got those quantities out?'

'Hullo, Bragg. I'm well on with them. The figures look big this time.'

'Yes, those slackers have got going at last. Seen Carey today?'

Carey was the contractors' chief resident engineer, Lowell's superior.

'No. Lowell was in the yard when I came in, but Carey didn't show up.'

Bragg went to the telephone and pressed the buzzer. 'Hullo, that you, Lowell? Is Carey about?'

The receiver barked so that Parry could almost hear the words.

'Oh, gone to Redchurch, is he? When will he be back? . . . Right, I'll go over after lunch.'

Bragg had appropriated for himself the smaller of the two rooms into which the hut was divided. He now pushed open the door and disappeared within. But he left it open and they talked spasmodically through it.

About one o'clock he emerged. 'What about a spot of lunch?' he suggested. 'Is Ackerley coming in for it?'

'He didn't know.'

'We'll not wait for him.'

The two men searched in coat pockets and knapsacks and produced sandwiches and sundry other foods. Then making themselves comfortable before the stove, they began their meal. Scarcely had they done so when the door opened and Ackerley appeared.

'At it again,' he greeted them. 'I've rarely seen you two when you weren't eating. Don't you ever do any work, Bragg?'

Bragg ignored this. 'What have you been up to all morning, young Ackerley?' he asked.

Ackerley hung up his dripping mackintosh and began washing at a small sink in the corner.

'That slip at Cannan's Cutting is moving.'

'Much?'

'It's come down about a foot at the top, and the bottom is bulging.'

Bragg nodded. 'We'll fix up something about it later.'

The three men chatted as they ate: a little shop, a little mild ragging, and a good deal of critical discussion on centreboard sailing, at which Bragg and Ackerley were adepts and Parry a keen learner. Then when a pipe and two cigarettes were going, Bragg turned back to business.

'I say, Ackerley, those figures for the pitching at Peg 110 don't seem to be right. They don't agree with the contractors' at all events. Ours show over 3500 yards pitched in the last four-weekly period. From a casual inspection there didn't seem to me to be anything like that done.'

'Three thousand five hundred yards,' Ackerley repeated slowly. 'You're right, Bragg, it's too large. Who measured it?'

'I measured that with Pole,' Parry put in, 'and I'm pretty sure what we did was right. Let's see the figures, Bragg.'

Pole was the contractors' junior engineer and ranked with Parry.

'They're on my desk. I didn't say you were wrong, young Parry. As you know, I get my figures by subtracting the total done at the end of the previous period from what you return as being done now. Conceivably there was an error in last month's return.'

'That wouldn't help Pole and me,' Parry pointed out, 'for we measured up last month's too. And what's more, I bet it was right also.'

'Well,' said Bragg, 'it's pleasant to deal with infallible people who never make mistakes. All the same, young Parry, you'll have to check it again. And I'll want it done this afternoon, because it must go into the certificate. Let's see, Ackerley; didn't you say you were going to walk through to Redchurch later on?'

'Yes, I've to see Potts about his right of way. Parry saw Potts and fixed it up.'

'I'd forgotten it was today. Better have a look at the slip again when you're passing.'

'Right, I'll do so.'

'What time shall you be starting, Ackerley?' Parry interposed.

'About half-past four, I think. I want to see a couple of things at the viaduct as I pass.'

Parry considered. 'That would just suit me. I'll walk out with you. I ought to get these quantities done by four-thirty.'

'"Ought to get" won't be enough, Parry,' Bragg declared. 'I must have them for the certificate if we stay here all night.'

Parry suddenly registered dismay. 'Oh, I say, Bragg,' he protested, 'I hope you won't want me to stay late. I have a "do" on, a very special affair, really.'

'So have I,' Bragg rejoined dryly, 'the certificate. What time do you want to get away?'

'I want to be in Redchurch by six-thirty. That would do, wouldn't it, Ack?'

Ackerley agreed.

'Well, look sharp and get your stunts done,' Bragg returned. 'We'll see how you get on. Is it still raining, Ackerley?'

'Yes, worse luck. But the wind's gone down.'

Ackerley, having resumed his mackintosh, which had left quite a respectable pool on the floor, went out, and Bragg and Parry settled down once again to their work. But they had not more than got under way when another visitor made his appearance. This time it was a tall stoutly-built man of middle age with a small dark moustache and wearing the inevitable dripping waterproof.

'Is the great man within?' he demanded in a rather high-pitched voice and with a mellow Irish intonation.

Parry leaned back consequentially in his chair.

'Yes, I'm here, Carey,' he replied condescendingly. 'What can I do for you?'

Carey advanced into the room.

'Sure what would I be doing talking to the likes of you?' he inquired. 'It's his lordship here I want to see.' With a jerk of his thumb he indicated Bragg, who had appeared at his door. 'You're after ringing me up, Bragg?'

Bragg agreed, and the two men disappeared into the inner office. As Parry worked he could hear scraps of conversation through the open door: 'held by the fox wedges,' 'three-eights inch camber,' 'meet the lateral thrust;' and then Bragg in a louder voice: 'When are you going to get a pump that'll clear out that blessed hole at Pier IV?' and Carey's protesting reply: 'Me dear man, the pump's one of the best. Sure didn't that idiot Hudson go and get it filled up with gravel and cut the valves out of it.' Another murmur and then Carey again: 'I declare to goodness that man'll have me demented, the way he's going on.'

The saga of the pump was still under discussion when there came a sound of movement, and the two men emerged into the outer office.

'Right,' Bragg was saying. 'That should get the water down.'

The door closed behind Carey, and silence fell in the hut as Bragg and Parry settled down to work. Both had a good deal to get through and neither wanted to be kept late. Then Ackerley turned up again, and going into Bragg's room, began to check with him certain figures for the certificate. For some time their voices came to Parry in low, indistinguishable murmurs. Then came Bragg's voice: 'I say, Parry!'

Parry got up and went to the door of the inner room.

'How long will it take you to finish?' Bragg asked. 'Bring in what you're at, will you?'

Parry collected his foolscap sheets.

'I'm pretty well on,' he explained as he laid them before Bragg, 'but I'm afraid it will take a bit of time still.'

'How long?'

'Most of an hour, I should think.'

'Well, Ackerley's ready to go now and you can't wait much longer or it will be dark. You'll be able to finish these when you get back.'

Parry's face fell, and Bragg, noticing it, went on impatiently: 'Oh, very well, very well. I forgot your blessed "do". See. We'll not get our train tonight, but we'll go by the ballast engine. Get me the comptometer and I'll finish the darned thing myself.'

'Oh, thanks awfully, Bragg. Very decent of you.'

With a gesture Bragg brushed his acknowledgments aside. 'Then you'll come back here as sharp as you can, Parry, with the check of that pitching, and you, Ackerley, will wait and see us at Redchurch. I'd like to hear about that slip, especially as I'll not be down tomorrow.'

It was close on half-past four when Parry and Ackerley left the hut and began walking down towards the railway.

'By the way,' said Parry, 'there's the ballast engine shunting that stuff for Lowell. I'll slip across and tell Blake we're going tonight. Ten to one Bragg'll forget.'

He crossed the sidings towards the engine. The driver stopped when he raised his hand.

'I say, Blake,' he called up, 'we're going to Redchurch with you, Mr Bragg and myself. Will you stop for us opposite the office?'

'Right, Mr Parry.'

'And I say, Blake,' Parry went on, 'are you going up to the station before you start?'

'Yes, we've to lift these wagons out of here and throw them into the goods yard for the early goods.'

'Then I wish you'd collect a bag of mine from the stationmaster's office—a yellow suitcase. I've not got time to go up for it.'

'Certainly, Mr Parry. I'll bring it along.'

Parry thanked him, and passing out of the gate, followed Ackerley along the line towards the viaduct. The weather was still unpleasant. Though the rain had ceased, it remained raw and cold. The sea, of a dirty lead colour, was white-flecked, and a dull roar came up from the beach and the base of the cliffs. Far out a small steamer, heading for Lydmouth, was making heavy weather of it, white water flying from her bows as she dipped into the swells.

The two young men, reaching the edge of the Whit Chine, descended to where the massive foundations of the new viaduct were going in beside the spindle-shanked piers of the old. Ackerley had a quick look at the work and a word with the various foremen, and then they climbed up the other side of the chine to where, a hundred yards ahead, loomed the black forbidding mouth of the tunnel.

'We'll not go into the tunnel,' Ackerley decided. 'I was through it yesterday and everything's going on all right. Besides, we've scarcely time.'

Dusk indeed was falling as Ackerley led the way off the railway to the sea side. A narrow path ran round the outside of the ness, joining the railway again at the far end of the tunnel.

'Are you coming down to the hockey on Saturday?' Ackerley asked as they stepped on the path.

Parry was pursuing thoughts of his own and did not want to talk about hockey. Vaguely he was aware of the white rocks on the right, sloping up out of sight above him, and on the left dropping quickly down to the foaming surf far below; of the race of white horses out on the heaving waters; of the wheeling sea birds with their melancholy cries. Vaguely he heard that the Redchurch goalkeeper was about as much use as a performing poodle; that Brenda played a better game than Mollie; and that Whitness would have to wake up and get busy if they were going to retain the cup. He wasn't interested, but he managed to reply with reasonable intelligence, and Ackerley speedily reverted to his customary shop.

They regained the railway at the Redchurch end of the tunnel, where for some hundreds of yards the line ran along a narrow shelf cut in the sheer cliff. Another half-mile brought them to Cannan's Cutting. A glance at the slip showed that no further movement had taken place and the men walked on to the end of the cutting where began a wide bay, Browne's Bay. At this point the work of the Widening was well under way. The base of the clay slope had been pushed out into the sea, and the new work was in process of being protected by stone pitching. Here it was that doubt had arisen as to the area completed.

'That's what you've got to measure.' Ackerley indicated the half-completed work immediately above the line of breaking waves. 'You'll get a bath if you're not careful. Start at this mile-post and work towards Whitness. You needn't be too accurate: pacing'll be near enough. Cheerio, then. See you at Redchurch.'

As in the days afterwards Parry thought over that parting, two things came back vividly to him, little things both of them, but significant. The first was the glimpse that he had had of Ackerley's ring. When Ackerley had said, 'That's what you've got to measure,' he had pointed with his left hand, and even in the dusk the glint of the stone in the ring had caught Parry's eye. Ackerley wore it on his little finger and Parry had seen it hundreds of times. It was a plain gold band bearing one small ruby, set in the simplest way without any chasing or ornamentation. Parry had often wondered why his companion wore it, but he had never asked, and Ackerley had seemed unconscious of its presence.

The second thing which Parry noticed was Ackerley's extraordinary fitness and good spirits. As he moved off he stepped out briskly with all the energy and vigour of a healthy young animal. He was whistling, too, something light and popular that went with a swing.

Bidding goodnight to the ganger of the length, who passed at that moment, Parry turned towards the pitching.

2

Tragedy

The Redchurch-Whitness Widening was a moderately big job, involving some heavy works. The main line of this particular area of the Southern Railway ran eastwards from Lydmouth, one of the most important watering-places on the south coast, till it joined the Exeter-Waterloo line about half-way between Templecombe and Salisbury. For the first fifteen miles, from Lydmouth to Redchurch, it ran along the shore, but at Redchurch it turned inland. Redchurch was a smaller but more fashionable resort, beloved of the Thank-goodness-it-hasn't-yet-been-spoiled-by-trippers type.

At Redchurch a line diverged from the direct London line, continuing eastwards along the coast through Whitness, and eventually reaching Bournemouth and Southampton. This line was double all the way except for one section, the three and a half miles stretch between Redchurch and Whitness. Here the cost of doubling had up till now been considered prohibitive. Very heavy earthworks and sea defences had to be dealt with, as well as widening nearly a quarter of a mile of tunnel and building a new viaduct. It was estimated that the cost would be upwards of a quarter of a million sterling.

These three miles of single line, however, had grown increasingly inconvenient. The stretch acted as a bottle neck which slowed up the traffic, causing endless delays and vexation. Though the times were so unsuitable for borrowing new capital, 'bus competition had forced the directors' hands and a contract for £320,000 had been let. Work had now been in progress for nearly a year.

When Parry arrived back at the engineers' hut he was more than a trifle breathless. He had underestimated the time it would take him to carry out what he had to do, and had had to hurry back as fast as he could. He did not wish to miss the ballast engine, and there was not much time to give Bragg his information and get the certificate completed before the engine was due. Parry was glad when he came in view of the lighted windows of the hut, shining like harbour beacons in the night.

He hurried to the door. Bragg was still bending over the certificate.

'Well?' Bragg grunted without looking up. 'What about that pitching?'

Parry threw his notebook down on the desk. 'I'm frightfully sorry, Bragg, the mistake was mine after all. I paced the thing over and every figure seemed to check out, then at last I found it. Pole and I measured it correctly, but I misread a figure in my book. The correct figure was 327 and I read it 827.'

'Then Pole's total is correct?'

'Yes. I'm not trying to make excuses, but what really

happened was that my book got wet and the figures weren't easy to read.'

'That's all right. Read me out the total. I've finished your earthwork.'

'Oh, good man, Bragg. Very decent of you.'

The entry of the pitching item completed the certificate. Bragg quickly monied it out, then added the total to that he had already obtained and signed the document.

'Get a sheet of brown paper, will you?' he said as he rolled up the papers and slipped a rubber band round them.

Parry produced paper and string, and the certificate and its attendant papers were parcelled up and labelled.

'You're going somewhere with Ackerley?' Bragg went on.

'Yes, to a dance.'

'Well, you'll have time to hand this over to the parcels people in Redchurch to send to the office. I don't want to bother taking it round. Come on, Parry. We'd better look sharp or we'll miss that blessed engine.'

Parry nodded. A moment later the two men were walking towards the wicket gate in the contractors' fence, put in close to the railway hut for their special convenience. This led out on to a branch road which passed through a little spinney behind the yard.

'For once I remembered my torch,' Bragg went on as a little circle of light began to play over the ground in front of them.

'It's not dark,' Parry declared. 'It's only coming out of the light makes it seem so.'

'The torch is a help when you're looking for a keyhole, young Parry.'

They passed through the gate and reached the line. As

Parry had said, it was not dark. The sky was heavily overcast, but behind the clouds there was a moon, and objects remained dimly visible. Though it was some time since the rain had stopped, the grass was still dripping and there were pools everywhere. A dull muffled roar came up from the sea, where the waves were dragging the shingle up and down the beach and breaking heavily against the base of the ness.

'Here she is,' said Parry.

From the direction of the station appeared lights, slowly diverging and growing brighter. Presently there showed behind them a dark mass, which resolved itself into the smoke-box of an approaching engine. Bragg showed his torch and with a clap the brakes went on, eased off and clapped on again. The boiler slid slowly past and the machine came to rest with the dimly lighted cab just above them. The fireman, a gauge lamp in his hand, stooped down and with a spongecloth gave a perfunctory rub to the steel handles above the steps. Then, stepping back, he made room for Bragg and Parry to climb up.

The driver was standing with his hand grasping the regulator. When his passengers were aboard he gently opened it, then reaching up to another handle, he gave a tiny whistle. With a faint quiver the engine began to move. A chink of the firebox door was open, and each beat drew the glowing coal up to a white heat which lit cab and crew.

The cab was roomy, as cabs go. Bragg, the most honoured traveller, had moved to the right-hand corner and sat down on the fireman's seat. Parry stood on the left side behind the driver, looking over his shoulder into the gloom ahead. They were now on the viaduct, and to Parry it seemed that they were hanging in space. To his left was a great gulf, for he was too high over the viaduct parapet to see it, and the nearest object was the shore and the beating waves some seventy feet below him. He grasped the upright rod which supported the roof, lest a jolt of the engine should tip him out, while to leave his hands free he dropped the parcelled certificate into the driver's box. Then the driver whistled again and with a waft of air which Parry felt at his eardrums, the roof of the tunnel slid back over their heads and the noise increased tenfold.

The experience of passing through the tunnel was impressive. The beam of light from the partly opened firebox door, now continuously white from the rapid beat, shone out on the front of the tender and up above it on to the roof of the cab. From these it was reflected back over the faceplate, or end of the boiler, showing up the maze of pipes and handles, gauges and dials, and bringing out unexpected high lights from polished brass-work. Bragg's figure, seated in the corner, showed dimly, with the fireman standing shadowy behind him, as Parry himself stood behind the driver. On each side between the tender and the cab the black walls of the tunnel quivered as they hastened by, while above the steam formed into a wide rolling coil, also hurrying backwards like an inverted wake.

Presently Parry turned and once again looked out ahead through the cab window, on which a great drop of water from the roof had just flattened itself. Faintly something curved began to show up. It was the 'high leg' or outside rail upon which they were travelling, reflecting dimly from its polished inside edge the light striking in through the approaching mouth of the tunnel. Then, as Driver Blake again whistled, the walls and roof slid back and they were out in the open.

For a few hundred yards they ran along the shelf cut in the cliff, with far below them the white horses showing up in ghostly smears. Then the cliff fell back. Another few hundred yards and they were traversing Cannan's Cutting, past the slip which had so much upset Ackerley. Then once again along the sea round the big inlet, Browne's Bay, and so to the next headland.

This next headland, Downey's Point, was blunt in plan, and the railway, instead of tunnelling or cutting through it, ran round it along by the sea. As they approached it, the line ahead, curving sharply to the right, slid behind the boiler out of sight of Parry and Driver Blake. From the right side of the cab no one happened at the moment to be looking out. The fireman had introduced the picker, or huge hooked poker, into the firebox, and was vigorously raking the fire forward up the sloping firebars. It had been let down very low, in fact to a mere layer of incandescent cinders thinly covering the bars, as the engine had really done work for the day, and after the fire had been cleaned of clinker, would lie banked until the next morning. Bragg, having lit his pipe, was absently watching the operation.

The furnace having been adjusted to the fireman's satisfaction, he withdrew the picker, its hook now white-hot, and laid it on the tender. A little spurt of flame and smoke sprang up where the glowing point came in contact with the coal, dying away as the iron cooled. Setting the firebox door to stand about an inch open, the fireman withdrew to the side of the cab, put his head out, and gave a perfunctory look ahead.

Parry, who happened to be watching him, saw him suddenly stiffen, for a fraction of a second peer earnestly ahead, and then swing round to the driver with a warning shout: ''Old! 'Old! There's something on the road!'

Parry's heart leaped as he watched the men's frantic movements. With one hand Blake threw over the regulator, shutting off steam, while with the other he dashed the vacuum brake handle down to the full on position. Then he whistled, several short sharp blasts. Simultaneously the fireman turned on the steam sanding and closed the firebox door, from which a burst of flames had come, due to the sudden cutting off of the suction from the blast. The engine gave a little shudder and the speed declined so rapidly that Parry had to cling on to the cab pillar to prevent himself from falling forward against Blake. Both Bragg and the fireman were now hanging out of their side of the cab, looking back.

The fireman swung in.

'We're over it!' he cried to Blake, as with a harsh grinding of the brakes and a sudden jerk the engine stopped.

The fireman had unhooked a gauge lamp and was already on the ground. Bragg and Parry followed as quickly as they could, each from his own side.

When Parry reached the ballast he stumbled backward past the tender, slipping about on the rough stones. The fireman was already some thirty yards away along the line, and was standing between the rails, bending over something dark. Instinctively Parry held his breath as he raced to the fireman's side. When he saw what was there his heart was pounding so that he could scarcely breathe.

The dark mass was a man, or what was left of a man. The engine had passed over him and the resulting injuries were terrible. That he was dead there could be no doubt whatever. Parry felt suddenly sick as he stared speechless.

Then he gave a hoarse cry. This man had been clothed in a waterproof and heavy boots. His left hand was stretched out and on its little finger was a ring, a plain gold band bearing a single ruby . . .

With a single blistering expletive Parry snatched the torch from Bragg, who had by this time come up, and held it close to the face. The features were only slightly disfigured and were plainly recognisable. This dead body, this awful wreck of what had been a man, this was all that remained of his colleague, Ronald Ackerley.

3

Inquest

Trembling as if from ague, Parry heard faintly the fireman's awestruck cry, 'My God, it's Mr Ackerley!' and Bragg's sharp horrified oath. All three, indeed, were overpowered by the ghastliness of the tragedy. And the fact that nothing could be done for the unhappy young man took away the stimulus of the need for instant action.

Presently Bragg swore again and with an obvious effort pulled himself together. 'He's gone, poor chap,' he muttered. 'We can't do anything. Here, Atkins,' he turned to the fireman, 'help me to lift him clear of the road. You, Parry, cut along and tell Blake what has happened.'

In a dream Parry stumbled back to the engine, realising in a numbed kind of way that Bragg had sent him on this message to save him from seeing more clearly the dreadful details of the tragedy. In a dream he climbed up on to the footplate and began telling the news to Blake. But he scarcely knew what he was saying, and when in the middle of his story Blake crossed the cab and answered someone on the ground, he felt no surprise. Presently he realised that Bragg and the fireman were there. Bragg was speaking from the step.

'Run in to Redchurch as quickly as you can, Blake,' he was saying. 'Tell the stationmaster to have an ambulance sent out. I'll wait here with the body.' Bragg paused and looked doubtfully at Parry. 'I say, Parry,' he went on hesitatingly, 'you know the Ackerleys, don't you? Think you can slip up and tell them? A rotten job, I know. If you don't feel like it, get Clay to 'phone. Go ahead now.' He stepped back on to the ballast and Blake once again gave his engine steam.

Parry had already been thinking of the Ackerleys. How could he force himself to take them this awful news? How could he go and see Pearl? She had always ragged Ronnie unmercifully, but Parry knew she idolised him. It would be a knock-out blow for Pearl. And for all of them. Indeed, Parry thought it would be even worse for the old people; Mrs Ackerley so fond of her son, Mr Ackerley so proud of him. How would it be possible to tell them? . . .

While these thoughts passed through his mind, Parry remained dimly conscious of his surroundings. The engine was now running at a high speed and already Blake had shut off steam for Redchurch and was sounding his whistle to announce his approach to the signalman. The yellow eye of the distant signal came up rapidly and slipped behind, and Blake began to apply the brake. That red light ahead was the outer home and at that, if it did not go off, they must stop. Though he could scarcely face what lay in front of him, Parry was now seized with impatience and felt that any delay would be unbearable. However, when they were still some hundred yards from the signal it changed to green, and Blake, releasing the brake, allowed his engine to coast forward. A further bunch of red lights approached, with a single green one at the extreme left. These drew near, passed slowly behind, and the engine turned gently to the left off the main line, and entering the locomotive yard, came to rest among some dozen of its fellows.

Blake wound his reversing wheel into middle gear. 'Come on, Mr Parry,' he said. 'We'll go and tell Mr Clay.'

Still in a dream, Parry followed the driver across the locomotive sidings and up the ramp of No. 1 Platform to the stationmaster's office. Clay was a small man with an alert manner. He heard the story, rapidly expressed a conventional horror, and took hold of the situation.

'If the poor fellow's dead there's not such a hurry,' he said. 'We'll let the 6.10 through and go out between her and the 6.25 goods. You, Blake, will work out the van.' He sat down at his desk and picked up one of its two telephones. 'Redchurch, one double-six,' he called, then, 'It that the police station? Clay speaking, Southern Railway agent. Is the superintendent there? . . . Good evening, superintendent. Yes, Clay speaking. It's just been reported to me that Mr Ronald Ackerley, one of the Company's engineers, has been run over and killed at Downey's Point, halfway between this and Whitness. What? Yes, the solicitor's son . . . What? I didn't catch? . . . Oh, yes, very sad. Well, superintendent, I propose sending out a special to bring in the body. It'll leave here on the arrival of the 6.10 from Whitness, say about 6.15. I'll be glad to know if this is in order from your point of view and if you'd like to be represented . . . Very good, if he comes down to my office I'll see that someone meets him.'

Mr Clay replaced the receiver and picked up that of the other instrument, pressing a buzzer in code. 'Who's that?

Yes, Clay speaking. Find Sparkes, will you, and tell him that a man has been run over between this and Whitness and that I want him to take a van out with the ambulance stretcher on the arrival of the 6.10. Blake will work it with the ballast engine. Get a couple of men to give a hand. Start from No. 1 Carriage Siding and don't go without me. That clear?' He rang off and then made another call. 'That the junction box? Who is speaking? . . . Oh, Harris,' and he explained what was to be done.

While these arrangements were being made, Parry had taken a firm hold on himself. 'What about telling the Ackerleys, Mr Clay?' he said in a low voice as Blake disappeared.

'I was going to speak to you about that,' Clay returned. 'Will you do it or shall I?'

'You better prepare them, I think, and say I'm going up to see them. And we'd better send a message to Mr Marlowe.'

Marlowe was Parry's chief, the Lydmouth divisional engineer.

'I'm going to wire the manager and I'll duplicate it; Yourself to Marlowe.' As he spoke Clay looked keenly at the other. 'If you'll not consider it a liberty, Mr Parry, I'd recommend you to call in the refreshment room and get a small pick-me-up. You'll find it pretty trying talking to the Ackerleys.'

It was good advice and Parry took it. He felt badly shaken and his heart failed him as he thought of the coming interview. However, there was nothing to be gained by delay and when he took a taxi he told the man to drive quickly.

Parry had frequently read of a 'stricken' household, but

he had always considered the phrase a piece of fanciful journalese. Now he saw that the adjective was just. No word which he could have supplied could more aptly have described the Ackerleys'.

The maid who opened the door was pale and startled-looking. 'I see you know, Ethel,' Parry said. The girl nodded in silence and Parry passed on into the hall. Mr Ackerley was just turning away from the telephone, and when he saw him Parry involuntarily shuddered. Why, this was an old man, ten years older than when he had seen him last. His face was gray and had somehow fallen in, and there were unwonted lines round the mouth. He came slowly forward to Parry, walking heavily as if a physical weight bore on his shoulders.

'How did it happen?' he said in little more than a whisper.

Parry felt overwhelmed. 'We don't know, sir,' he answered, also in a low tone. 'All I can say is that it was instantaneous; there was no suffering. But we don't know how he came to be on the line. Unless he tripped and struck his head on the rail,' he added as an afterthought.

'They're bringing him in,' went on Mr Ackerley dully. 'I must go down.'

'I'll go with you, sir.' Parry hesitated. 'What about Mrs Ackerley and—and Pearl?'

'They know; I've told them.'

Still Parry hung back. 'I was wondering, sir, if I could do anything. Could I ring up your guests, for instance, and put them off?'

'Guests?' Mr Ackerley stared uncomprehendingly. 'Oh, yes, there was to be a dance.' He spoke as if in a dream. 'Thank you, Parry; it's good of you to think of it. Ethel will get you the list. Call Ethel. I must go.'

Fumblingly he began looking for his coat. Parry found it for him and was holding it when there came a diversion. A slight, pale-faced girl came running downstairs.

'No, Clifford,' she said. 'I heard what you were talking about. Don't mind about the people; we'll see to that. Go with him to the station.'

'I will, of course,' Parry returned. He would have gone on, but she raced upstairs as quickly as she had come down.

'A taxi,' Mr Ackerley directed. 'It would take too long to get the car.'

Parry had kept his, and a few minutes later they reached the station. Here they learned that the engine and van had gone out, but had not yet returned. On the way down, Parry had given the old man all the details he knew. Silence had then fallen between them. Once only Mr Ackerley's lips moved. 'Oh, Ronnie, Ronnie,' Parry heard him whisper. 'Oh, my son, my son.' Parry did not think he was conscious of his presence.

Presently lights appeared approaching the platform, and the engine and van came slowly in. News of the accident had spread and a little crowd of railway people had collected, though the public had been rigorously excluded from the platform. Bragg and Clay stepped from the van and under the latter's directions the side doors were opened and while caps were doffed two men slowly carried out a stretcher on which lay a figure covered with a white sheet. A space had been cleared in a store near Clay's office and there on a table the stretcher was laid. Mr Ackerley pushed forward, deferential way being made for him.

'Can't he be taken home, Mr Clay,' he asked.

Clay hesitated. 'I'm afraid, sir, there'll have to be an

inquest and we thought it might be more convenient to hold it here at the station. What do you say, sergeant?'

A sergeant of police had followed Clay from the van. He now saluted Mr Ackerley.

'It would be better, sir, for all concerned, if the remains were left here till after the inquest. You need not be afraid. Everything will be done with the greatest reverence.'

'The room will be locked, Mr Ackerley,' went on Clay. 'No one will be able to enter.'

'Very well,' Mr Ackerley returned slowly. 'I see it can't be helped. Thank all of you for what you have done.'

Clay began to murmur some words of sympathy, while the sergeant saluted again. Then Clay bent over to Parry.

'Take him home, Mr Parry. He's upset from the shock.'

But Mr Ackerley wanted all details, and Parry introduced Bragg and the fireman, though they could not add to what he had himself already stated. No one was able to say how the accident had happened, or how Ackerley came to be where he was found.

In the end Parry went back with the old gentleman. But he did not see Pearl. The ladies were upstairs and could not be disturbed. Mr Ackerley murmured something about his staying for dinner, but Parry excused himself and came away.

When he reached the station he found the sergeant waiting for him. Respectfully the man asked for a statement, and Parry described what had taken place. Bragg had by this time gone on to Lydmouth, and Parry, left alone in Redchurch, took a sharp walk before making his way back to his rooms.

The inquest had been fixed for eleven o'clock on the following morning, and shortly before that hour Parry found himself once more on No. 1 Platform at Redchurch. With him were Mr Ackerley, Bragg, Clay, Driver Blake, Fireman Atkins, and three or four other men. One of the waiting-rooms had been commandeered and the police were busy arranging it for the inquest. A crowd of the curious stood round, staring at everyone concerned.

Mr Ackerley, though still pale and aged-looking, had regained his normal composure and stood talking to a short, middle-aged man with a thin, legal-looking face. This was Mr Loxton, his partner, who apparently was going to appear for him. Talking to Bragg was Hugo Graham, the chief assistant engineer in the Lydmouth office, and the Railway Company's local solicitor, Mr Kenyon. With the driver and fireman, who seemed somehow incongruous in their best clothes, was a sharp-looking man in gray tweeds. This, Parry knew, was George Thompson, the local representative of the Associated Society of Locomotive Engineers and Firemen.

Clay had been hovering over the group as a hen mothers her chickens. 'Now, gentlemen, if you please,' he said at last. 'The coroner's waiting.'

A move was made across the platform and the party filed into the waiting-room. It was a large room with a table down the centre and chairs along each side. At the head of the table sat the coroner, Mr Latimer, a local solicitor. The chair next him was kept vacant, but in the second and third places Mr Ackerley and his partner, Loxton, sat down. Then came the Company's representative, Graham and Kenyon, with Bragg and Parry behind them. Thompson of the A.S.L.E. & F. sat next to Kenyon, with Driver Blake and Fireman Atkins behind him. Beside the fireman was a permanent-way man, Mutch, the ganger of the Whitness length, though what he was there for Parry didn't know. At the table beyond Thompson were two or three reporters. Clay, after hovering anxiously round, had at last subsided behind Mr Ackerley.

The chairs at the opposite side of the table had been kept vacant, and now Sergeant Hart, the man who had gone out with the special, called the jurors to those places. When they were sworn the coroner glanced round and said that before they proceeded to business he was sure that all present would wish to join with him in tendering to Mr Ackerley and his family their sincere sympathy in this most distressing affair.

Upon this up jumped Mr Kenyon. He said that on behalf of the Railway Company he wished to associate himself with all that the coroner had said, and to add that the Company was anxious to assist the inquiry in every way possible by producing all the evidence available. 'We have the driver and firemen and several officials here, and if there is anyone else you would like to have present, you, sir,' he bowed to the coroner, 'have only to say so.'

Sergeant Hart did not look too well pleased at this calm taking of the credit for what he had done, but he refrained from putting his feelings into words. Thompson then rose and said that on behalf of the men of the Locomotive Department he also wished to associate himself . . . Mr Ackerley, obviously struggling with emotion, briefly returned thanks and the coroner bowed and said, 'Horace George Ackerley,' adding, 'Don't trouble, Mr Ackerley, to move. You're quite all right there.'

Mr Ackerley, sworn, said in a low voice that he had seen the remains and they were those of Ronald George Ackerley, his son. He gave some details of the young man's career, explaining that for the last four years his work had permitted him to live at home. Ronald was unmarried, and so far as Mr Ackerley knew, was not engaged. Witness had last seen his son at breakfast on the previous morning, and he then seemed in perfect health and in his normal good spirits.

Mr Grahame, the chief assistant engineer, was then called. He corroborated the details of the deceased's career since he joined the railway staff, adding that since Ackerley had come to the Lydmouth office he had worked steadily and well, and that his appointment as resident engineer in charge of the Whitness Widening was promotion and an outward and visible sign of the confidence which his superiors reposed in him. Deceased had fully justified this confidence, having carried on efficiently since his appointment. So far as Grahame knew, Ackerley had no worries, was keen on his job, got on well with his colleagues and seemed to enjoy his life.

'Clifford Parry.'

Parry, feeling more nervous than the occasion appeared to warrant, moved forward to the chair beside the coroner and was sworn. Mr Latimer began with a number of general questions, then came to the previous evening.

'About half past four you and the deceased left your office at Whitness in company and proceeded along the railway in the direction of Redchurch?'

'That is so.'

'What was your purpose in doing so?'

'The inspection of certain works. Mr Ackerley wished to see a slip which was giving trouble at Cannan's Cutting and also he intended to have an interview with a Mr Potts about a right of way. I wanted to check the measurement of some sea pitching at the Cannan's Cutting end of Browne's Bay. We walked together up to this point.'

'Where did you separate?'

'At the pitching.'

'At what hour was that?'

Parry hesitated. 'It must have been a few minutes past five,' he said at length. 'I don't remember exactly, but I should estimate about ten minutes past five.'

'Quite so. As a matter of fact another witness will prove it was at twelve minutes past.'

Parry was a little taken aback. He had not known they were overlooked. Then he remembered Mutch, the ganger who had passed just as he and Ackerley separated. This, of course, was what the man had been brought for.

'Was the deceased in a thoroughly normal condition when you parted?'

'Absolutely, so far as I know.'

'What was the last you saw of him?'

'He was walking on towards Downey's Point as I began to pace the pitching.'

Mr Latimer took a fresh sheet of paper, making a little pause as if at the end of a chapter.

'What then did you do?' he resumed.

'I paced the dimensions of the pitching and in a few minutes found the error I had been looking for. I walked back then to the office at Whitness.'

'How long did that take you?'

'The pacing took seven or eight minutes. It's a mile back and I took, I suppose, fifteen minutes: probably less, for I ran part of the way. Say, twenty-two or twenty-three minutes altogether.'

'That would bring it to half past five or twenty-five minutes to six when you reached the office?'

'It was thirty-three minutes past,' Parry returned. 'I noticed the time particularly because I had hurried back so that there would be time to deal with the pitching figures and catch the ballast engine at 5.50.'

'Quite so. Now, just one other question. Was it dark when you parted with the deceased?'

'It was dusk, but not dark. I could see to pace the pitching, but I could not read my book without an electric torch.'

The coroner paused. 'Does any gentleman wish to ask the witness a question?' he asked presently. No one evincing such a desire, Parry stood back and Bragg was called.

Bragg came forward and took his place on the vacant chair at the coroner's left hand. In reply to the coroner's questions he said he was the chief design and executive assistant, under Mr Grahame and immediately above the deceased. Owing to the deceased's comparative lack of experience of such important works, he Bragg, had been instructed to assist and supervise him to the best of his ability. In accordance with these instructions he visited the works three or four times a week and kept in close touch with their progress.

'You visited the works yesterday?' went on Mr Latimer.

Bragg had visited the works. He explained in detail about the four-weekly certificates, stating that it was upon this work, the completion of the current certificate, that he had been engaged on the previous day.

'Now, Mr Bragg, you have heard the statement of the previous witness that he and the deceased left the office about half past four with the intention of carrying out certain inspections. Did you instruct them to do so?'

Bragg moved uneasily. 'Yes and no,' he answered. 'The interview with the farmer, Mr Potts, had been arranged some time previously in the ordinary course of work. The idea of inspecting the slip on the way was the deceased's, but he set out to do both of these things with my knowledge and approval. I definitely instructed the last witness to check the pitching, but so long as it was done that day I left the time of doing it to himself. From what he said, I think he chose the time in order to have the deceased's company so far.'

'I follow. Now, Mr Bragg, you say that you told the deceased to meet you here in Redchurch on the arrival of the ballast engine. At what hour should that have been?'

'A minute or two before six.'

'Very well. Now, if the deceased parted from Mr Parry at the point where this pitching was measured at 5.12, as we shall prove, and was due in Redchurch about six, at what hour should he have passed the place at which the accident occurred?'

'Downey's Point? It was seven or eight minutes walk from the pitching. About 5.20, I should say.'

'At what hour did your engine pass Downey's Point?'

'About 5.55.'

'That's what I've been coming to. How do you account, Mr Bragg, for the deceased not having been farther on when the engine came?'

'I can't account for it at all. That was one of the things which overwhelmed me with surprise, that he was there when he should have been at Redchurch.'

That ended the examination and Mr Kenyon took advantage of the coroner's invitation to ask a question.

'Tell me, Mr Bragg,' he said, 'was it quite a normal thing

for you to arrange with the deceased to walk over the Widening?'

'Absolutely normal. We were doing it every day. It was part of the deceased's duty.'

'Quite so. But what about walking the line in the dusk or dark?'

Bragg shrugged. 'That was not so pleasant, of course, but at this time of year one can't help oneself.'

'I don't mean that, Mr Bragg. I mean, was it usual and was it safe?'

'It was both,' Bragg returned firmly. 'Besides you will remember that last evening was not dark. There was a moon behind the clouds.'

'There was no reasonable fear of the deceased meeting with an accident?'

'None, I think. He was thoroughly experienced and knew every inch of the way, and he could easily see where he was.'

Mr Kenyon intimated that that was all he wanted and sat down.

Mr William Potts deposed that he was a farmer living some half a mile on the Redchurch side of Downey's Point. He had had a business appointment with the deceased for half past five on the previous evening. He had duly come down to the railway, but after waiting till after six had assumed the deceased had been detained, and had returned home.

Driver Blake was the next witness. After giving evidence about the fatal run of the ballast engine, he was questioned in detail as to the conditions obtaining on the footplate just before the accident. He was standing in his place, looking out ahead. Mr Parry was standing behind him.

Mr Bragg was seated on the fireman's seat and the fireman was occupied with the fire. No, there was no talking going on, and all concerned were carrying out their duties carefully and normally. He did not see anyone on the line. He could not do so because of the curve. The first intimation he had that anything was wrong was a shout from the fireman, and he stopped as soon as it was physically possible.

Fireman Atkins corroborated the driver's evidence. The fire was low and wanted raking up and he did this work as they approached Downey's Point. When he had finished he stepped to the side of the cab and looked out ahead. He had no special reason for doing this. It was merely a precautionary measure, as he knew the driver's view would be bad. When he had looked out a moment he saw something black on the line. He shouted to the driver, who immediately stopped. He went back and found they had run over Mr Ackerley.

'When you saw this black object,' resumed Mr Latimer, 'did you know it was a man?'

'No, I didn't know what it was. But whatever it was I knew we should stop.'

'Quite so. Now, where exactly was the object?'

'Just about halfway round the curve.'

'I don't mean that. Was it between the rails or across the rails or outside them?'

'As far as I could see, it was lying across the low leg.'

'What do you mean by the "low leg"?'

'The inside rail.'

'That is the right hand rail because the curve was turning to the right?'

'That's correct.'

'Can you swear he wasn't standing up?'

The fireman didn't think so, but he wouldn't swear to it. He had seen Ackerley as a dark mass and in the gloom he was not sure in what position the unhappy young man had been.

'Now,' Mr Latimer went on, 'after the engine had passed was the position of deceased altered?'

Of this there was no doubt. The engine had struck the body and carried it along, leaving it between the rails. The right arm had been severed and it lay outside the right hand rail.

'Did you examine the engine afterwards?'

It appeared that there were bloodstains on the right life guard and leading bogie wheel. It was clear, therefore, that the accident had occurred with the ballast engine and not with some previous train.

On the coroner giving the usual invitation, Mr Thompson of the A. S. L. E. & F. sprang up.

'With regard to the lookout that was kept from the engine can you say that this was adequate?'

The witness was positive that it was entirely adequate.

'As good and complete as is ever kept?'

'Yes, quite up to the normal.'

'As a matter of fact, could you under any circumstances have seen the deceased sooner than you did?'

'Not except in daylight.'

Mr Clay was then questioned as to the hour at which the previous trains had passed Downey's Point. It appeared that one left Redchurch at 5.0 and stopped specially at Downey's Point to pick up the workmen, reaching Whitness at 5.10. It there crossed a train from Bournemouth, which left Whitness at 5.10 and arrived at Redchurch at 5.16.

There was no other ordinary train then till the 6.10 from Whitness. On the previous evening there had been no special except the ballast engine leaving Whitness at 5.50.

Permanent Way Ganger Mutch was next called. He stated that while walking home on the previous evening, at the pitching between Browne's Bay and Cannan's Cutting he had passed Mr Ackerley and Mr Parry. They were just separating. As he went on he happened to glance back and he saw Mr Ackerley walking towards Downey's Point and Mr Parry stepping off the line down over the pitching on the sea slope.

'At what hour did they part, Mutch?' the coroner inquired.

'About 5.12.'

'Now, will you just tell the jury how you happen to know that so well?'

'I know it by the 5.10 from Whitness,' the man returned. 'She passed about a minute after they parted. That would be about 5.13 or 5.14 at the outside.'

'It has been estimated, ganger,' said the coroner, 'that the deceased must have reached the point at which he was killed at about 5.20. You know the place and you saw the speed at which he was walking. Do you agree with that estimate?'

Mutch thought it would be about right.

'Would it have been possible for him to have been killed by that 5.10 from Whitness of which you speak?'

About this the ganger was positive. It would have been utterly impossible for the distance to have been covered in the time.

'Then he wasn't killed until 5.55. Can you suggest what he might have been doing in the interval?'

Mutch had no idea and was allowed to leave the witness chair. Sergeant Hart bent down.

'I think, sir,' he said confidentially, 'that I can put forward a theory to account for this. It is, of course, only a theory.'

The coroner nodded. 'Very good, sergeant, we'll hear it in due course.'

Dr Cripps, the police surgeon, testified that he had examined the remains. He described the injuries till Parry felt sick. The face was slightly disfigured from contact with the stone ballast and there had been a blow on the right side of the head behind the temple, fracturing the skull. This was probably due to the deceased falling against the rail, as the skin was but slightly damaged. The right arm had been severed. In the doctor's opinion these injuries were consistant with the deceased having fallen and having been run over by a railway engine. Death had been instantaneous.

Sergeant Hart was the last witness. He deposed that he had accompanied the engine and van out to Downey's Point on the previous evening, when the remains were being brought in. He had examined the line with a torch and from the marks on the ballast he believed he had been able to reconstruct the tragedy. Firstly, he was of opinion from the nature of the injuries that the deceased had been lying across the rail before the engine approached. Just behind where the young man's foot would have come was a cross drain, due to the workings, where the ballast had been sunk between two adjacent sleepers to a depth of nine or ten inches. It appeared to the witness that the deceased might in the dusk have slipped into this drain and fallen, striking the side of his head on the rail and being stunned. This, of course, was only the witness' theory and he had been unable to obtain actual proof of its truth.

This being all the evidence, there was a short pause while the coroner adjusted his notes. Then he made a summary of what had been stated, very clearly and fairly, as Parry thought. Finally he gave a short exposition of his own views.

'I do not think, members of the jury,' he ended up, 'that you will have much difficulty in reaching a verdict in this unhappy affair. You may consider that this unfortunate young man lost his life as the result of an accident, for which neither he nor anyone else was to blame. If you do so you will return a verdict of accidental death. On the other hand, if you are not satisfied with this view, you will consider the alternatives. There are only two; suicide and murder.

'Now, with regard to suicide, the whole of the evidence tends to show that the deceased was in good health, bodily and mentally; that he was happy in his work and with his associates; that he was ambitious and working hard for advancement and success; and that he was free from pecuniary embarrassment and from unhappy love entanglements: in fact, he had every reason to live and none to die. In the face of this evidence, the theory of suicide seems to me to present grave difficulties.

'There is one piece of evidence, however, which might at first sight be held to support the theory of suicide: that the deceased must have been for a considerable time, about half an hour, at or near the point at which he was killed. It might here be argued that he was waiting for the engine in order to throw himself before it. Sergeant Hart, however, has put forward a theory to account for this delay, which you may consider adequate. There was a drain across the line; in the dark the deceased did not see it; he put his foot into it, tripped over the next sleeper and fell forward, striking his head on the rail and becoming insensible. There at all events you have what might have happened. That it did happen cannot be proved, but still less can it be disapproved.

'But if the evidence for suicide is unsatisfactory, I think you must agree that no evidence has been given which in any shape or form suggests that murder has been committed. I do not think I need labour this point.

'Now, members of the jury, I would ask you to retire and consider your verdict, and if there is any point in which I can assist you in your labours, I shall be glad to deal with it to the best of my ability.'

The jurors, looking important, whispered among themselves. Then the foreman, standing up, said that the members didn't require to retire to consider their verdict, that their minds were made up, and that they found that deceased had met his death through an accident and that no blame attached to any person therefore.

4

Enter Inspector French

Early on the morning of the day after the inquest on Ronald Ackerley Superintendent Rhode and Inspector Dawe of the Redchurch police were seated in the former's office in the police station of that town. Two men less alike in personal appearance than the superintendent and his assistant it would not have been easy to find. Rhode was a big heavily built man with a domineering expression and a curt manner. Dawe on the other hand was thin and nervous looking and seemed chronically ill at ease. Rhode reached his results by sheer driving force which refused to recognise any obstacle, Dawe by his alert mentality. Both were good men, respected by each other and by their superiors.

They were not discussing the inquest. They were not interested in the inquest except to load it with imprecations for having occupied a day of Sergeant Hart's time, a day which both they and he had been very reluctant to spare. For the Redchurch police force was at the moment working at high pressure. No less than three serious crimes, a murder and two burglaries, had recently occurred in that usually peaceful area, and these were proving just a little more than the staff could handle with comfort. In fact, the calling in of the Yard to help with the murder case was under consideration.

This was indeed the point on which Rhode and Dawe were now engaged. They were about to draw up a report to their chief constable, giving a considered opinion for or against applying to London. Dawe was against it, Rhode on the whole in favour of it, but willing to be convinced.

'If we could get a line on Farjeon,' Dawe was saying, 'we could get ahead. That's what's holding us up.'

'A week's work of far more men than we can spare has gone into it already,' Rhode answered, 'and we don't seem much further on. If we could have got those men on to the burglaries we'd probably have had them squared by this time. I'm afraid, Dawe, if we don't do better by tomorrow or next day we'll have to get help.'

Dawe's reply was cut short by a knock at the door. A constable put in his head.

'Coastguard Wilmot of the Whitness station is here, sir, and would like to see you about the death of Mr Ronald Ackerley.'

Rhode and Dawe exchanged glances. 'Good Lord,' said the former, 'more trouble. Show him in, Braithwaite.'

Wilmot proved to be an elderly and intelligent looking man bearing the obvious stamp of the Royal Navy. He wished the officers good morning and took the chair to which Rhode pointed.

'Well, Wilmot,' said Rhode, who knew him well. 'What's bitten you? Something about the Ackerley case?'

'Sorry to trouble you gentlemen,' said the coastguard, 'partic'larly as I ain't certain if there's anything in wot I 'ave to tell you. But I thought to myself, if so be that it's important, why then it should be told, and if there ain't nothing in it, why then mentioning it won't do no 'arm.'

'A profound truth,' Rhode declared dryly. 'I subscribe to your philosophy and so does the inspector. Well, let's hear the worst.'

Wilmot evidently took this for encouragement.

'It were just something I saw,' he explained. 'On Monday afternoon, the day Mr Ackerley was killed, I 'ad an inspection along the coast. I left Whitness about 'alf past four to walk to Redchurch. I kept on the top of the cliffs where there ain't no road till I got to Downey's Point, then I took the road round the Point, and after that went along the railway into Redchurch. When I were about 'alf way round Downey's Point I saw the lights of a steamer going up Channel, and I stopped to 'ave a look at 'er. Well, there weren't nothing interesting about 'er and I turned to go on, but before starting I 'ad a look back along the road to Whitness; just sort of by chance, if you understand.'

'I understand,' Rhode said patiently as the coastguard paused.

'As I were looking back I saw a man. 'E appeared at the back of the mound fence on the sea side of the road. As you know, sir, the road runs about eighty feet above the railway at that place, and if this man weren't climbing up from the railway, I'm jiggered if I know where 'e was coming from. 'E stopped and 'ad a good squint up and down the road, but I don't think 'e saw me for I were close behind a small thorn bush: about the only one that grows on the sea side of the road. Then 'e climbed over the mound fence and ran across to the small shrubberry that's on the other side of the road. You know, sir, there's just a little bit of flat ground before it starts to slope up again to the top of the ness, and it were into that 'e went.'

'I know it well. Get along, man.'

'I wasn't 'alf surprised,' Wilmot continued, 'seeing 'im come up like that in such a 'urry, and run across the road kind of stealthy. Something stealthy in the way 'e ran, like as if 'e were trying not to be seen, if you know wot I mean.'

Rhode's foot was marking time with irritable persistence, but he controlled himself and said quietly, 'I know.'

'I weren't in any 'urry and I thought I'd watch and see wot 'appened. In a moment 'e came out of the shrubbery wheeling a bicycle, a push bike. 'E jumped on it and rode off as 'ard as 'e could towards Whitness.'

'Well?'

'That were all,' the coastguard returned. ''Is 'urrying and 'aving the bicycle there 'idden, so to speak, it seemed kind of suspicious to me. But there ain't maybe nothing in it.'

Rhode moved impatiently. 'I don't get your idea,' he declared. 'Why should this have had anything to do with the Ackerley case?'

'I don't say as 'ow it 'as,' Wilmot returned irritatingly, 'but it seemed to me kind of suspicious because of the time.'

'The time?'

'Yes, sir. It were just on to quarter past five.'

For a moment there was silence, and then Wilmot resumed. 'Of course, sir, you understand that I didn't think nothing about it at the time, excepting just wot I've told you: that it seemed a bit queer. But when I read about the inquest in last night's paper I wondered if so be there weren't something in it. 'Ere were a young man got to

Downey's Point about 5.10 and were killed. But there weren't no reason why he should 'ave been killed at that time. The engine didn't pass till 5.55, and nobody couldn't explain wot 'e were doing between 5.10 and 5.55.'

Rhode glanced at him keenly. 'What's all this?' he asked. 'Are you suggesting that Ackerley was murdered?'

The coastguard shook his head. 'No, sir, I ain't suggesting nothing. But I thought I'd better tell you wot I'd seen. If you think there ain't nothing in it, why then, that's all right.'

Rhode frowned and glanced at Dawe.

'How are you so sure of the time?' he asked.

'I looked at my watch. I thought the thing were a bit queer, and I thought if anything came of it I might as well know the time.'

For a moment there was silence in the little room, then Rhode struck a bell.

'Has Hart gone out?' he asked the constable who appeared. 'If not, send him in.'

In a moment Sergeant Hart entered.

'Sit down, Hart. Here's Coastguard Wilmot with a story of something he saw at Downey's Point on the night Ackerley was killed. He says,' and Rhode briefly repeated the statement, ending up: 'What do you think? Anything in it?'

Hart did not immediately reply. He seemed impressed. He gave a lifelike representation of a man thinking, then said hesitatingly that he didn't know.

'That means you think there might be, I suppose?' Rhode returned. 'Why?'

'That half hour, sir,' Hart said, still with hesitation. 'It was commented on at the inquest. And then of course,' he paused again, 'there was that blow on the head that was supposed to have been caused by falling on the rail.'

Rhode moved irritably. 'Good Lord, man, are you starting now to build up a murder case after you yourself explaining the whole thing away at the inquest?' He frowned, then went on: 'Look here, go out now with Wilmot and see just where this man came up. See if it was directly above where the body was found. And get anything more from Wilmot that you can. Then come back and report.' He looked at the inspector. 'That's the best thing, Dawe?'

Dawe agreed. 'That'll about put the lid on doing without a man from the Yard,' he went on when the other two had left, 'that is, if this Ackerley case has to be reopened.'

Rhode nodded gloomily. 'You know,' he said, 'though I didn't give it much attention, the thought did pass through my mind that it was extraordinarily careless of a railwayman getting killed like that. It was a single line; there was no other train that he could have been getting out of the way of or that was making a noise to distract his attention. I don't know. I'm afraid if Hart can't clear the thing up we'll have to go into it.'

'If so, we get someone from the Yard.'

'If so, we get someone from the Yard,' Rhode repeated. 'Yes, I think we'll have to. However, let's wait till Hart comes in.'

They turned to other work until in a couple of hours Hart's return brought them back to the matter.

'It looks baddish,' the sergeant declared. 'The place where the man came up is immediately above where the body was found. I had a look at the bank between the road and the railway. You know it's pretty steep. There's the railway cutting about forty feet high, then the slope of the Point, running on up nearly as steeply, but with little shrubs on it. I was able to find marks nearly all the way where someone had slipped back in climbing up. None of them clear enough to be useful, but just proving that someone did climb it recently. Then I had a look among the shrubs on the inland side of the road. I saw the mark of the bicycle. It had been pushed in between the double stems of a birch, like into a bicycle rack. I couldn't see any clear footprints nor anything else.'

Rhode whistled below his breath. 'Do you know anything about this fellow Ackerley? Any enemies?'

'None, sir, that we've heard of, but as you know, we didn't make very detailed inquiries.'

Rhode nodded. 'Very well, Hart; that'll do. I'll have a word with the chief constable. You get on with that Farjeon business.'

It was as a result of a protracted conference, at which the chief constable was present, that Detective-Inspector Joseph French of the Criminal Investigation Department, New Scotland Yard, stepped late that afternoon from the train at Redchurch Station.

French had for the past few months been working continuously at the Yard and had led a comparatively humdrum life. Since he had finished up the Grinsmead affair at Ashbridge, in Kent, he had been engaged on smaller and less thrilling cases, cases which meant plenty of work, but in which, owing to their sordid and commonplace nature, he found it impossible to take a great deal of interest. He had investigated two burglaries, a forgery, and a murder of a wife by her drunken and jealous husband. In two of these crimes he succeeded in putting his hands on the guilty parties, but one housebreaker eluded him, and as the drunken husband made no attempt to escape, his apprehension could not be said to represent any very signal triumph of the detective art. At the moment French had been free. He had been hoping to be sent to Brussels, where a gang of international criminals, badly wanted by the London police, were believed to be in hiding. This application from the Dorset Constabulary had, however, queered his pitch so far as Belgium was concerned, and he had been told to proceed by the first train to Redchurch.

Hart met him at the station.

'The station's only a few blocks up, sir,' he explained. 'If you'll give me your bag I think we might walk.'

'By all means let's walk, sergeant. But hadn't I better give the bag to one of these hotel people?'

A room having been reserved, the two men walked to the police station. French, in accordance with his invariable rule, chatted pleasantly about his journey and the locality, and the sergeant, expecting to be kept severely in his place by their distinguished London visitor, became at once human and friendly and anxious to assist.

Rhode was awaiting them in his room. He shook hands with French, and after a somewhat curt greeting, got to business.

'You better remain, sergeant,' he directed. 'The inspector may want to ask you some questions. Sit down, both of you. You know nothing of the case, I suppose, inspector?'

'Nothing, sir. The Home Office simply advised us that you wanted a man.'

'Then I'd better run over the salient features; they're very simple. We've done practically nothing on it because we've no men to spare. We were busy on two burglaries when we got that Farjeon case on the top of us; you know, the case in which Mrs Farjeon and Captain Higgings were found shot.'

'I read of it. Admiral Farjeon was suspected, I gathered.'

Rhode shrugged. 'That's as may be,' he answered shortly. 'At all events we haven't the staff for anything else. The chief constable decided we must concentrate on the Farjeon affair and apply for help from the Yard for the railway case. So there it is, inspector; that's why you're here, and you start with a free hand in your own way.'

'I understand, sir,' French answered politely, though inwardly he smiled. His country cases usually began with some such preamble. Never yet had he been told that the local men had tried a problem and found it too big for them. Always they were prevented by other work from giving it their attention. However, this was only human nature. French had made it an invariable rule to save the faces of the local men in this connection, and he had found it to pay him.

Rhode leant heavily back in his chair.

'It's the case of a young man being run over on the railway,' he went on. 'They're doubling the line between here and Whitness, that's a small town three and a half miles along the shore to the east. This young man that was killed, Ronald Ackerley, was the resident engineer for the Company,' and he went on to tell of the apparent accident, the inquest, and the visit of Coastguard Wilmot with the sinister suggestion resulting from his story. 'So you see,' he concluded, 'the facts, so far as we know them, are few and simple, and all we want you to do, inspector, is to clear up the doubt. If you can prove the death to have been an accident, your work's done. If it is murder,' Rhode shrugged, 'it'll be just beginning.'

'I see that,' French agreed. 'Has the case not been gone into at all? Is it known, for instance, whether the young man had enemies?'

'I may say that it really has not been gone into. The sergeant went out and saw the place, and as I have said, checked up about the man and the bicycle. But that's all that's been done. With regard to enemies: we've not heard of any, but then we've not inquired. I tell you, inspector, better have a talk with Sergeant Hart. He knows the case better than anyone else. Take the inspector to the other office, Hart.'

French, thus dismissed, got up. 'I'll be glad of anything the sergeant can tell me,' he observed. 'Also I should like the depositions made at the inquest. I'll go over them tonight and be ready to make a start in the morning.'

The discussion with Hart having proved unfruitful—the sergeant was unable to add anything material to Rhode's statement—French returned to his hotel and after dinner settled down to study the *dossier*, so far as it had been compiled. A very little thought led him to the conclusion that it would be a waste of time to try to evolve theories until he had more detailed information. He must go over the ground and get statements at first hand from those concerned, so as to be sure he understood the affair thoroughly. He would then be in a better position to reach a considered opinion.

Accordingly next morning he took an early train to Whitness, and walking out to the engineers' hut, presented his card to Parry.

'I'd be much obliged, Mr Parry,' he said after some introductory remarks, 'if you'd come out with me to Downey's Point and show me where the body was found.

It was seen by you and Mr Bragg and the fireman, was it not?'

'Yes.'

'Would it be possible to get either of those other two also?'

'When do you want to go?'

'As soon as possible. Now, if you can manage it.'

Parry considered. 'Mr Bragg is not here today, but I think I could get the fireman.' He made a telephone call. 'You're in luck, inspector,' he went on. 'If we walk down to a siding just beyond the tunnel we'll get an engine to take us out, with the fireman you want on board. Will you come along?'

They left the hut and walked down past the viaducts, old and new, and along the path on the slopes of the headland outside the tunnel. The day was fine and the sea, a pale greenish blue, was calm and beneficent looking. Far out on the horizon, which showed hard and dark against the clear sky, a large steamer was heading up Channel. Nearer inshore two or three white sailed pleasure boats heeled over as they tacked against the breeze. To French it was a delightful change from London. He was interested also in what he saw of the work of the Widening and made up his mind that before he left he would get Parry to take him over it and explain just what was being done.

On the siding, which was on a widened portion of the rocky shelf beyond the tunnel, stood the ballast train. Miggs, the ballast guard, and Blake, the driver, were on the ground beside the engine.

'You're waiting till the 9.50 clears to get out, I suppose?' asked Parry.

Miggs said that was so and that she wouldn't be long.

'Mr French is making some inquiries into Mr Ackerley's death. I want you, Blake, to run us out to where the accident took place. I told Mr Pole that we'd delay you a bit.'

The men murmured 'Very good, sir,' and shot interested glances at French.

As they spoke a train which French had neither heard nor seen approaching, suddenly materialised. It ran slowly past, whistling as it disappeared into the tunnel.

'You have to keep your eyes skinned here,' French remarked, considerably surprised at its unexpected appearance.

Parry agreed. 'If the wind's the wrong way trains come up on you very quietly. A lot of men have been knocked out because of it. Better get up, inspector. We'll be ready to start in a moment.'

Parry climbed on to the footplate and French, immensely interested, followed. He had never been on an engine before and was like a child in his eagerness: so much so that he had sternly to remind himself that he was here on business, and that in his enjoyment of a new sensation he must not forget his job.

Miggs, having hooked off the engine, now went to the occupation box, obtained a tablet from it, and unlocked and threw open the points. They ran out along the shelf of rock, passed through Cannan's Cutting and round the long curve of Browne's Bay, pulling up just short of the fatal spot, about halfway round Downey's Point. Parry clambered down, followed by French and Fireman Atkins.

'Now, gentlemen,' French began, 'will you please show me how the poor young man was lying.'

The medical and police evidence suggested that Ackerley

had not been knocked down by the engine, but had been lying on his face on the line when it came up. The face was only slightly disfigured and the clothes were not cut in front, as they would have been had Ackerley been dashed forcibly down on the sharp-edged stone ballast. The slight wounds on the face would have resulted from his being pushed a little forward, as he undoubtedly had been. On the other hand the injuries caused by the engine were terrible, but local. The unfortunate young man had apparently been lying partially across the rail, and the wheels had crushed the chest and severed the right arm and shoulder.

French found this view strengthened by the evidence of his two witnesses. Had Ackerley been knocked down, not only would the face and clothes in front have been torn, but the back where struck by the engine would have been crushed into pulp. Such injury to the back was entirely absent.

French had brought the *dossier* and he re-read the medical evidence. In addition to the injury to the arm, Ackerley's skull had been fractured by a blow behind the right ear. It had been admitted that this blow could not have been caused by the engine, as the skin was but slightly damaged. French saw that this was correct. Had the engine struck the head, it would have crushed it like an egg-shell. The blow, the sergeant had suggested, had been caused by Ackerley's striking his head against the rail as he fell.

French did not feel particularly happy about this explanation. For some moments he stood thinking, then as best he could he went through the motions of stepping into the drain, tripping over the adjoining sleeper, and falling forward on the rail.

It was as he had thought. If the side of his head struck the rail, it would be a mere glancing blow. A direct blow would come on the forehead. French doubted whether even the most direct blow received from such a fall would fracture the skull, but he felt positive that a glancing blow would be insufficient.

Parry's voice broke into his thoughts. 'We mustn't keep the engine,' the young man pointed out. 'There's only six minutes to clear the road for the next train.'

'Thank you, I've finished with the fireman, but I'd be obliged if you could wait with me, Mr Parry.'

The engine backed off and French resumed his cogitations. A further point had occurred to him, a point of the simplest, but most convincing kind. If Ackerley had really tripped over that sleeper, he would have saved himself by putting out his hands. He might have fallen, but he never would have fallen with sufficient force to fracture his skull.

French felt a growing certainty that the blow had been struck before the engine came up. If so, there could be but one deduction. The tragedy was no accident. Ackerley had been murdered: murdered in a cold-blooded, deliberate, premeditated way which included the faking of an accident to cover up the crime. French saw that his case was only beginning.

For a moment he was inclined to think hard thoughts of the doctor who had reported in favour of accident. Then he saw that had he been in the doctor's place, he would probably have done the same thing. The man had no suspicion that the affair might not be an accident. He had not come out to the site and made a reconstruction, as had French. It was only when French had followed in his mind what must have happened, that he saw the flaw. No, the doctor could not be blamed.

French thought his conclusion was pretty well proven, but as he stood looking round he saw something which strongly confirmed it. The railway track with its broken stone ballast was rough and unpleasant walking. But beside it, between the ends of the sleepers and the top of the sea pitching, was a space of some six or eight feet, and down the middle of this ran a smooth well-trampled path.

'Tell me, Mr Parry,' French said as he took in these details, 'Why would Mr Ackerley have been on the railway at all? Would he not rather have walked on this path?'

The point had evidently not occurred to Parry and it obviously puzzled him. It was Ackerley's habit to walk on the path. Parry had been with him scores of times and he had always done so. Parry did not believe he would have walked on the line, though he suggested that he might have stepped on to it for some reason just before the ballast engine came along.

French nodded absently. All this evidence was cumulative, and French knew that there is nothing in the world so convincing as cumulative evidence. When to what he had now discovered were added the three other facts which pointed to murder, first, the unlikelihood of an experienced railwayman being run over under the circumstances in question, second, the chronological discrepancy in any other theory, and third, the hurried departure of the unknown man on the bicycle, French felt he had enough to establish this part of the case.

There being nothing else to be seen on the railway, he turned to his companion.

'How can we get back to Whitness, Mr Parry?'

'Walk it, or if you like, get up on the road and wait till a 'bus passes.'

'I'd rather walk, if you don't mind.'

They set off in the pleasant sunshine. French improved the opportunity not only to see the pitching which Parry had been sent to measure up, but also to make inquiries about the *personnel* of the Widening. Then he turned to the question of who had known that Ackerley would be on the railway at Downey's Point on the evening of his death.

'I should think that everybody knew it,' Parry returned. 'I knew it, for I parted from him a few minutes before. Bragg knew it, for he was aware of what we proposed to do. The contractors' men, Carey, Lowell and Pole, knew that he was walking through that evening. They mightn't have known the exact time he would have passed Downey's Point, but they could have guessed it approximately. Potts might also have guessed it: that's the farmer Ackerley had to meet. Ganger Mutch of the Whitness length could have deduced it, and also other railwaymen who might have seen us walking out.'

This did not seem a very promising line of research. French therefore dropped it and set himself to pick up as much of the railway politics as he could, finally getting Parry, on reaching Whitness, to introduce him to the other members of the office staffs, so that he might form his own opinion of their personalities. His somewhat veiled inquiries, however, threw no light on possible motives for desiring Ackerley's death.

Having thanked Parry for his help, French walked out again to Downey's Point, this time by the road. The coastguard officer had been sworn to silence about the man he had seen, and French had not wished to give away that he was working on any special line. Hence his revisiting the place alone.

It was a striking enough view that he looked out on from the road. Away to the horizon stretched the sea, a great flat plane of deepest blue, with in the middle distance a small coaster threshing along, probably making for Lynmouth. On each side were bays round which ran the railway. That to the left ended in a headland, in the side of which showed the V-shaped cleft of the entrance to Cannan's Cutting. To the right were several low lying points, one behind the other and reaching away to near Lydmouth, each fainter and bluer than the last. Below, showing here and there through gaps in the shrubs which covered the slopes, was the permanent way, its sleepers looking from the height tiny and placed with extraordinary neatness. As French gazed down a train passed—a toy on a model line. He followed its passage rond the curve of Browne's Bay till it disappeared into Cannan's Cutting.

He climbed down the slope to the railway, first through the shrubs, and then down the rather poor grass of the cutting. How long, he wondered, would it have taken a potential murderer to escape? A man in a hurry could, he thought, run up to the road in about two minutes. One more minute to retrieve a bicycle from the shrubs at the opposite side of the road would make three altogether from the leaving of the victim to the departure on the bicycle. French was now strongly of opinion that some unknown man had on the night of Ackerley's death spent three minutes in just that way.

The marks of the man's hurried climb discovered by Hart were still visible, but though French examined them with great care, they were too blurred to afford any clue. He then crossed the road and soon found the tracks of the bicycle, crossing a small patch of loose sand thrown up by a rabbit at the root of a small birch tree. This tree, as Hart had stated, had two stems about four inches apart, and the front wheel of the bicycle had been thrust between them, as into a stand. The patch of sand was very small and it bore no footprints.

French examined the ground all about in the hope of finding some little object which the unknown might have dropped, but without success. He did, however, discover a mark which for a short time puzzled him. On the left hand stem of the birch, about a foot from the ground, was a small cut or scrape in the bark. It showed first on the back and dragged round to a point almost opposite the other stem.

A little thought, however, told French what it was. A cyclometer evidently. The bicycle had been hurriedly withdrawn and the cyclometer had caught in the tree. Considerable force had obviously been used and French wondered whether the cyclometer had not been broken off. If it had, the unknown must have seen and removed it, as it was not anywhere to be found.

French stood thinking. Here at last was a clue: a push bicycle with a bent or broken cyclometer. To find it was surely a job for the local men. Would it be dealt with by Rhode and Dawe and Hart, or by the local staff at Whitness? He felt sure there must be a local staff at Whitness, and as the bicycle had disappeared towards that town, it was probably there that he should apply.

He set off to walk back and immediately had a minor stroke of luck. A 'bus appeared behind him. He got on board and ten minutes later was entering the police station at Whitness.

Sergeant Emery, the officer in charge, greeted him with surprise and respect. He was evidently keenly interested in French's statement and eagerly promised to do what he could to help. Yes, he would certainly try to find anyone who had been on the road between Downey's Point and Whitness on the evening in question and would make inquiries as to a push-bicycle having been seen. Yes, he appreciated the fact that the man was pedalling hard, and it should certainly have drawn attention to him. Emery thought also he could find out, by having the arrivals and departures at the contractors' yard unobtrusively watched, how many bicycles belonged to the workers there, and he was sure he could make some excuse to examine closely any with cyclometers, or which had lost cyclometers. Also he would try to pick up as much of the gossip of the Widening as he could, and if he came on anything which seemed worth while following up, he would tell the inspector. And if there was anything else the inspector had only to ring him up.

'Good man,' said French heartily, 'that's just what I want. Now about the inquiries along the roads: how will you set about it?'

'Our own men first, sir. Then coastguards, postmen, 'bus drivers, doctors, the district nurse, workmen cycling home to Redchurch: there are a good many people to ask.'

French was pleased. This Emery was evidently an efficient man. 'That's the style, sergeant. Peg away on those lines and you're bound to get results. You'll ring me up at the hotel if you've any luck?'

French turned away with the man's cheery 'Good evening,

sir,' ringing in his ears. There would, he thought, just be time for one more inquiry that night. Returning to the engineers' hut, he managed to get Parry to agree to his searching Ackerley's desk. Here, however, he had no luck. There was nothing in it which gave him the least help.

Having called in to tell Rhode the result of his first day's work, French returned to his hotel to write up his notes and consider his next step.

5

Concerning a Bicycle

French, having reached virtual certainty on the fundamental question of his new case: Had Ackerley been murdered? went on to consider the two which immediately followed: Who had a motive for the crime? and, Who had the opportunity to commit it?

The answer to the original question had been reached very easily: he had been lucky in finding facts which, if they did not absolutely prove it, at least made it so likely as to amount to very nearly the same thing. Certainly these facts had shown that murder was so likely that no doubt was possible as to the need for going further into the affair.

But it was most improbable that the answers to the second and third questions would be come by so readily. These would be reached, if they were reached at all, by hard work; detailed, uninspiring, monotonous work. To find the motive would mean going carefully into Ackerley's life, as well as the lives of those with whom he had come in contact: the sort of slow, patient investigation which French hated, but of which he had to do so much. The same applied to the question of opportunity: he would have to learn where all the possibles were at the time of the crime; who had alibis and who hadn't; also a tedious and wearisome process and as often as not unproductive.

However, it was his job, and the sooner he got on with it the sooner it would be done. He therefore set himself to make a list of all the lines of inquiry he could think of. Next morning he set off on the first.

Going to the Ackerley's house, he caught Mr Ackerley as he was starting for his office.

'I'm sorry, sir, to delay you,' he began, handing over his official card, 'but if you could give me a few minutes before you leave I think it might be more convenient for both of us.'

Mr Ackerley was obviously surprised, but he led the way to his study. 'What can I do for you, inspector?' he asked.

'I'm afraid, Mr Ackerley, that what I have to say may cause you pain, but I think it is better to tell you what is in my mind. The authorities, to put it bluntly, are not entirely satisfied about the death of Mr Ronald Ackerley. They are inclined to question whether so experienced a man would really have met with an accident as Mr Ackerley was supposed to do. Somebody suggested a doubt, and as suicide appeared to be out of the question, it was asked whether by any possibility there could have been anything in the nature of foul play. I have been sent down to make sure.'

Mr Ackerley was so obviously taken aback that he could scarcely speak.

'My God,' he murmured brokenly, staring at French with haggard eyes, 'what are you saying? Foul play? Oh, no! Surely such a thing is not possible.'

The old man's distress was pitiable, but he agreed that if any uncertainty existed it must be removed. Slowly he controlled himself, then asked what the suspicious circumstances were.

'"Suspicious circumstances" is rather too strong a term,' French told him. Then he went on to explain the points suggestive of murder which Rhode had made, though he did not mention what he himself had discovered. Mr Ackerley seemed far from convinced, but he presently shrugged his shoulders hopelessly and repeated his former question: 'What can I do for you, inspector?'

'I want you, sir, first to tell me everything you can about your son: who, as far as you know, his friends were; whether he had any enemies; whether he was engaged or about to become so; how he spent his leisure; those sort of matters and others of the same kind. Anything that may help me to find if anyone wished him ill.'

Mr Ackerley shook his head. 'There was no one; I'm sure there was no one. Ronald was a general favourite. No one, I'm positive, could have wished to harm him.'

'All the same, sir, I would like you to tell me in detail what you can. Now, about his friends?'

French was comprehensive and persistent in his inquiries, and the old gentleman was evidently anxious to answer them as fully as he could. But he was unable to tell French anything which gave him the slightest help. In fact, everything he had to say told against the theory of murder. Ackerley was popular in his own set, a good set of clean-living, hard-working young men and women. He had no enemies, at least, so far as his father knew. He was not engaged, nor, again so far as his father knew, anxious to become so. With the same reservation, he neither owed nor was owed money. His interests were concentrated on his job, and when he came home in the evening he was tired and did not often go out.

French, having obtained all the information he could, asked to see the young man's room, so that he might ascertain if any of his possessions could be made to reveal a secret. Mr Ackerley agreed at once, also giving French a note to Ronald's bank manager, authorising him to give French all details as to his son's finances.

Both of these lines of investigation, however, proved unproductive. Neither from old letters nor other papers, nor from an examination of the deceased's clothes, nor yet from his finances, was there anything to throw light on the affair.

Information, however, was closer than French anticipated. He had advised Rhode as to his movements, and at the bank he received a telephone message from the superintendent, asking him to return immediately to the police station.

He reached it to find Rhode in conversation with a small, stout, consequential-looking man, whose tiny features were bunched close together in the middle of his huge, round, red face.

'Come in, inspector,' the former greeted him. 'This is Mr Charles Ewing, and he has called to give us some information which may possibly interest you. Perhaps, Mr Ewing, you would tell Inspector French what you found.'

The little man looked at French with obvious interest.

'You are Inspector French from Scotland Yard, are you not?' he said, twisting backwards and forwards in his chair. 'I've heard of you. At least I've read about you. I'm glad to meet you.'

'Very kind of you to say so,' French returned with a somewhat dry smile. 'I shall be glad to hear what you've got to tell me.'

'Yes,' went on the other seriously, as if giving a weighty opinion which must of necessity impress his hearers, 'I've read about you. I've read several of your cases. I've been much interested.'

French laughed outright. 'You will embarrass me, sir, if you're not careful,' he declared. 'This surely is fame.'

Mr Ewing nodded several times with quick, bird-like movements. 'Fame,' he repeated. 'Yes. I'm very much interested to meet you.'

With the corner of his eye French observed that Rhode was not appreciating this conversation as much as he might. There was no use annoying the superintendent, even in joke.

'This is very nice of you, Mr Ewing,' he said, 'but I'm afraid it won't help us with our business. Perhaps you will tell me what it was that you found.'

Again the little man twisted in his seat. 'Nothing much,' he returned; 'only a bicycle. It looked to me like an accident, you understand, or I'd never have mentioned it. But it certainly seemed like an accident.'

A bicycle! No wonder Rhode had given French an urgent call to hear the story. There were few things at that moment which French would be more pleased to discuss. But his interest could not have been deduced from his manner as he quietly asked: 'Where did you find it, sir?'

'It was this morning,' said Mr Ewing, frowning slightly. He was not going to have his story minimised by any unseemly haste. 'I am, you should understand, a writer: I write critical articles on shells; conchology, you know.'

'I know,' said French.

'I frequently walk along the shore in the search for specimens to illustrate my articles. I photograph them and make lantern slides and all that sort of thing. It involves a great deal of work.' The little man shook himself importantly. 'For some time I have wanted certain specimens for a little *brochure* I have recently completed. These are usually to be found just below low water. Now, as you are doubtless aware, it is low spring tides today, and I decided to go down and have a look among the rocks.'

'Dash it,' French thought, 'the pompous little ass has found a bicycle on the shore. Why can't he say so and be done with it?' To Mr Ewing, however, he merely said: 'Quite so, sir. I follow.'

'You are also doubtless aware—or perhaps you are not, inspector, if you are a stranger to the locality—that there is a section of the cliffs to the west of the town, about a mile out, where the beach is only uncovered during low springs, and then only in calm weather. It is a place where the particular shells I required are likely to be found, but unfortunately it is a place to which one can but seldom obtain access. Today, as being low spring tide and a perfectly flat calm, I decided to have a search. I went, and about halfway round the cliff I found the bicycle.'

'Where was it sir, exactly?'

'It was in a pool, just at the base of the cliff. It was completely covered with water, and I should not have seen it had I not stopped at the place to look for shells. It had evidently come down over the cliff, for it was buckled. I noticed also that it must have fallen quite recently, for the handles were quite bright.'

The little man was evidently extremely proud of his

observation, and French did not fail to compliment him upon it.

'Yes,' he went on complacently, 'I noticed that at once. Then it occurred to me that it was unlikely that a bicycle should have fallen over the cliff alone. I mean that some person had probably fallen also. That was why I came in here to tell the superintendent; lest there should have been an accident.'

'I think, sir,' said French, 'that you acted very wisely. Don't you think so, sir?' he turned to Rhode with the suspicion of a flicker in his left eye.

Rhode grunted and French went on: 'How high is the cliff at this point, would you say, Mr Ewing?'

The little man cocked his head on one side and assumed an expression of thought. 'Let me see,' he begged, 'quite high. I should say almost two hundred feet, and quite sheer.'

'Is there a road near it?'

'Yes, there is. The main road from here to Lydmouth runs along the top of the cliff, I suppose within a hundred yards of the edge. Would you say a hundred yards, superintendent?'

Rhode somewhat gruffly agreed.

'At that point,' Mr Ewing went on, 'the railway and the road have changed places. Most of the way to Lydmouth the railway runs along the shore and the road is inland. Here the railway goes inland to avoid the range of hills which makes the cliff.'

French nodded. Really, the little man wasn't doing so badly. His statement, if long-winded, was at least clear.

'I think, Mr Ewing,' French said, 'we must have a look at that bicycle. Is it likely to be still uncovered?'

Mr Ewing shook his head. 'Oh, no, you couldn't possibly go near it now. You won't get it for a fortnight, and then only if it's fine.'

French looked at Rhode. 'I'd better have a boat, sir, and perhaps Mr Ewing wouldn't mind coming out with us and showing us the place? Will you do that for us, Mr Ewing?'

'Certainly, but it's only fair to tell you that you won't find anyone very willing to take a boat out there among the rocks.'

French got up. 'Then we'd better go at once lest the wind should rise. What do you say, sir?'

Rhode nodded briefly. 'Yes, you'd better go now. You can get a boat from John Nesbit. If you tell him I'll guarantee any damage to his boat he'll raise no objection about going.

'You see, Mr Ewing, he'll not guarantee anything about our lives,' French smiled, as he shepherded the conchologist out of the room.

Though he had not shown it, French was extraordinarily interested in this story of Mr Ewing's. That this should be the bicycle which had been used by the presumed murderer of Ronald Ackerley seemed more than likely. French, indeed, wondered whether such a thing would not be too good to be true. To get so valuable a clue just as he was beginning to feel up against it would certainly be better luck than he was accustomed to. Yet for two distinct bicycles to be involved simultaneously in episodes interesting to the police would be perhaps an even greater coincidence.

He listened impatiently to what amounted almost to a lecture on conchology as he walked with his new friend to the harbour. At another time he would have been interested; the little man spoke well, but now he found it a strain even to make intelligent comments. The distance, however, was short, and soon he had made a bargain with John Nesbit for what was wanted.

French enjoyed that row, for there was not enough wind to make it worth while putting up a sail. The sky was clear, and the sun, though a little thin, made the sea an exquisite turquoise and whitened the chalk of the cliffs. There was scarcely a ripple on the water, and the air was almost warm. Another phenomenal piece of luck! At this time of year French might easily have had to wait several days for a chance to look for his clue.

Their two oarsmen rowed with that apparent absence of effort which always makes the landsman who tries an oar marvel at its weight. A few minutes brought them opposite the cliff, and then the bowman, passing his oar to his mate, took up a boat-hook and began to sound with it over the bows. Slowly they worked inshore, carefully avoiding the sharp spines of rock around which, even on this day of flat calm, the water lazily swirled and eddied.

'A little farther,' Mr Ewing directed; 'a little farther in and a little farther to the right. That's better. I should think this is about the place.'

While the oarsman pulled slowly backwards and forwards, Nesbit lowered a small three-pronged anchor overboard and began to move it up and down just above the bottom. It was a slow process, the hooks continually catching in rocks and seaweed and having to be painfully disentangled.

'I'm sorry,' Mr Ewing explained, 'that I wasn't able to

mark it. If I had had a cork and some string in my pocket I could have done so, but I hadn't. In any case I didn't think you would come out like this to get it.'

For a couple of hours they worked without result and then Nesbit pointed to the horizon, which had darkened somewhat.

'Wind out there,' he declared, 'and the swell's rising. If we don't get it soon, we won't get it at all. Sure it's not farther in, Mr Ewing?'

Mr Ewing believed not, but of course could not be sure to a yard.

'We'll try a little farther in if I don't get it this time,' Nesbit went on, tapping his anchor along the bottom. Then suddenly he called out: 'Hullo, what's this? By gosh, we've got it!'

He drew in his rope, and there, with its diamond frame hooked over one of the anchor prongs, was a bicycle with a badly buckled front wheel.

French could not wait till it was taken off the hook. He swung it round and glanced at the bottom of the left front fork.

Attached to it was a cyclometer, bent forward out of place.

Making no attempt to conceal his satisfaction, French congratulated Mr Ewing and the men, and their return to the harbour became a sort of triumphant progress. Arrived at the wharf, French telephoned for a police car to be sent down. On to this the bicycle was loaded.

'Can I run you home, Mr Ewing?' French asked politely.

The little man glanced at the car and declined. French, outwardly regretful, thereupon wished him good-day, and instructed the driver to run down to Downey's Point. There he fitted the cyclometer to the mark on the tree. It exactly registered.

Leaving the bicycle in the police station at Redchurch, French drove out along the Lydmouth road till he came to the cliff immediately above the spot at which they had carried out their salvaging operations. The road was bounded by a sod bank, and between it and the edge of the cliff the surface was covered with rough grass. Here French spent another couple of hours going over every inch of the ground across which the murderer might have passed, but again without result. He thought he saw where the bicycle had actually been thrown over, a slight scrape on the very edge, undoubtedly fresh, but there was nothing pointing to the man who had abandoned it.

To French it seemed that this finding of the bicycle removed the last shadow of doubt that Ackerley's death had been due to murder. The murderer, indeed, would have had to get rid of the machine. He had left it in the shrubbery above Downey's Point, possibly for some time, and there was always the chance that it might have been seen. If the finder were an observant person he might have been able to identify it again, and if a doubt arose as to the cause of Ackerley's death, such identification might have proved extremely awkward for the murderer. On the other hand, if the bicycle were secretly and finally disposed of, such a danger would be removed.

French returned to the police station in Redchurch and began a meticulous examination of the bicycle. As he did so he experienced a growing disappointment which became as keen, or keener, than his delight when the machine first appeared above the sea. After all, he did not think he was any farther on. There was here, he feared, no clue to the murderer. The bicycle, it was true, was not new, but it was of a standard make and there was nothing about it, save the bent cyclometer, to distinguish it from the thousands of other similar machines on the roads.

Then an idea suddenly occurred to him at which his depression fell away and he felt once more keen and eager.

Would it not, he wondered, be as dangerous for the murderer suddenly to get rid of his bicycle, as to keep it? More dangerous even? To keep it would at least not call attention to it, while to dispose of it would do so effectively.

If he were right in this, that the murderer had felt it would be dangerous not only to keep the bicycle, but also to get rid of a machine he was known to possess, did it not follow that he must have specially obtained the bicycle for this particular purpose? No doubt, if so, he had obtained it in some way in which he did not think he could be traced, but leaving that for the moment, would he not have obtained it?

French spent some time considering this point, during which a good deal of his keenness fell away. He was not so sure. It would probably be as dangerous to buy the bicycle as to get rid of it. He tried putting himself in the man's place, and he had to admit that he was not sure what he would do.

It was, however, certain that he *might* have bought it. And if so, would it not be worth while trying to follow up such a purchase? French did not hesitate long over the point. It would be worth while. It was a legitimate, indeed, a promising line of inquiry.

It was the kind of job French liked to delegate to subordinates. But on this occasion he could not do so; Rhode's men were too much occupied as it was. The next three days, therefore, French spent in painfully going round all the dealers in secondhand bicycles of whom he could hear, the suspect machine hidden in the back of his police van.

Though he did not think the murderer would have been such a fool as to put through his deal in a small place like Whitness, or even Redchurch, he combed these towns thoroughly before going farther afield. Lydmouth, he believed, was more hopeful. It was the largest town in the district, with a population of something over 50,000. Drychester, a few miles inland, was another possibility, and so was Exeter. In fact, as French grimly reminded himself, so was any town in Dorset or the surrounding counties.

Armed with a local directory, he set to work in Lydmouth. From shop to shop he drove his van, asking the proprietors to come out and inspect the bicycle and say whether they had ever seen it before. But when closing-time came and he had to knock off, he had had no luck.

Next morning he was early at work, going on from where he had left off on the previous night. For some hours longer he continued without result, then suddenly his search was rewarded.

Mr Peabody, principal of the small firm of John Peabody & Son, recognised the machine as one he had sold on the previous Saturday week, the Saturday previous to the murder.

'It was a good machine,' Mr Peabody declared, 'a thorough good machine, in first-class order and with all accessories, but secondhand, you know. It was easily worth five pounds, but I let it go for four. You have to let these secondhand machines go for less than they're really worth.'

'I suppose you have,' French said sympathetically. 'Whom did you sell it to, Mr Peabody?'

Mr Peabody shook his head. 'It may sound strange to you,' he answered, 'but I know no more than if it was the man in the moon.'

This was what, in a way, French had hoped to hear. At least it showed him that he was on the right track.

'How was that?' he asked.

'Never saw the man. Never laid eyes on him.'

'Ordered by letter?'

'Letter? No, not a stroke of writing about it.'

'Then how?'

'Telephone. I'll tell you. Will you come into the shop?'

French followed him through the small and dingy shop into the smaller and dingier office behind it. Mr Peabody lifted a stack of catalogues off the only chair and motioned French to sit down. French produced his cigarette-case. Mr Peabody waved it aside.

'Thanks; only smoke a pipe.' A cold pipe was lying on the paper-littered desk, and he thrust it into his mouth and after some difficulty lit it.

'About, let me see, about seven-thirty or a little later last Saturday week evening,' he went on, 'I was called up by someone whose voice I didn't know, asking if I sold second-hand bicycles, and if so, what was the best I could do for four pounds? I said I had a good Rudge-Whitworth, in first-class order, in fact, practically new and fitted with all accessories complete down even to the carbide in the lamp. The man said it sounded like what he wanted and could I let him have it at once for cash?'

'Did he give his name?'

'Yes; Mr Howard Wiliams, but he said I shouldn't know him as he was a stranger in the town. He said my shop had been recommended to him by a friend.'

'Any address?'

'No.'

'What sort of voice had he?'

'What sort of voice?'

'Yes: was it high or low-pitched; clear or throaty; or peculiar in any way?'

'It was a high-pitched voice; not very high, but higher than ordinary.'

'Any accent? Could you tell what part of the country he came from?'

Mr Peabody shook his head. 'Not except that it wasn't from anywhere I've ever been.'

'Disguised perhaps?'

This had not occurred to Peabody, but on consideration he somewhat hesitatingly admitted that it might have been.

'Very well. What happened then?'

'The man said he had started on a walking tour, but had decided to continue on a bicycle. He was leaving the town on the Monday and he would like to try the machine on the Sunday. He was engaged at the moment himself, but he would send a messenger for it at once. The messenger would have the four pounds and I could hand the machine over to him. If it turned out to his satisfaction, well and good; the deal would be over. If he didn't like it, he would bring it back on Monday morning and I would refund him his four pounds, less one day's hire and less cost of damage done, if any. Would I agree to that?'

'And did you?'

'Certainly I did. Why shouldn't I? It was fair enough.'

'Sounds perfectly fair. Well?'

'Well, I gave the bike a bit of a rub and set it aside and then in twenty minutes or so—about eight o'clock—a boy came in and said he was come for Mr Williams' bicycle and handed me an envelope. There were four notes in it, four Bank of England one-pound notes. That was all right. I gave the machine to the boy and he wheeled it out and that was the last I saw of it till you brought it back.'

French nodded. It was the kind of story he had expected to hear.

'Was the envelope addressed?'

'No, there was nothing on it.'

'I suppose you didn't keep it?'

Mr Peabody smiled a trifle crookedly. 'We keep some things that we maybe don't want,' he declared, glancing round the little office with its masses of dusty papers lying higgledy-piggledy over everything, 'but we draw the line at used envelopes.'

French grinned. 'I suppose it's natural,' he admitted. 'Who was the boy, Mr Peabody? You didn't by any chance know him?'

'Never set eyes on him before or since.'

'Well, I've got to find him. I'd be obliged if you'd give me the best description of him that you can.'

Mr Peabody's descriptive powers were not on a par with his gift for narration. French had to do a lot of detailed questioning, not only of the principal, but also of his two assistants, before he was able to form in his mind's eye an adequate picture of the messenger.

He was, it appeared, a youth of about twelve, of the labouring classes, if not what used to be called a street arab. He was tall and thin, with pale face, made paler still by his dark hair and eyes. A good-looking boy, dressed fairly neatly, though in patched clothes.

There was not much help in all this, and French was

therefore thankful when a further question brought out what really might prove a clue. The boy spoke in a very thin, high-pitched voice, as if his throat was somehow constricted.

'You would know him if you saw him again?'

Oh, yes, Mr Peabody would know him all right. Moreover, he would agree to see and if possible identify any boys whom French would present for his inspection.

On the whole not dissatisfied with his progress, French snatched a bit of lunch at a tea shop and immediately plunged into a second inquiry. This time schools were his objective. From his directory he made a list of all those in the neighbourhood of Peabody's shop. He hurried in order to get round as many as possible before they closed.

At the first school he saw the principal and put the case to him. The principal, as soon as he was assured that none of his pupils was 'wanted' on any charge, became helpful. It was on his suggestion that French, in the rôle of a school inspector, made a tour of the building and asked questions in history and mathematics of tall pale youths of about twelve. But none of those whose physical peculiarities answered the description spoke with a squeaky voice. Nor were any absentees tall and thin.

French's inquiries at the second school produced a similar negative result, but at the third he struck oil.

Here a thin, pale boy, asked if he knew a town on the River Mersey, replied in a squeak. French passed on, but when he left the class he had the boy sent for.

'This gentleman wants to ask you a few questions, Langton,' said the principal. 'Do your best to answer them. There's nothing wrong; you need not be in the least alarmed. I'll leave you here, Mr French. I have to get back to my class.'

'No, son, there's nothing wrong,' French said with a smile. 'I just want you to give me a bit of help. It really hasn't anything to do with you. Do you remember last Saturday week doing a job for someone? Something about a bicycle?'

The boy nodded and French breathed more freely. Then, with the aid of a good many questions, the story came out.

It appeared that about eight o'clock on the night in question he was walking past the corner of the street close to Messrs Peabody's establishment. The corner, in fact, was not more than twenty-five or thirty yards from the shop. A man was standing at the corner, and he called Langton over and asked him would he like to earn a tanner? The boy said he would. The man said: 'Well, take this note into Peabody's shop and ask for Mr Williams' bicycle and bring it out to me here. I'd go myself,' the man went on, 'only I have to meet a friend here, and if I went into the shop I might miss him.'

Langton thereupon went into the shop and delivered the envelope and message. A bicycle was handed to him and he wheeled it out to the man. The man thereupon gave him the tanner and he went home rejoicing.

'Had you ever seen the man before?'

'No, sir.'

'Then I want you to describe him.'

As in the case of Mr Peabody, the description was more easily asked for than obtained. French put in a tedious half-hour, at the end of which he had not a great deal to show for his work. The man was wearing his collar up about his ears and the brim of his hat turned down over his eyes, and Langton could not see much of his face. There was, moreover, a lamp-post at the immediate spot, and the light came down so directly that what was visible of the face was in shadow from the hat brim. The man, however, was tallish and stout, and was dressed in a fawn-coloured waterproof and soft sports hat. He had a black moustache and wore black-rimmed spectacles. His voice was rather high-pitched and he spoke in a queer sort of way, though French's most painstaking efforts failed to discover wherein the queerness lay.

Though all this was not as much as French would have liked, he recognised that it was more than he could reasonably have expected. He did not know how far it would help him to trace the unknown, particularly as several of the items of his appearance suggested a disguise, but at least there was something on which to work. On his way to the station he visited the Lydmouth telephone exchange to ask that all calls for Messrs Peabody's establishment between 7.20 and 7.50 p.m. on the previous Saturday week should if possible be traced. It was an inquiry from which he did not expect much result, feeling that a man who had so well covered his traces in other particulars, would not have given himself away in this simple manner. However, there was always hope, and in any case it could not be neglected.

Tired, but pleased with his progress, French returned to Redchurch.

6

Progress

When, that evening, French came to compare Langton's description of the purchaser of the bicycle with his recollections of the engineering staffs on the Widening, he found the result was not particularly illuminating. If the unknown were really tall and stout, and not merely made up to appear so, it could not have been Parry, who was of medium height and slight, nor yet Pole, who was the same. Nor could it have been Templeton, the contractors' time-keeper, who, though tall, was very thin. On the other hand, Bragg, Carey, and Lowell were all big men. While, therefore, it by no means followed that the unknown was one of these three, they were the most likely persons who had yet come into the picture, and French felt that they should be the subjects of his preliminary inquiries. French discounted the moustache and glasses as being too like a disguise to be taken seriously. Carey, it was true, wore both, but his moustache was small and his glasses were *pince-nez*, not spectacles. Neither of the others had a moustache.

Incidentally these glasses and moustache might, if they were really part of a disguise, prove useful clues. French took a note that if he did not soon get what he wanted, he would try to trace their sale.

Another obvious point that would no doubt be helpful was that the murderer, so far as present information went, was down in the working quarter of Lydmouth at eight o'clock on the Saturday evening prior to the crime. Where were all the possibles at this hour? French saw that the investigation of this alibi would be quite as important as that for the time of the murder itself.

Well, then, to get down to it.

Of the three, Bragg, Carey, and Lowell, with whom he had decided to start, Bragg at a guess seemed the most promising. He had come more closely in contact with Ackerley than had either of the others, and was therefore more likely to have become involved with him in some nefarious association. With Bragg, then, he would begin.

A telephone to headquarters revealed the fact that Bragg was at Whitness, and half and hour later, thanks to a convenient 'bus, French was knocking at the office door. Bragg himself opened it. He invited French in and nodded when he heard his business.

'Parry told me you were looking into the affair,' he said. 'Would it be indiscreet to ask what's supposed to be amiss?'

French hesitated. 'The chief constable is not very satisfied that the affair was an accident,' he explained. 'I have been instructed to make sure.'

'But what does he suspect? Not suicide surely?'

'No, not suicide.' French looked very searchingly at the engineer. 'As a matter of fact, he wants to be sure it was not foul play.'

Bragg was apparently very much impressed. He stared incredulously. 'Foul play? Good Lord, inspector! Do you mean *murder*? You don't really suspect that?'

French shrugged. 'That was what occurred to him, Mr Bragg. I'm trying to pick up information about it. Hence my visit.'

'But,' Bragg seemed almost bereft of speech, 'but who would want to murder Ackerley? Why, he was a general favourite. Everybody liked him. I can't imagine anyone wishing him harm.'

'If the truth be told, neither can I,' French admitted. 'However, orders are orders, and I must make my inquiries. Now, Mr Bragg. I want you, please, to answer a few questions.'

'Of course, inspector. I'll tell you anything I can. But you mustn't mind my saying that I'm sure you're on the wrong track. What exactly do you want to know?'

French wanted to know a great deal. He began with a series of questions about Ackerley himself, his character, habits, associations and peculiarities, following these up with similar inquiries about those with whom the deceased had been brought in contact by his work. Bragg answered freely enough, but nothing that he said seemed of much help. Most of it simply substantiated what French had already learnt from other sources, and what was new was unimportant.

These questions, however, while potentially useful in themselves were really only preliminary. To his vital inquiry French now turned: Where was Bragg at the time of the murder?

Bragg's expression, which up to this had indicated surprise and interest, now changed subtly. It became alert and watchful, and the man seemed to French to be weighing his answers as he had not done at first.

'I can tell you that quite easily,' he replied with only a slight hesitation. 'I was here.'

'Here?'

'Yes. I was in the office all that afternoon up till the time the ballast engine left.'

'I understand, sir. You were working?'

'Of course I was working. I was finishing the certificate. Do you know what the certificate is?'

'I have an idea.'

'Well, Monday was the day the certificate had to be finished, and it was because it was not finished at the usual time that Parry and I missed our train and went by the ballast engine.'

'Quite so.' French paused, then went on: 'Now, we officers are not allowed to take unsupported statements. Can you give me any confirmation of this?'

Bragg was now looking definitely uneasy. His pause this time was very distinct.

'I don't think I can, inspector,' he said slowly. 'I was alone, you see. I was here about half-past four when Ackerley and Parry left to go out along the Widening, and I was here about half-past five when Parry returned. Parry can prove these statements. But for the time between . . .' Once more Bragg sat in silence. 'No, I'm afraid no one came in during that time. You'll have to take my word for it . . . or do the other.'

French also sat in silence. 'It's rather important, Mr Bragg,' he said at last. 'I wish you could think of something.'

Bragg shrugged. 'You don't wish it as much as I do. But it's too late. If I could have foreseen that the information would have been required, nothing would have been easier than to have got it. I had only to go over and chat with the men in the contractors' office. But then, I didn't know.'

'I see the difficulty,' French admitted. 'What were you doing during that hour?'

'What I told you; working at the certificate.'

'Can you not tell me in more detail?'

'Yes, if you want me to. It was Parry's job at that time to take out the quantities of earthwork, cut and fill. He summed these and gave me the figures. I entered the figures in the certificate, priced them and extended them. You understand?'

French nodded.

'Now, in checking over the amount of sea pitching which had been laid during the period of this certificate, it seemed high. I thought a mistake might have been made and I was afraid to include it. I sent Parry out to check over the measurements. But this involved Parry's leaving the office before he had completed the earthwork. I finished it for him. That occupied me during most of the hour, though I also did some more work on the certificate itself.'

French felt grimly amused at the turn the conversation was taking. Actually it seemed as if he, French, was trying to prove his suspect innocent against the man's own will. French, however, was really out for truth, not for a victim, and if Bragg was innocent the sooner he was off the list of suspects the better.

'Can you prove that you did that work during that hour?' he asked.

Bragg shrugged. 'How could I? I was alone.' He paused, then went on: 'Wait a minute; perhaps I can. Would Parry's testimony constitute proof?'

'It might, under certain circumstances,' French replied cautiously.

'Parry ought to be able to prove it. He knows how much he had left undone, and of course he knows I finished his work.'

'We'll ask him. In the meantime, I want you to show me exactly what you did.'

Bragg had at last seemed to realise what was in French's mind. It was with some eagerness that he went to the cupboard and produced a book of cross-sections. He must, French thought, have been more anxious than he appeared. He dumped down the book before French and turned over the pages.

'Here it is,' he said. 'You see these cross-sections, taken all along the railway, one at every hundred feet? Now, you see these little coloured areas on them?'

French saw them.

'These coloured areas represent the amount of cutting or filling removed or deposited during the four-weekly periods for which the certificates are issued. There's a separate colour for each period. Now let's see.' He turned over the pages. 'Here,' he pointed to Section 118, 'is where Parry stopped. I finished from 119 to the end. You can see that from the work. We always keep the original sheets.' From the cupboard he got a sheet of foolscap paper covered with calculations. It showed two handwritings. Up to Section 118 it was in one, and from 119 on in another. 'That first work is Parry's, the second is mine.'

French nodded. 'I'm going to ask you, Mr Bragg, to do that work again. I think it would be worth your while: just to repeat exactly what you did that evening while Mr Parry was out of the office.'

Bragg was very willing. 'While you time?' he said. 'I'll be delighted. All the same I don't think it is going to help you. How do you know that I won't do it twice as slowly this time?'

French smiled. 'I'll take my chance of that,' he declared.

Apart from the point at issue, French was interested to watch Braggs's proceedings. He got some foolscap paper and took from a box a strange-looking little instrument consisting of polished rods, pointed feet, and a small graduated wheel. 'A planimeter,' said Bragg, answering French's look.

'Now,' said Bragg, 'you needn't count the time of preparation, because all these things were ready to my hand. Start now.'

French noted the time, then watched the work. Bragg, having written down the number of the section on a sheet of foolscap, took the planimeter, planted it on the sections on its sharpened feet, then pushed a stylus round certain coloured areas. The wheel, being thus dragged about the paper, rotated backwards and forwards as it moved, and the reading on its scale before and after the operation enabled Bragg to obtain the area. Very quick and ingenious, French thought.

Bragg, having entered his result, went on to the next section. When all were done he summed them up with the comptometer, added two noughts, reduced the cubic feet to yards and entered it on a large blue form.

'I have to suppose now that all these squares contain figures of money,' he said. 'There are seventy-two of them. I add with the comptometer. Then I complete this part of the certificate and also complete a duplicate.' He went through the motions, wrote in a number of other details and signed his name; all twice over. 'How long, inspector?'

'Fifty-seven minutes, Mr Bragg.'

'Well, there you are. I couldn't have done that and left the office.'

French was satisfied enough as to that. If Bragg had really done all that work in the period in question, he certainly would not have had time to ride out to Downey's Point and murder Ackerley.

But had Bragg done it?

'Now, Mr Bragg, without your speaking to him, I'm going to ask Mr Parry to do the same job. Will he be in here this morning?'

Bragg laughed. 'I see,' he said. 'I wondered how you'd satisfy yourself. Yes, Parry's due at any time and you can get him to do what you like. There's the paper, if you care to sit down and wait for him.'

'Thank you, but there's one other question that I may as well ask when I'm here. Where were you, Mr Bragg, between half-past seven and eight on Saturday evening week, that was the Saturday before Mr Ackerley's death?'

French, though usually exceedingly sharp in such cases, could not tell if this came as a shock to the victim. Bragg's manner certainly expressed just the surprise natural under the circumstances.

'Saturday evening week,' Bragg repeated. 'How do you expect me to be able to answer that now? Let's see.' He thought or simulated thought. 'On that Saturday afternoon I went out sailing and in the evening—yes, I remember. My wife and the child went out to her mother's; there was some children's do on. I was asked, but I hate those sort of things and I didn't go. I stayed at home and read a novel: I was tired after the sailing.'

'Were you alone in the house?'

'Yes, the servant goes out on Saturdays.'

'And can you let me have any confirmation of that?'

Bragg was now making little effort to hide his uneasiness. 'No, I'm afraid I can't. My wife and the child can prove I was there when they went out about seven and when they came back about ten, but I can't prove anything about the time between.'

'Where do you live, Mr Bragg?'

'In Howard Street, Lydmouth.'

While French had to admit to himself that Bragg's statement was reasonable and might well be the truth, it was equally evident that it might be an invention and that he might have bought the bicycle. Moreover, if he were guilty he would doubtless have devised some kind of alibi for the time of the murder, but it would probably not have occurred to him to do so for the time he was making the purchase. He would not have believed that the transaction would become known. There was, however, nothing more to be said for the moment and French read his paper till Parry appeared.

'Look here, young Parry,' Bragg greeted him, 'the inspector wants you to do tricks for him. I'll leave you this office, inspector. I have to go down to the viaduct.'

Parry came in and French explained what he wanted. Parry was no fool and obviously realised what was behind the request. He whistled below his breath, washed his hands and sat down before the sections.

'Where exactly did you stop work that afternoon when you went to measure the pitching?' French began.

'We can see that,' Parry returned. 'The actual work for the certificates is always kept in case some question should arise. It's in this book.' He turned to the sheet Bragg had already exhibited. 'The work in that handwriting is mine,' he explained, 'the rest is Bragg's.'

'Very well, Mr Parry. Would you mind doing what Mr Bragg did. I want to see how long it takes.'

Parry worked in the same way as Bragg, though not so quickly. He was evidently doing as well as he could, yet he took sixty-five minutes. Here was convincing proof that Bragg had worked fairly. French was satisfied that the work could not have been done in much less than an hour.

'Now,' French went on, 'do you know of your own knowledge—this is very important, remember, and you may have to swear to it in court—do you *know* that Mr Bragg had finished that work when you came back from measuring up the pitching, and before you left for the ballast engine?'

'Oh, yes, I know that all right.' Parry spoke confidently. 'He had inked in the earthwork total on the certificate. He couldn't have done that without finishing the sections.'

This seemed pretty conclusive to French. He turned it slowly over in his mind, searching for loopholes. Parry's voice interrupted him.

'There's a way in which you can be quite sure that Bragg finished the certificate, inspector,' he was saying. 'I forgot about it until just now. Bragg gave me the certificate that night and asked me to send it to the divisional offiice, as he didn't want to spend the time going round there on arrival in Lydmouth. I put it in the driver's box on the ballast engine. In the upset of Ackerley's death I forgot about it and left it there. It was found by the driver when he was going off duty and handed first thing in the morning to Mr Clay, the stationmaster at Redchurch. It was labelled, of course, and Clay forwarded it to the office. The driver told me about it next day and I at once made inquiries as to whether it had been safely received. So you see Bragg had no opportunity of altering it after he left the office. If it hadn't been complete then the accountant would have raised hell about it.'

This, if true, settled the matter. French was, however, leaving nothing to chance and he took a note to see Driver Blake and Stationmaster Clay before finally accepting the alibi. In the meantime he might take the opportunity to get Parry's statement as to his own movements during the two periods in question.

But Parry had very little to tell him. With regard to the Monday afternoon of the murder he simply repeated his statement at the inquest: he had parted from Ackerley at the sea pitching, had carried out his measurements, and had then hurried directly back to the office. Unfortunately he was not seen on the way. The working day being officially over, the line was deserted.

The previous Saturday evening he had spent, so he said, in his rooms. He had taken a long walk in the afternoon and like Bragg, being tired, he had remained in after supper. He thought his landlady could vouch for this, but he wasn't absolutely sure.

Though French took a note to interview the landlady, he did not really suspect Parry, principally because of the evidence of the boy, Langton.

On his way to his hotel French saw Clay, the Redchurch stationmaster, and obtained complete confirmation of Parry's statement about the sending in of the certificate.

As after dinner that night French sat considering his day, he gradually came to the definite conclusion that Bragg's alibi was sound. At half-past four on the afternoon of the crime an hour's work at the certificate remained undone. At half-past five this work was finished. It must have been complete then, because it was impossible that it could have been done later. There was no one but Bragg to do it. Therefore Bragg was in the hut during the critical period. Therefore, Bragg was innocent.

That same evening French received news that what might have proved a useful clue had petered out. The telephone call ordering the bicycle from Peabody had been traced. It had come from a box at the railway station, and the report said that this box was placed in such a dark corner that it was most unlikely that the caller had been seen entering or leaving.

Though French decided that he would inquire among the station staff, he felt he need not hope for a favourable result.

Next morning French took an early train to Whitness to resume his inquiries into the alibis of his suspects.

He reached the contractors' office to find that both Carey and Lowell were out, though working in the technical office were Pole, the junior, and Templeton, the timekeeper. For the same reason as in the case of Parry, that they did not comply with Langton's description, French did not really suspect either of these men. However, not only for the sake of thoroughness, but to distract attention from his real suspects, he asked both of them his questions.

Templeton, according to his own story, had alibis on both occasions. On the Monday he was working in the office till after six, and as some of the clerical staff had also worked late that night, they could vouch for the fact. On the Saturday he had supper in his rooms in Whitness about seven, going out about eight to some billiard rooms. Several people saw him there between eight and half past.

French noted these particulars in case a check became necessary and turned his attention to Pole. Pole didn't think he had any alibi for the Monday night. After leaving the office he had gone straight to 'Serque', the house at which he and Carey and Lowell shared rooms. He had not, however, seen anyone on arrival, and he did not think anyone knew that he was there. But on Saturday he had an alibi. He had dined with Lowell at 'Serque' at seven o'clock, and though they had afterwards gone out, this had not been till nearly eight o'clock.

If this were true both Lowell and Pole were cleared.

From Templeton, confirmed as far as he was able by Pole, French then obtained a note of the movements of the other members of the staff. On that afternoon of Ackerley's death Carey, Lowell, Pole and Templeton were all working in the office. About five o'clock Carey went out. Lowell followed almost immediately and Pole a few minutes later. Templeton, as already stated, had not finished and remained on, working alone. About six Carey returned, saw that nothing had come in, and left again almost at once. Both Carey and Lowell, Pole stated, were present at dinner at 'Serque' at seven.

From both men French also learned that while Lowell was in a perfectly normal frame of mind, Carey had that afternoon seemed irritable and as if some trouble was weighing on his spirits. Contrary to his habit, he had gone without any remark as to where he might be found. Next day this irritation had again been in evidence, in fact, Carey had never completely recovered his normal good humour. In answer to another question Pole stated that

Carey had not been in to dinner on the previous Saturday and had mentioned afterwards that he had gone to a theatre in Lydmouth.

All this made French prick up his ears hopefully. He determined to be specially careful in his approach to Carey.

At this point Lowell appeared. He stared in a rather unfriendly way at French, but led the way to Carey's private office when the latter asked for an interview.

Lowell made no difficulty about answering French's questions and his answers confirmed what Templeton and Pole had said, so far as they covered the same ground. While Lowell had a complete alibi for the Saturday evening, he had none for the Monday. During the time the murder took place, Lowell, according to his own story, was walking along the Whitness front. He had, he said, been working in the office practically the whole of that day and had got a headache. Instead, therefore, of going straight to 'Serque' he had taken a walk. Unfortunately no one, so far as he knew, had seen him and he was therefore unable to prove his statement.

French had scarcely finished questioning Lowell when Carey entered the office. Lowell introduced French and with a 'That all I can do for you, inspector?' vanished, leaving French alone with Carey.

With the first glance French noted how completely the contractors' chief resident engineer answered the description of the boy, Langton. His pronounced Irish accent also might well have represented what the boy called speaking in a queer way, moreover, his voice was rather high pitched. When French remembered that Carey had seemed preoccupied immediately before and since the crime, and had vanished between five and six on Monday and during the whole of the evening on Saturday, he felt himself looking forward with keen interest to his interview.

Carey professed no surprise at the questions, saying he had heard that inquiries into the matter were in progress. Nor did he seem to resent the personal nature of the questions. His eye, however, grew extremely wary and he obviously gave careful thought to his answers.

His story accounted for the facts, but left French very far from convinced. He said that on the Monday of the accident he received a letter from a friend, a lady, asking him to meet her at the Whirlpool Cave at quarter past five that night, in order to discuss some private business. This Whirlpool Cave was situated at Blackness, a headland of dark rock along the shore about a mile east of Whitness, that was, in the opposite direction to Redchurch. It was reached by a cliff path, a favourite walk in the summer, but deserted at this time of year. As the business was somewhat unpleasant, Carey had been a good deal worried during the day, but he never questioned that it was his duty to keep the appointment. He left the office, therefore, a minute or two before five and walked out. He reached the cave in good time, but there was no one there. Thinking that the lady was late, he waited. He waited for half an hour, till quarter to six. Then he supposed she had changed her mind and wasn't coming, though he felt rather surprised as it was unlike her not to keep her appointments. He returned to the office, made sure that nothing of importance had come in, and went on to 'Serque', where he dined with the others.

French then made his second little speech about the need for confirmation. Carey shook his head.

'The boys'll tell you when I left the office and when I got back,' he said, 'or Templeton will anyway, for he was there both times. But if it's confirmation about me being out at the Whirlpool Cave you're wanting, I have me doubts about your getting it.'

'Did no one see you either there or on the way?'

'Never a one, at least not so far as I saw.'

French leaned forward and his manner became more urgent. 'This is an important matter, Mr Carey,' he declared, 'an important matter both for you and for me. It's necessary that I should have some confirmation of your story. That doesn't mean that I doubt it; it means that this is a murder case and that every statement connected with it must be tested. Please think again. Try and remember something to help.'

Carey shrugged. 'Sure now, inspector, you wouldn't be having me remember things that never happened? I would give you all the confirmation in the world, only there isn't any.'

'Did you get into communication with the lady afterwards?'

'I did.'

'And what did she say about not turning up?'

'It was all a mistake. She hadn't written the letter at all.'

French glanced at him sharply. 'Not written it? Then who had?'

'Ah, now, if I could tell you that you'd know more than I do meself.'

'You've no idea?'

'No more than the babe unborn.'

'Have you got the letter?'

For the first time Carey hesitated. 'I might have,' he

admitted unwillingly, 'but it hasn't anything to do with what you're asking me.'

'Nothing to do with it? It seems to me it has everything to do with it.'

'It has to do with me going out to the Whirlpool Cave, but it hasn't anything to do with Ackerley's death.'

'You don't know that,' French returned with some sharpness. 'I'm afraid, Mr Carey, I'll have to ask you to show me that letter.'

Carey drew back and again shook his head. 'Sure now, you wouldn't be asking me to show you a lady's private letter and it be totally beside the point at issue?'

'But you've just said she didn't write it,' French pointed out.

'Neither she did.'

'Then it's not her letter and she couldn't object to your showing it to me.'

Carey wouldn't admit this reasoning and an argument ensued. Carey said that the lady would object because the letter was about her. French said he didn't mind whether she objected or not, that the letter might be about the case and he must see it.

'You don't realise the position, Mr Carey,' he said at last with grave emphasis. 'Mr Ackerley has been murdered. Someone is going to be charged with that murder. On the chance of that person being yourself, you have a right to refuse to answer my questions. On those grounds do you wish to avail yourself of that right?'

This was an approach to bluff on French's part, but Carey took it seriously.

'Will the letter be kept confidential?' he asked.

'No,' said French, 'not if it should prove to be material

evidence about the murder. If it proves not to be connected with the murder, I can give you my word it will be kept secret.'

Carey was clearly shaken. He considered for a moment, then slowly took a letter from his pocket and handed it over. It was typed on a sheet of medium quality note paper headed 'Serque, Whitness, Dorset,' with in smaller print in the left hand corner, 'Telephone Whitness 73,' and read:

> 'DEAR MR CAREY,
>
> 'I am in very great trouble through one of your assistants and wonder if you would be so good as to help me with your advice. I shall be at the Whirlpool Cave, Blackness, at 5.15 tonight and would be so grateful if you could meet me. I should not keep you long. Please keep our meeting private for obvious reasons.
>
> 'Yours unhappily,
>
> 'BRENDA VANE.'

The signature was written in a woman's hand.

That this effusion was not genuine appeared obvious to French upon the face of it, and when he examined the signature with a lens he found his idea substantiated. The writing was a mass of tiny shakes, showing that it had not been written boldly, but slowly and laboriously; in other words, it was a forgery. He could indeed scarcely imagine how anyone could be taken in by it.

'Who is Brenda Vane?' he asked.

'Miss Vane is the daughter of the lady who runs "Serque"; the younger daughter; there are two of them.'

'And is that her handwriting?'

'I thought so till she said it wasn't.'

'It's "Serque" paper all right?'

'It is certainly.'

'And did you really believe that the lady was in trouble as she suggests and that she wanted to see you about it?'

Carey hesitated. 'Well, I'll tell you,' he said confidentially. 'I didn't believe she was in the sort of trouble you mean. I thought it was maybe something about money; not paying the bill or something of that kind.' He moved uneasily, then continued: 'I may as well tell you, inspector, that I was bothered about it. I didn't know whether she had written it or whether she hadn't. But anyway, I thought I'd best go out for fear she might have.'

Put like this, Carey's action seemed reasonable enough. His statement might be quite true. On the other hand he might as easily have written the letter himself to account for his absence from the office during the critical period. French nodded.

'With your permission I'll keep this letter. I might be able to trace the sender.'

Carey agreed without protest and French, seeing there was no more to be made of that line, turned to the Saturday evening.

Here Carey's statement was equally reasonable and equally unsatisfactory. He had, he said, gone in the Widening car to Lydmouth on business with his tailors and he had seen the bills of a variety show in the Lydmouth Empire and stayed on for it. He had acted out of mere whim because there was nothing to bring him back to Whiteness.

With regard to confirmation, his tailors could, of course, check up the call. The attendant at the park where he had left his car should also remember him. He had bought a ticket for a stall and it was conceivable that someone in the theatre had noticed him. He could not tell. The inspector doubtless would make inquiries if he thought it worth while.

French noted all possible lines of inquiry, then set himself to dispel any uneasiness the interview might have aroused in Carey's mind. He put forward the idea that the murderer had planted the letter on Carey to destroy his alibi, in the hope that Carey might be suspected, and tried to make him believe that it was on these lines that he was going to work.

He was slightly surprised at Carey's reaction all through. Carey had not at any time appeared to grasp that the affair might have serious consequences for himself. He evidently considered it important and as such gave it his grave consideration, but he seemed to do this impersonally, as if the importance was for someone else.

Leaving the contractors' yard, French walked up the town to the police station and saw Sergeant Emery.

'We got the bicycle all right, sergeant,' he said pleasantly. 'You had my message cancelling your investigations on the point?'

'Yes, sir, but I'm continuing the other inquiries.'

'Good man. Can you tell me anything about "Serque" and the people who live there?'

'Not a great deal I'm afraid, sir. "Serque" is situated on the sea front, towards the west end of the town and stands in its own small grounds. It's not a very large house, but it's very well run and attracts a good class of visitor. Mrs Vane, who keeps it with her two daughters, was the wife of a dean and is well connected. Messrs Carey, Lowell and Pole are staying there. As far as is known, all three are hard working, good living gentlemen, and are well spoken of in the town. They're members of the local club and go there a good deal in the evenings. Constable Morton got in touch with the servant; went out in plain clothes and took her to the pictures, and he gathered from her that there's trouble there; that two of the gentlemen, Mr Carey and Mr Lowell, are soft on the second daughter, Miss Brenda. How much there's in that I don't know.'

'She must be an attractive young woman.'

'She's attractive looking right enough,' Emery admitted cautiously.

For the next few days French busied himself in the tedious work of checking, so far as he was able, the statements he had listened to. First he called at 'Serque' and saw Brenda Vane, coming at the same time to the conclusion that both Carey and Lowell were men of taste. Brenda absolutely denied knowledge of the letter. She had not written it, and she had no idea who might have done so or its possible object.

None of French's efforts to trace the author bore fruit. The paper anyone could have got. A call on someone known by the caller to be out and a request for a sheet of paper on which to write a note, would have been followed by an invitation to the writing-room, and any number of sheets could have been secreted. It was true, however, that Brenda did not know that such a call had been made. Samples from Brenda's typewriter and from those in the railway and contractors' offices proved that the letter had not been done on any of them. Nor did searches of his suspects' rooms bring to light any hidden machines. Carey unfortunately had not kept the envelope and the postmark was, therefore, not available.

A painstaking search for anyone who was on the cliff walk to Blackness about the time of the murder, and who therefore might have met Carey had he gone to the Whirlpool Cave, produced no result. This left Carey's alibi in the air so far as the Monday was concerned. There was, however, a considerable amount of confirmation as to his story of his movements on the Saturday. The tailors stated that he had called with them at half-past four, leaving shortly before five. A waitress in a teashop remembered his coming in for tea, she believed, shortly after five. The attendant at the car park testified that he had parked shortly after four, removing the car shortly after eight. Pressed as to the exact time at which Carey had returned, the attendant became vague. He could not say exactly; it might have been as early as eight or as late as nine. Finally, the door attendant at the music-hall remembered seeing Carey enter for the first or 6.15 house.

All this testimony confirmed Carey's statement in general, but not on the particular point that mattered. So far as French had learned, there was nothing to have prevented Carey from going to the bar during an interval, and instead of returning to his seat, slipping unseen from the building and purchasing the bicycle. He might have ridden it to a quiet quarter, hidden it in some convenient place, gone back for the car and then either put the bicycle into the car and taken it to Downey's Point, or made two journeys, one with the car and the other with the bicycle. On the other hand, there was not the slightest scintilla of proof that he had done so.

Nor was there any proof as to the truth of Carey's statement about the letter; whether he had really received it through the post or written it himself. That it had been typed on an old machine was obvious from certain defects in the type, but French was unable to find the machine. On the whole he was inclined to believe the story. Supposing Carey were anxious to build up an alibi, would he not have chosen someone to help him other than the girl with whom he was in love? Firstly, he would never have exposed her to the annoyance of testifying on his behalf in a police court, and secondly, he would recognise that her statement there wouldn't carry much weight. He would see that it would be argued that she was in love with him and was perjuring herself to save him. Further, if he really were in love with her, would he not have thought of some other reason for her meeting him than that she was in trouble through one of his assistants?

As the days passed on French grew very worried. Here was a murder, and on the first and most important question, that of motive, he had drawn a complete blank.

On the second question, that of opportunity, he had done a little better. Carey was a possibility. He was indeed, French believed, the only possibility, though even in his case the evidence was far from satisfactory. Of all others who from *a priori* reasoning might be guilty, there was either definitely negative evidence or no evidence at all.

Finally he decided to go to town and pursue his inquiries at the contractors' headquarters. It did not seem a very promising line, but some chance remark might be dropped which would give him the idea for which he was in search.

7

The Day's Work

While French was engaged thus unprofitably in his researches into the death of Ackerley, work on the Widening was steadily progressing. For Parry indeed these last few days had been outstanding. A great event had happened in his life which, to do him justice, he had neither expected nor foreseen. Marlowe, the chief, had called him to Lydmouth and asked him if he thought he could take Ackerley's place as resident engineer, and ten minutes later Parry found himself appointed. To replace Parry a new junior had to be taken on, a man named Ashe, fresh from college.

A second event which was to prove of more importance to Parry than at first he realised was his making the acquaintance of Brenda Vane. A couple of days after his appointment he had unexpectedly to work out all night at a slip, and to save his going back to Lydmouth Lowell asked him to dine and spend the evening at 'Serque'. Parry accepted thankfully.

After dinner in the large first floor sitting-room which

the three contractors' men had in common, Carey and Pole went out, leaving Parry and Lowell alone. They sat on either side of the blazing fire and had just started a desultory discussion on the prospects of that season's rugger, when the door opened and Brenda Vane entered, a tray in her hand.

She was a pretty girl of about five and twenty. Tall and with a really remarkable carriage, and she had the fair hair and blue eyes of the northern races. Her expression was pleasant and kindly, but her slightly too heavy chin showed that she was one who would get her own way or know the reason why.

Lowell sprang to his feet. 'Brenda!' he exclaimed delightedly. 'This is goo—' Then remembering his visitor, 'This is my friend, Parry. Miss Brenda Vane.'

The girl came forward and held out her hand.

'How do you do, Mr Parry? I've often heard your name being—what does Mr Carey say?—miscalled.'

'Sure what else? That's what old Carey would say. Yes, I'm afraid Parry's not been reverenced as you'd expect now you've seen him. Has the excellent Kate gone out?'

'She's gone to a bun worry, again according to Mr Carey. A social connected with her church.'

'Good for Kate,' said Lowell heartily. 'I say, Brenda, it's a lovely night,' He paused and entreaty shone in his eyes. 'There's a clinking moon and the roads are dry.' Another pause. 'Parry and I were going for a walk, but we want someone to take care of us and hold our hands. What about it, Brenda? A good tramp round Blackness; the three of us?'

Brenda was dubious, but finally agreed, and fifteen minutes later the three young people strode off along the deserted front, their footsteps ringing out sharply above the gentle murmur of the waves. Round the ness the path twisted and turned through the broken rocks, now rising, now falling, now bridging the entrance to a gully or cave in which the water swirled lazily. Of these openings, the biggest was the Whirlpool Cave. The path was no place for a dark night, but the moon gave just enough light for safety. Then the walkers climbed the four hundred odd feet to the top of the cliff, stopping to look at the lights of a steamer far out in the bay and to watch the winking eyes of the lighthouses on the adjoining headlands, east and west.

This walk seemed to draw the three together and when Parry bid the others goodnight on his way to the station, he felt as if he had known Brenda as long as Lowell.

On the Tuesday morning following this meeting with Brenda, Parry set off to work at his usual hour. He had just moved into rooms in Redchurch, Bragg having insisted that Lydmouth as a headquarters was too far off for the Widening resident engineer, while objecting to Whitness on the ground that he didn't want Parry to see too much of the contractors' men in the evenings. As Parry paced the platform waiting for the 8.20 a.m. from Lydmouth, he thought how completely he had stepped into Ackerley's shoes and Ashe into his. Here he was waiting at Redchurch as Ronnie had waited, and Ashe would be in the train, as he himself had formerly been. They would travel together to Whitness as he and Ronnie had travelled, and then he would take the interesting jobs as Ronnie used to do, leaving the measuring and dull calculations to Ashe, who was proud and glad to get them.

They reached the office at Whitness and set to work.

Having attended to the correspondence, Parry took out his notebook and considered his plans for the day. If he walked through the Widening he could get lunch at Redchurch and return with Bragg, who was coming down in the afternoon. He had several small things to look at and he saw that if he were to get through his programme he must start at once.

It was a bright sunny morning, though very cold. There had been frost and the ground was still hard. The wind was northerly and the sea, sheltered by land, showed scarcely a ripple. Parry thought he had never seen the horizon so sharp. Right out on it a big steamer was creeping up Channel.

Parry walked smartly, stopping at intervals to inspect the work and talk to the foreman in charge. At one place he came on the contractors' entire engineering staff.

Some quarter of a mile beyond Downey's Point the railway bank cut off a small and unclean swamp from the sea. This swamp had been euphemistically named 'The Lily Pond.' It was drained by a small bridge through which the sea ebbed and flowed at spring tides. To save the cost of widening the bridge it had been decided to replace it by a three-foot culvert and valve. The putting in of this culvert was in progress.

Instead of shoring the line up on timbers, cutting down through the embankment, building the culvert in the old-fashioned way, and refilling the earth on the top of the work, pipes to form the culvert were being jacked through the bank. The first section of pipe had a steel cutting edge, and the remaining lengths, of reinforced concrete, were added one by one as the pipe lengthened. Inside the pipe, as it slowly advanced, a man cut out the earth core and worked it out in tiny trucks. The job was interesting to Parry, as he had never seen anything like it done before.

Standing watching the work were Carey, Lowell and Pole. Carey hailed Parry.

'Here's another of these blessed jacks after giving up on us,' he complained, pointing to the offending implement. 'I never saw the equal of the muck that Loco. Department of yours sends out under the name of tools.'

'Don't look a loan horse in the mouth, Carey,' Parry advised, climbing down the embankment. 'One thing'll be all right at all events, and that's the bill you'll get for breaking it.'

'Breaking it?' rejoined Carey. 'Sure the thing would break if you put it under a tin of biscuits, and it supposed to lift the quarter of an engine. What are you going to do about it?'

'It's not my job to do anything,' Parry returned. 'But I'll tell you: I'm going into Redchurch now and I'll try and borrow you a couple from the Loco people there.'

'I wish you would. And get them out to us.'

'How's the pipe?' Parry asked as he took his note.

'As well as can be expected when all it gets to help it on is dud tools,' Carey returned.

As he spoke Pole came over. 'Going to Redchurch, Parry? I'll go with you part of the way.'

They tramped on while Pole poured out a lamentation. 'They're a bright pair, Lowell and Carey,' he complained. 'They're just the same; always smelling out some mistake which doesn't exist. I had to come out with them to check those pegs for the retaining wall at Peg 61. I checked them last week and made sure they were right;

but, no, that wasn't good enough. I had used the soft tape. I must check them again with the steel tape. Rot! But I needn't worry; I got a walk out of it. I was fed up with the office. Been doing concrete costs since I can't remember.'

'You needn't grouse,' Parry returned. 'There's nothing in concrete costs.'

'That all you know about it?' replied Pole with disdain. Then with a change of tone, 'I say, Parry, I promised to go with Lowell and the Vane girls to a show tonight and now I find I want to slip over to Redchurch. I suppose you wouldn't care to take my place? It's only fair to tell you you'd be stuck with Mollie Vane, for if Lowell's about you won't get a word in with Brenda.'

'Can't,' said Parry. 'I'm going to a show at Redchurch myself. Wouldn't Carey go? I thought he was as wax where the Vanes were concerned.'

'Carey? Do you want to have murder done? You're a nice little bit of tact, you are, to suggest Carey and Lowell going out with Brenda Vane.'

'Has Carey really fallen for her?'

'Sure thing, bo. Carey *and* Lowell. Interesting situation. As I say, unless she decides between them soon, there'll be murder done.'

'Go on, Pole, pile it on. And which does the lady favour?'

'Personally I'd go nap on Lowell, but you never know.'

For another half mile Pole babbled, then saying, 'Well, here's where I get off,' he stopped to take his measurements.

Parry tramped on alone. He was now approaching the station. The railway ground widened and sidings containing coaching stock appeared at each side of the line. Then came the loop points, and two or three hundred yards farther, the junction with the main line from London. Parry turned off to the left into the locomotive yard.

Parry always enjoyed a visit to a locomotive depot He liked seeing the engines, and though in the approved professional way he pretended to be unconscious of their presence, he was nevertheless excited by their very proximity. He had read something about them and could recognise the types. There was one of those Continental looking machines, a 2-6-0, with the bead round the chimney top instead of a flange and the outside cylinders and Walschaert's gear. And there was one of those old South Eastern tanks, an 0-4-4, with the driver underneath her packing a valve spindle gland. And here creeping slowly past him, with a little whispered remonstrance from her snifting valves, was a Lord Nelson. Her boiler towered so high above Parry that he cold not see her chimney, but her huge smoke deflection plates—Parry wasn't sure of their correct name—made up for it. They were designed, he knew, to create an air current which should carry the steam from her chimney high above the cab, and prevent it blowing down and obstructing the men's view. There was something impressive in her massive coupling and connecting rods, which slowly rose and fell above and below the level of his eyes. Parry felt thrilled, as with a wisp of steam at her injector exhaust, she passed on to the turntable.

He entered the shed. Here it was gloomy and smoky. Engines were standing on many of the roads. Some were being washed out. Men in high boots were watching cascades of water pouring out from firebox shells, while on the brick floor beside these streams were the countless little flakes of brown scale which had been removed from the plates. Other engines were in the hands of the cleaners, having their paintwork rubbed up with oily cloths and the rust taken off their bright parts . . .

'Good afternoon, Mr Parry,' said a voice. It came from a stout good-humoured-looking man, the shed foreman.

'Oh, I was just looking for you, Mr Floyd,' Parry answered. 'I want to know if you can do something for me,' and he went on to explain the tragedy of the broken jack.

'Why, certainly,' Floyd returned. 'I can let you have a couple of fifteen tonners. Will they do?'

'First rate, Mr Floyd. Will you send them to Whitness by the 1.40 and I'll get Blake to take them out to Mr Carey.'

As Parry left the shed he noticed that the Lord Nelson had gone and that a big 0-8-0 goods engine was swinging round on the table. Then he saw the Lord Nelson again. She had stopped at the sand furnace and was getting her sandboxes filled. Her driver, a long oil feeder in his hand, was reverentially probing at one of her bigends as a priest might perform some sacred rite. Parry half envied him.

After a leisurely lunch in the refreshment room Parry walked down to the signal cabin, from which he could ring up Miggs to tell him to call for the jacks. He had a few minutes to kill before his train and after putting through his message stood for some moments watching the life of the box.

This Redchurch Junction Box was of medium size, containing some eighty levers. They stretched in a row along the back of the box, their ordered line being broken by the dozen or so which were pulled forward to the front of the frame. Above them ran a shelf groaning with instruments. Over a number of the levers at the ends were little boxes containing model signals. These were the repeaters which electrically indicated the positions of signals which were too far away from the box to be clearly seen by the signalman. At the ends also were the block instruments, showing whether the line in each direction was clear, was about to be entered upon by a train, or whether the train was actually on the line. These were operated by plungers, and every now and then the signalman plunged, while bells rang, indicators moved, and the times were entered in a book.

In the centre of the frame, stretching across a number of other dials and plungers and indicators, was the illuminated diagram. This was one of the features added recently, when the place was resignalled. It was a huge plan of the yard, the main line portion of which was divided up into small numbered sections, each lit from behind by a small electric lamp. So long as the particular part of the line corresponding to any one of these sections was unoccupied, the light shone. But should a vehicle pass over the rails, the light went out. The passage of trains through the yard was, therefore, indicated by corresponding shadows moving across the diagram, while an engine or vehicle standing at any point was shown by a dark patch.

Parry stood listening to the various sounds inside and out. Puff—puff—puff—puff, while the box trembled and steam floated up before the windows: an engine slowly backing a set of carriages to the platforms. One two, pause, one two three; a bell ringing imperiously, followed by the softer sounds of the plunger repeating the same code. Crash—crash—crash—crash, as levers were pulled over and thrown back. Rattle, rattle, rattle, rattle from behind; a rake of goods wagons jingled past. The telephone bell: 'Hullo? . . . Into No. 4? Right. Yes, she warned at thirty-eight.' Puff, puff, puff, puff, loudly and smartly, followed by the heavy rolling sound of coaches; a train going out. The telephone again . . . So continuously it went on.

'The Belle,' said the signalman suddenly.

Parry looked out. Round the curve from London a train was racing towards them. It was the Lydmouth Belle, which daily did the run to and from Waterloo without a stop. Parry could see the engine rolling. It lurched heavily as it slipped through the junction points, rushing on madly towards the station. With a roar like a shipyard it was opposite the box. Parry got a glimpse of the driver looking steadfastly ahead and with his hand on the regulator, then he was gone and the long green smooth-sided coaches were whirling past. In the windows were white-clothed tables and the shadowy suggestion of travellers. Then the van swung its end round towards the box, hurried between the platforms, vanished.

For a moment there seemed to be almost silence, then Parry realised that the signalman was speaking. '. . . fifteen miles to go and sixteen minutes to do it in,' he was saying, as he threw back his levers and plunged the departure to the next station.

Parry nodded. It was nearly time for his train and with a word to the signalman he left the box and regained the platform. Bragg was in the train and they travelled to Whitness together. That afternoon they had set aside to finish a special report on some joint suggestions for the improvement of the work.

'I must slip down to the viaduct before we start,' Parry

declared. 'I forgot to tell Blenkinsop about those concrete samples.'

'Don't be long,' Bragg returned. 'I want to be done by six as I'm driving over then to Drychester. I brought the car down yesterday.'

'I'll hurry.' Parry had his own reasons for wishing the work finished in good time. He had no objection to waiting till six, but he did not want his entire plans for the evening to be spoilt.

As he was leaving the viaduct, Parry stopped for a moment to inspect the concreting. Shortly before a controversy had arisen with Carey relative to the crushed stones or aggregate of which the concrete was being made. Bragg had objected that the mixture was dirty, that it contained too much dust, which Carey denied.

Standing by the mixers as Parry approached was Carey.

'Is it dust you're trying to smell out?' he grumbled, following the direction of Parry's gaze. 'Sure you may save yourself the trouble, for there isn't any. If you and Bragg want to have the mix full of voids, you can. Are you going back to the yard?'

'Yes, I'm on my way.'

'I'm going meself. Come on away from those blessed stones and don't be after making more trouble.'

Carey, it appeared, was perturbed about many things. Amongst others, the slow rate at which the rock cutting over the tunnel was progressing. He wanted to see Bragg about it and asked where Bragg was.

'Look in on your way home and you'll see him,' said Parry, who did not want Bragg to be interrupted till the report was done.

'About half-past five?' inquired Carey.

'About that.'

'I don't know what Bragg would do—' began Carey, then hearing a sound, he turned round, stopped, stared, and began to laugh.

The ground surrounding the viaduct was a veritable booby trap. It was trodden into muddy pools and littered with planks, ropes, ladders, wedges, wire and other objects calculated to bring discomfiture on the unwary. Carey heard the sound of a foot striking steel and looked round just in time to see Parry performing windmill evolutions with his arms. But these efforts did not save him and he fell heavily on his side right into a particularly virulent looking pool.

Carey laughed more and more and more, till he could scarcely stand. Then as he listened to Parry's language, his features took on an expression of unwilling respect.

'Holy saints, Parry!' he exclaimed, 'you've been in the army all right. Why don't you look what's in front of your feet?'

Parry picturesquely explained why he didn't look what was in front of his feet as he tried to rub the mud off his trousers with handfuls of grass.

'Sure you're only making it worse, doing that,' Carey pointed out. 'Go away and dry it at the fire in your office and then it'll brush off. Or some of it will anyway,' he added consolingly.

It was in no very sweet temper that Parry reached the office. He found Bragg alone, Ashe having gone back to Lydmouth.

Bragg stared, then he also exploded into peals of laughter. 'Say, young Parry, what have you been playing at?' he implored between his paroxysms. 'Tell us about the game. Was it rugger with Miggs?'

He roared again, then seeing that Parry was trembling, he stopped. 'Any the worse, old man?' he asked.

'Of course I'm none the worse,' Parry returned, beginning to wash in the sink. 'Tripped on a blinking bar at the viaduct.' He began to laugh himself in a queer, high-pitched way. Bragg didn't like the sound of it. The man must be more shaken than he admitted.

'Stop that,' said Bragg sharply. He opened the cupboard and took out the whisky. 'Here, you ass,' he said. 'Drink that.'

Parry gulped down the liquid. It pulled him together.

'Sorry, Bragg,' he said. 'I don't know what came over me. 'I'd be all right if I could get some of this confounded mud off.'

'It'll dry,' Bragg comforted. 'Come on and get at this blessed job.'

'I typed out a couple of suggestions for Section II last night,' Parry remarked, laying some sheets of paper on the desk before Bragg.

'Good,' said Bragg, running his eyes over the paragraphs. 'I thought you wouldn't use your machine for railway purposes?'

Parry gave a sickly grin. 'It wasn't that. Pearl Ackerley has had it for the last three weeks. Besides I look on this as our own private job.'

'So it is in a way. I like that paragraph two, but,' and Bragg went off into technicalities. The work proved easier than Parry had expected and they finished it comparatively early.

'There,' said Bragg, throwing down his pen, 'thank the Lord that's done. Go through it, Parry, will you, and see that all the corrections are clear so that Miss Redfern can type it straight off in the morning.'

Parry pulled the sheets in front of him.

'I had a look at that aggregate at Pier IV as I came along,' he remarked. 'I didn't tell you, because I thought we'd be busy till quitting time. But I thought it was damned bad stuff; just as dirty as ever. I was wondering if you'd care to have a look at it, seeing you won't be down in the morning.'

Bragg glanced at his watch. 'Twenty-five past. I suppose I might.'

'I met Carey,' went on Parry. 'He wanted to see you. I told him to call on his way home.'

'What's he want?'

'Something about the output of rock from the tunnel.'

Bragg stood up. 'I'll go to the viaduct,' he said. 'I've heard about that blessed output of stone till I'm sick. If I'm not back when he comes, tell him I'll see him next day I'm down.'

Parry grinned. He had expected just this reaction. Bragg put on his coat. 'When are you going?' he inquired as he opened the door.

'By the 6.10.'

Parry settled down to collate his sheets. There was really not much to be done and in a few minutes time the alterations were checked and the sheets made up. As Parry was writing the address there was a knock at the door and Carey entered.

'You're feeling better after your bath, I hope?' he inquired solicitously, looking Parry up and down. 'Sure the mud's caking the very best.' He put his head into the other room. 'I thought Bragg was to be here now?'

'He's gone down to Pier IV to look at the dust in the aggregate.'

This also produced the expected reaction. Carey gave an excellent imitation of a man gibbering with rage. 'I'll wait till he comes back,' he went on, 'and let him know what I think of him. And you too,' he added as an afterthought.

He drew the most comfortable chair he could find up to the stove, lit his pipe, and began to talk. Parry pulled his stool round beside him and to the best of his ability did the honours of the office. Presently there was a sharp footstep and Bragg appeared.

'I've been waiting for you, Bragg,' Carey said, swinging round in his chair. 'This imp of wickedness told me you'd be in. I say, Bragg, I want to see you about getting in another couple of blasts in the day at the tunnel. There's twenty min-yits between trains in the forenoon and seventeen in the afternoon when we don't blast. Why couldn't we fire then?'

Bragg glanced at his watch and moved impatiently. 'Look here, Carey, I've got to go over to Drychester. Let's postpone the thing. I'll be down on Thursday morning and we can fix it then.'

Carey agreed 'so long as it wasn't overlooked' and presently took his departure.

'I had a look at that aggregate,' Bragg went on when they were alone. 'I don't know what you were thinking about, Parry. There was nothing wrong with what I saw.'

'Then they must have changed their minds,' Parry returned. 'What I saw was damned dirty. I expect they saw me looking at it and thought we'd come up and take a sample.'

Bragg grunted. 'Got that report finished?'

Parry pointed to his letter.

'Well, see it gets to the office early so that it can be typed ready to put before Marlowe at eleven. I'd take it myself only for going over to Drychester.' He paused and looked keenly at Parry. 'What's wrong?' he went on. 'You're trembling.'

'I don't know,' Parry answered irritably. 'I suppose I'm getting a chill from that damned wetting.'

'Well, get home as quick as you can. You said you were going on the 6.10? You'll just get it if you hurry.'

'I think I'll wait for the 6.25 goods,' Parry returned. 'I didn't get that plan out of Holford and he'll want it in the morning.'

This was a plan of the foundations for a small shed which was to be erected in the goods' yard at Whitness. Parry had obtained a print of the portion of the yard in question, but the shed had to be shown on with the necessary dimensions to enable the inspector to peg it out.

'Oh, yes, that's important,' Bragg agreed. 'Is the plan ready?'

'No, but I can do what's wanted in fifteen minutes.' He opened a drawer and produced a plan, spreading it out on the desk. 'Just have a look at it, Bragg, will you? The shed's twenty feet from this corner of the store, isn't it; not from the back?'

'Yes, from the front corner. Right. Then you'll get your 6.25.' Bragg nodded and left the office and Parry heard him starting up his car in the adjoining shed, used as a garage.

There was quite a collection of vehicles in the shed. Cars were represented by Bragg's two-seater and a large Morris belonging to the contractors, theoretically for the use of the staff, but in practice monopolised by Carey for pleasure excursions. Carey justified this arrangement by pointing out, first, that as the road between Whitness and Redchurch ran at a considerable distance from the railway, the car was no use on the job, and second, that anyone else who could drive it could have it. Besides the cars there were four motor bicycles, belonging respectively to Lowell, Pole, and two members of the clerical staff.

Parry's job finished, he hurried to the station. The plan, complete with its added information, he handed to the stationmaster, to be given to Inspector Holford first thing in the morning. He was cold and shivering as he climbed into the van of the 6.25 goods, and when he reached his rooms he found he could not eat. He had an invitation to a dance, but he felt so badly that instead he mixed himself a stiff glass of grog and went to bed.

8

Tragedy Again

Next morning Parry felt miserable, though better than on the previous night. He decided he was not sufficiently ill to stay in bed, and breakfast with plenty of hot coffee made him feel more his own man. In due course he reached the station at Redchurch to get his usual train to Whitness. There Clay, the stationmaster, beckoned him over mysteriously.

'Heard the news, Mr Parry?'

'No,' said Parry, 'not that I know of.'

Clay leaned forward. 'Mr Carey,' he said in a low tone. 'He's dead.'

Parry stared. 'Dead?' he repeated incredulously. 'You're not serious, Mr Clay?'

'It's true enough. The news has just come through. They found him hanging in his office this morning.'

'Good God!' Parry cried weakly. 'Suicide?' he added almost in a whisper.

Clay shrugged. That was all he knew. No doubt Mr Parry would hear all details when he got to Whitness.

As in a dream Parry watched his train come in. Neither Bragg nor Ashe was coming down this morning, and still as in a dream Parry got into an empty compartment. A feeling of horror was weighing him down. It was a feeling he was growing accustomed to. He had felt it during the War—practically continuously, if for the most part subconsciously. He had felt it at the time of Ackerley's death. That tragedy had shaken him to the very marrow. And now he was feeling it again. He shivered.

As he sat gazing unseeingly at the passing landscape, he reviewed the occasions on which he had seen Carey on the previous day. Whole days sometimes passed without a meeting between the two men, but yesterday they had encountered one another several times. First at the culvert in the Lily Pond, then at the concreting of Pier IV, and finally before he, Parry, left Whitness. Perfectly well and perfectly normal Carey had seemed when he left Bragg and himself in the railway hut. It was true he had appeared to be slightly annoyed; in the morning by the failure of the jack, in the evening by the suggestions that there was dust in the aggregate. But Parry was certain that he was not really annoyed. That was Carey's manner, that continual assumption of a grievance. Really, he was half joking. A little tiresome, perhaps, but it meant nothing. Parry had once seen him really angry and it was a very different thing.

At Whitness, Parry had a word with the stationmaster. Yes, the news was only too true. The storesman had found Carey in the office when he went in to light the fire. He had given the alarm and the police were now in charge. Yes, it was supposed to be suicide, but the stationmaster didn't believe any one knew for certain.

Parry hurried down to the contractors' yard. At the door of their office a police constable was standing. Parry went up to him.

'Are Mr Lowell or Mr Pole about?' he asked.

'Both inside, sir. The sergeant's talking to them. Your name, sir?'

'Parry; Clifford Parry. I'm the Railway Company's resident engineer.'

'You knew Mr Carey, then?'

'Of course I did. I saw him only last night.'

'In that case, sir, the sergeant will want to get some details from you. Will you wait a moment?'

'Certainly, I'll be over in my own hut. Come over if you want me.'

Parry felt too much upset to settle down to work. He made a pretence of going through the letters, but he found himself reading them over and over again without in the least grasping their meaning. His thoughts remained centred in that office in the other hut.

Parry did not know much about Carey. None of them did. It was rumoured that his father had been a labourer and that he had started with the firm as a clerk, working himself up to his present position by sheer merit. But of his present family circumstances no one knew anything, not even if he was married. His name and his accent proclaimed the country of his birth, but had it not been for these tell-tale clues, probably not even that would have been known.

Parry wondered if it was not this secretiveness, not only in connection with himself, but in all matters, which made Carey disliked. Disliked, perhaps, was too strong a term; not very popular, would be nearer the truth. Carey's reaction was to keep everything dark and in his own hands. Even as contractors' engineer the same inclination came out. It made him essential, of course, which might have been his motive for adopting it. But it was bad for the work. He tended to become a bottle-neck which slowed everything up.

On the other hand, Carey had his good points. Indeed, he had many of them. He knew his job and he could get work out of his men while still treating them decently. He was fair and he was a worker. If he asked others to pull out he was ready himself to do the same. He was always—

There was a knock at the door, and a sergeant of police entered.

'Mr Parry?' he said, halting on the threshold.

Parry got up. 'That's my name. You wish to see me? Won't you sit down?'

The sergeant advanced, followed by a constable. They took the seats Parry pointed out.

Parry's feeling of horror intensified as he thought of discussing the affair in cold blood, but he resolutely pulled himself together and answered the sergeant as collectedly as he could.

'It's about this unhappy occurrence,' the sergeant went on. 'You, sir, knew the deceased?'

'Yes, I knew him well, though it was as a business acquaintance rather than as a personal friend. We were on good terms, but not specially intimate.'

'I understand, sir. What is your exact position here?'

'Resident engineer for the Railway Company.'

'Quite so. How long have you known the deceased?'

Parry told him all he knew of Carey; history, character,

activities, reputation: it didn't amount to much. Then he recounted his three interviews with the dead man on the previous day. No, Carey didn't seem excited or depressed or in any way unusual. He, Parry, had no idea of anything which might have been weighing on the deceased's mind or which could have influenced him to take his own life. Quite the contrary. So far as he knew, Carey had occupied a position with which he ought to have been well satisfied. It was responsible and, Parry supposed, lucrative, and his holding it was proof of the esteem in which his firm held him. His prospects, Parry thought, were good. No, he didn't know if Carey was married, or whether he had any amatory or financial or other trouble.

The sergeant looked over his notes. 'I think that's all, sir,' he said slowly. 'It seems to me that you and Mr Bragg were the last persons to see the deceased alive. He left here, you say, about six last night, or a few minutes before it. And that was the last time you saw him?'

'Yes, the last time.'

While he spoke, Parry was trying to solve a secondary problem. He was wondering whether he should volunteer a statement: something about last night: something which—

The sergeant brought his ruminations to an untimely end. He had apparently noticed Parry's change of expression, for he spoke in a somewhat sharper voice than he had yet used. 'Something has occurred to you, sir. What is it, if you please?'

Parry hesitated. Then he shrugged. 'As you will, sergeant. It was just a little thing I saw last night. I'm afraid I didn't observe it very carefully. Naturally I considered it not only not my business, but also of no importance. Besides, I was suffering from the beginning of a chill and was feel very cheap and sorry for myself.'

'Never mind that, sir. Tell me what you saw.'

'It was when I was leaving this office. That would be about quarter-past six, for I caught the 6.25 goods, and I always allow ten minutes to go to the station. I passed, as you can understand, within forty yards of the contractors' hut. It was in darkness except for Mr Carey's office, which was lighted, though the blinds were drawn down. The evening was fairly light; no moon, but bright stars. I saw someone walking towards the hut. He passed between me and the lighted window, and I saw the silhouette of his head and shoulders. He went on to the door and I heard him knock.'

'Was the door opened for him?'

'No,' said Parry; 'he opened it himself, but not at once.'

'He opened it himself? Then it wasn't fastened?'

'It was fastened. He had a key.'

The sergeant looked a trifle puzzled. 'I don't think I understand,' he said. 'Why did he knock if he had a key? Just to give notice of his approach, I suppose?'

'I don't know,' said Parry. 'I thought it a bit strange myself.'

'How long elapsed between the time he knocked and his opening the door?'

'I couldn't say. I told you I wasn't paying much attention to the matter.'

'What I mean,' said the persistent sergeant, 'is whether he just gave a knock merely to announce his approach, or whether he knocked and waited, as it were, to see if anyone was going to open?'

'Oh, he waited. I can't say how long he waited, but it was an appreciable time.'

'Did he close the door behind him?'

'Yes, he went in and shut the door.'

'Did he see you?'

'I don't think so.'

'Humph,' said the sergeant judicially. 'This might be important enough, and again it might not. Now, tell me,' he leaned forward and became impressive, 'who was it?'

For the fraction of a second Parry hesitated. This was the question he was expecting. 'I don't know,' he answered.

The sergeant looked at him keenly.

'That you shouldn't know, sir, under the circumstances, I can well understand,' he said smoothly. 'But I should be very much surprised indeed to hear you say you had no suspicion.'

'I'm afraid, sergeant, that's what you're going to hear. I neither know nor suspect.'

The sergeant made a movement as if settling himself more permanently in his chair.

'Now, sir, I'm afraid I must ask you to help us better than that. You will see for yourself that we must find this caller. He may have brought news to the deceased which caused him to take the action he did. I'm sure the man would come forward with his information if he realised its importance. But in case he may not, we must go ahead and find him. Think again, Mr Parry. Have you no idea who it might have been?'

'It might have been anybody; that's just the trouble. I didn't see the face, and I don't know.'

The sergeant turned to his companion. 'Slip over to that other office, Forster, and get me a list of everyone who has a key for it.' Then, to Parry. 'An unfortunate business, this, sir, particularly coming on the top of that other tragedy, the accident to Mr Ackerley.'

'I know,' Parry said in a low tone. 'He was my greatest friend on the railway.'

'I'm sorry, sir.' The sergeant spoke sympathetically. 'I think—Are you not the gentleman who was on the engine?'

'Yes, Mr Bragg and I.'

The sergeant shook his head. 'It must have given you a nasty shock, and I'm therefore the more sorry to have to trouble you over this affair.' He paused as the constable entered and laid a sheet of paper before him, then continued: 'Now, I'm depending on your help in this, Mr Parry, and we'll try elimination. This list is headed by Mr Lowell's name. Can you,' he looked very searchingly at Parry, for all his suave manners, 'can you say definitely that the figure was not Mr Lowell's?'

Parry hesitated as he considered the question. Then he answered firmly: 'I can't say it was not, sergeant, but still less can I say that it was.'

The sergeant was very persistent. He went through every name on the list, engineers, clerks, timekeeper, and storesmen. In every case Parry returned the same answer. Once again the sergeant shook his head.

'I think you ought to able to do better for me than that, Mr Parry,' he declared. 'Now, see here. How high up the window did the man's head come? Don't you see? Some of the men on this list must be as much as six feet and others can be little over five—I've seen them all. Come now, that should be a help to you. If you can't eliminate from memory, I'll light up that window tonight and get all these people to walk past it tonight while you look on.'

Though Parry had been interrogated by the police on the occasion of the Ackerley tragedy, he was impressed with the thoroughness with which the sergeant was making his inquiries. On the officer's suggestion he went out and looked at Carey's window while the constable walked past it. 'I hadn't thought of that question of height,' he declared. 'The man was pretty tall; nearly as tall as the constable.'

This, then, eliminated Pole and two of the clerical staff, leaving Carey himself, Lowell, Templeton, and one clerk as possibles. The sergeant then got on to the question of the shape of the hat, but Parry could give no information as to this. Finally, the sergeant, with a civil word of thanks, took his leave, first telling Parry to hold himself in readiness to attend the inquest on the following day.

When he had gone, Parry went again to the contractors' office. He had not yet heard the details of the affair, and he wanted to see Lowell or Pole. The police, however, were still in charge. An ambulance had arrived and was standing beside the hut, and it was evident that the remains had just been moved into it, for the door was being closed. Two cars were also drawn up close by and, as Parry approached, a man whom he knew by sight as a local doctor named Willcox, emerged from the hut and drove off in one of them. Immediately after the ambulance followed. Then the police got into the other car and also drove off.

Parry crossed to the hut. In the drawing-office were Lowell, Pole, and Templeton. They looked worried and upset and were talking together in low tones. They nodded to Parry.

'Tell me about it,' Parry said in a similar low tone. 'I've not heard any details as yet.'

Lowell indicated the private office with a twist of his head. 'It was in there,' he said, speaking as if with an utter repugnance and distaste. 'He had taken the rope off one of those bundles of big pegs—you know, the three by three centre line pegs—and hanged himself to the beam of one of the roof principals. He had evidently stood on his stool and then kicked it aside. We didn't see him, thank goodness. When we got here the police were in charge and had cut him down.'

'But you saw the body?'

'Yes, and I don't want to talk about it.'

Parry glanced at Lowell with a feeling of slight surprise. He seemed very much upset. A considerable amount of agitation was, of course, natural, indeed inevitable. He, Parry, felt it himself. But somehow Lowell appeared to be struggling with more emotion than Parry would have expected. He seemed not only shocked and sorry, but also nervous, as if he foresaw the possibility of trouble for himself arising out of the tragedy. Parry ignored his somewhat short manner and asked when the affair was supposed to have taken place.

'Last night, they think. Several hours ago at all events.'

'Then he came back here in the evening?'

'Came back?' Lowell returned. 'Why do you say that? Do you know where he was?'

'I? No. Did he not dine with you?'

'No. We never saw him all the evening. We supposed he had met someone and had gone to dine elsewhere.'

'And he didn't come in later?'

'No, but no one knew that till this morning. Everyone went to bed, you see. Carey had his own latch-key.'

'Of course.' Parry seemed a little bit puzzled. 'Then it is

supposed that he never went anywhere last night, but did it when he got back here from our office?'

'I believe so,' Pole returned. 'The police didn't say so, but from their questions it looked as if they thought so.'

This, Parry thought, would explain the sergeant's interest in the silhouetted figure. He glanced involuntarily at Lowell.

'It'll upset the Vanes,' he said presently, 'particularly Mrs Vane. Lucky it didn't happen there.'

'I think,' said Lowell, 'now that the police have gone and we're free, I'll slip down and give them the details. They only just know that it had happened.' He swung out of the door and they heard his quick footsteps as he tramped off.

'It's upset Lowell too,' Parry remarked.

'Well, of course it has,' Pole returned. 'It has upset us all. What gets me is this, it's so surprising. There was no reason, so far as any of us know, why Carey should have wanted to commit suicide. He wasn't unhappy. He wasn't in trouble. He had plenty of money. He liked the work and the people. There was nothing wrong. All that, of course, so far as we know. That's what gets me: why did he do it?'

'It's what gets me too,' said Templeton, who had not yet spoken. 'I knew Carey longer than any of you, and since ever I've known him he's been the same. I mean, there's been no change of manner lately or anything of that sort. He was absolutely normal up to the end.'

Parry wondered if he should tell them of the silhouetted figure. He thought it better. Why make a mystery out of nothing?

'Neither of you chaps were back in the office last night, I suppose?' he said.

'That's what the sergeant asked us,' Pole replied. 'We weren't.'

'Nor Lowell?'

'No.'

'Well, someone was,' and Parry went on to tell his story.

Both men seemed impressed. 'Dash it, I wonder who it could have been?' said Pole, while Templeton believed that it proved that there was something more going on than anyone had suspected. 'You know,' continued Templeton, 'Carey was a bit of a dark horse. None of us knew much about him.'

'That's what I had to tell the sergeant when he was pumping me,' Parry said.

'We all had to,' Pole admitted.

'Well,' said Parry, turning away, 'this'll settle Lowell's trouble about Brenda Vane at all events. Unless she thinks because of this that she was fond of Carey.'

'I don't believe Brenda ever cared tuppence for Carey,' Pole declared. 'Lowell thought she did, but I believe it was only panic and jealousy.'

'He was jealous, was he?'

'Jealous as they make them. A silly ass about it, threatening to murder Carey and all that.'

'He didn't.'

'Didn't he, though.'

'In joke, it must have been,' Parry suggested.

'Precious little joke about it, if you ask me,' Pole returned. 'What do you say, Templeton?'

'Did you hear it too?' put in Parry.

'Everyone in the office heard it,' Templeton answered. 'They had a row; not the noisy sort of row, but a deep, silent, cursing-beneath-the-breath row. Lowell was a silly goat. He lost his head and said things he never should have. For the moment he was all worked up, but of course when he cooled down it was all right. Then it happened a second time at "Serque"'.

Parry moved close to the others.

'I suppose,' he said confidentially, 'this thing couldn't have happened because of Brenda? What if Carey had proposed and she had refused him? Was he far enough gone to take it to heart like that?'

'Not my idea of Carey, at all events,' Templeton declared. 'Carey was too fond of Number One to injure himself for a thing like that. Though he was fond of Brenda, all right.'

'Well, anyone might be that. She's a damned fine girl.'

'She's all right,' Pole admitted. 'But there's just about an ocean of difference between being fond of her and committing suicide because of her. I say, I'm a bit bothered about whether we oughtn't to close down for today because of this affair. Lowell thought not, but he wasn't very sure.'

'I shouldn't, if I were you,' Parry declared. 'I think the less fuss you make in the case of a suicide, the better.'

'I agree with Parry,' said Templeton. 'In any case, it's Lowell's say.'

'That's right in a sense,' Pole returned, 'but it doesn't seem quite the thing to take no notice of it. For instance . . .'

Parry left them arguing, and returned to his own office. There he rang up Lydmouth, got through to Marlowe, and gave him all the details he had learned. Finally, with a despairing sort of effort, he settled down to deal with his correspondence.

During the whole day, Parry was haunted by the thought of the tragedy. He finished the essential portions of his clerical work, then finding he could not settle down to his usual routine in the office, he went out on the job. But he did not see a great deal of what was going on. That swinging figure in the contractors' hut held his attention.

Only twice, however, was he actually reminded of what had happened. After lunch a constable arrived with a summons for him to attend the inquest at 10.30 on the following morning. It was to be held in the carpenters' shop, which would be cleared for the occasion. The second time was in the afternoon, when he called for a moment at the Vanes, formally to express his regret at what had happened.

When he joined his train at Redchurch next morning he found Bragg in it. Bragg had been interviewed by a constable on the previous afternoon and had also received a summons to be present at the inquest. Bragg seemed a good deal upset by the tragedy. Of all the railway officers he had known Carey best, and of all those on the Widening, he had probably liked him best. His comments were much the same as those of Pole and Templeton.

'The last man in the world to do such a thing, I should have said,' he declared. 'It shows how one may be mistaken in people. Suicide is usually the coward's way, and whatever Carey was, he was no coward. I tell you, Parry, I can scarcely believe it. I didn't know Carey extraordinarily well, but I thought I knew him well enough to swear he would never have committed suicide. And what possible cause could there have been?'

'That's what everybody's asking,' said Parry.

'When we were talking to him that night there were no signs of anything being wrong, and from what we hear, he must have done it just after leaving us. I tell you,

Parry, it's incredible. There's something more behind it that we don't know.'

'Did you hear that I had seen someone going into his office?'

Bragg heard the story with interest. 'There you are,' he declared when Parry had finished, 'that's what I said. There's something more in it than we've heard.' He paused, then went on with a little side glance. 'There was something about one of those Vane girls, wasn't there?'

'The others were talking about that. They said there was nothing in it.'

'But they didn't know?'

'I suppose not, but they seemed pretty sure of it.'

Bragg shrugged. 'Well, I expect we'll hear in an hour or so. By the way, Marlowe has agreed to give that notion of ours a trial,' and he went on to talk business.

Shortly before half-past ten they walked over to the carpenters' shop.

9

Inquest Again

As Parry's thoughts went back to that morning at Redchurch station some four months before, when the inquest had been made into the death of Ronnie Ackerley, it seemed to him that history was about to repeat itself. The carpenters' shop, the one large room in the immediate neighbourhood, had been prepared for the occasion. The benches had been removed to one end and a trestle table erected in the centre, while chairs, lent from the station, were arranged about it. But though the place was different, the atmosphere was the same as at Redchurch. Similar little groups of people stood about, waiting uneasily; the police were busy superintending everybody and everything and holding hurried conversations among themselves, and everywhere an identical air of expectancy was manifest.

The coroner was the same Mr Latimer who had held the inquest on Ackerley. Only, instead of Sergeant Hart and the Redchurch constables, there were here the Whitness men, Sergeant Emery and his myrmidons. This time, moreover, beside the police sat Inspector French.

The opening formalities of the previous occasion were repeated, except that here no polite speech of condolence was made. The jury were called to their places and sworn. They elected not to view the body and at once the proceedings began. A word or two of introduction from the coroner, and the first witness was called: Hugh Bertram Spence.

'You, Mr Spence,' said Mr Latimer, 'are the junior partner of Messrs John Spence & Sons, the engineering contractors who are carrying out this work on the railway?'

'I am.'

'You have seen the remains upon which this inquest is being held?'

Mr Spence had seen the remains, morever, he identified them as those of Michael John Carey, the firm's resident engineer in charge of the Widening.

'Now, Mr Spence, will you give a short sketch of the deceased's career?'

Carey, it appeared, had entered the service of the firm twenty years previously as a lad of eighteen, which would make him at the time of his death thirty-eight years old. He had started as a pupil in the drawing-office. There he had given such satisfaction that on the completion of his pupilage he had been offered a junior post with the firm. While carrying out his work efficiently, he had spent his evenings in study, with the result that he had qualified for Associate Membership of the Institution of Civil Engineers. From time to time he had been advanced in both position and salary until, when the contract for this railway widening had been entered into, he had been put in charge. Though not the first, it was the largest job of which he had had charge, and he, Mr Spence, was glad to be able to testify as to the completely satisfactory way in which he had carried out his manifold duties.

'What, so far as you know, was the state of his health, both bodily and mental?'

'Both excellent: I wish mine were as good.'

'You never noticed any tendency towards melancholy or depression?'

Mr Spence had never noticed anything of the kind. Nor had he ever suspected that the deceased might have some secret worry preying on his mind. He could not think of any reason why he might have committed suicide; on the contrary, so far as he could see, Carey had every reason to live and none to die. His prospects were good and his life should have been happy.

'Did you know anything of his being in financial difficulties?'

'Nothing, and I don't believe he was.'

'Will you tell the jury what salary your firm paid him?'

'Seven hundred and fifty,' Mr Spence answered after a slight hesitation, 'but there were certain variable allowances which brought the actual sum considerably above this figure.'

'Was the deceased married?'

'Not to my knowledge.'

Mr Spence, in fact, could not give any real help to the inquiry, and no one wishing to ask him a further question, he stood down.

The next witness was an elderly man in workman's clothes, who gave his name as Albert Bradstreet.

'You are employed by Messrs Spence?' began the coroner.

'Yes, *sir*. For five-and-thirty years, day in, day out, I—'

'In what capacity?' interrupted Mr Latimer.

'Assistant storesman: weighing out stuff, measuring liquids, keeping the store tidy; I knows it all and I—'

'Quite so. Now, is it part of your duties to sweep out the offices in the mornings and to light the fires?'

'That's right, sir. I 'as a general tidy up to do before the gentlemen comes out, I 'as; I pulls up the blinds, an' sweeps the floors, an' 'as a dust round, an' empties the waste-paper baskets, *an'* lights the fires, an' brings in coal, an'—'

'Now, look here, Bradstreet, just confine yourself to what you're asked. D'you see? Just what I ask you and no more.'

'Well, so I am, but I was just going to—'

'Never mind what you were going to do. Listen to me and answer my questions. Now, on yesterday morning did you carry out your work at the office?'

'I did an' I didn't, if so be that you understand me. I began to work as usual, but w'en I found the boss I stopped pretty quick. I didn't do nothing more after—'

'You found the boss? You mean the deceased, I suppose?'

'I mean Mr Carey. After I'd found 'im I wasn't on for work, as you might understand. It didn't 'alf—'

'Now, will you tell the jury just what you found?'

'Well, the blinds was down, like they always was, an' I went for to raise them so as there'd be light for me to do the fire. An' w'en I raised them, there didn't I see the boss, 'anging there from the roof.'

'And what did you do?'

'I sez to myself, "Oh, my, oh, my," or words to that effect, an' I went over to look at 'im for to see if maybe 'e might he alive. But 'e weren't. 'E were dead, an' 'e'd been dead for some time, for I felt 'im an' 'e were cold, as cold as ice.'

'And what did you do then?'

'W'y, I stood an' thought wot I'd best do, an' then I thought I'd—'

'Look here, Bradstreet, did you tell anyone what you'd seen?'

'That's right, sir. I ran out, shutting the door after me, an' I ran to Alf Whitaker, that's the storesman, an' I said, "I'll be jiggered, Alf, if the boss ain't been an' 'anged 'imself." An' Alf said—'

'Did you then go back to the office?'

'Yes, as soon as Alf Whitaker 'ad rung up the police, we both went back. 'E couldn't scarcely believe 'is eyes, Alf couldn't. 'E—'

'Did you remain in the office till the police came?'

'That's right, we waited—'

'Now, one other question, Bradstreet. From the time you first made the discovery until the police arrived, was anything touched in the room?'

'No, there weren't nothing touched. I felt the body for to see if it were cold, but there weren't nothing else touched. I—'

The coroner looked round. 'Does any gentleman wish to ask the witness a question?'

No one else desiring to restart the flood of Bradstreet's eloquence, he was told to stand down, which he did with unwillingness and an aggrieved expression.

Sergeant Emery was the next witness. On the coroner's suggestion he gave his evidence in the form of a statement.

'Yesterday about 8.5 a.m.,' he began, 'I received a telephone message from this yard, informing me that the chief engineer had just been found dead in his office. I proceeded to the place and found the deceased as stated. He was hanging by a rope from the beam of the roof and had been dead for a considerable time, the body being quite cold. His toes were swinging about three inches above the floor. A tall office stool lay on its side on the floor beside the body, just out of reach of the feet. It looked to me as if the deceased had stood on the stool while fixing the rope about his neck, and had then kicked away the stool.'

'There were no other marks of violence, either on the body or in the room?'

'No, sir. I didn't see any marks on the body, but Dr Willcox is here and will tell you definitely. There were no traces of violence in the room.'

'Yes, sergeant. What did you do then?'

'I had telephoned for Dr Willcox before leaving the station, and he turned up shortly. We cut the body down and he made his examination of it while I went over the room. I found nothing to disprove my belief that the deceased had committed suicide. On the other hand I found nothing to suggest his motive for doing so.'

'And then, sergeant?'

'Then, sir, I made certain inquiries. I did not learn a great deal, but as a result I have some other witnesses to put before you.'

'Well, sergeant, we'll hear them now.' Mr Latimer went on asking questions, but the sergeant had evidently told all he knew, and presently Dr Willcox was called.

The doctor had not much to say. He had been summoned to the contractors' office on the previous morning and had there found a man hanging from the roof, as the previous witness had described. The man was dead, and had been dead, so far as he could estimate, for about twelve hours. He must, however, point out that this figure was quite approximate and that is was not possible to state definitely the hour of death. The man had died from asphyxiation, and his condition and the injuries to his throat were consistent with death from hanging. There was no other wound upon the body or sign of any struggle.

Lowell was next called. He described briefly the life in the office and the excellent relations which had obtained between the deceased and the other members of the staff. He was with Carey off and on during the day of the tragedy. Carey seemed absolutely normal and he, Lowell, had no inkling that all was not well with him.

Lowell then went on to describe the events of the previous evening. Shortly before closing time all the members of the staff were in the office. About half-past five the deceased said he was going over to the railway hut to see Bragg, and if the others were done before he returned they need not wait for him. He went out and shortly afterwards Templeton put away his papers and followed. Lowell completed his work about a quarter to six and left the office, Pole, who had not quite finished, remaining behind. Having a headache he, Lowell, went for a short walk before returning to 'Serque', the house where the three of them were staying. He was troubled with these headaches and often found a walk helped them. When he reached 'Serque' Pole had already arrived, having walked direct from the office. As Carey did not turn up they waited dinner for a few minutes, then supposing he had gone to dine elsewhere, they went on without him He, Lowell, and Pole stayed in all the evening, reading novels. Next morning at breakfast Carey did not appear, and on Lowell going up to look for him, he found that his bed had not been slept in. Even then no suspicion that anything was wrong entered their minds; they simply supposed Carey had met friends and stayed with them all night. The first intimation he, Lowell, had of the tragedy, was his finding the police in charge at the office.

Lowell had been led through this evidence by questions from the coroner, and now a juror asked him whether Carey had ever before failed to turn up for dinner without sending a message. Lowell thought not: at least, he could not remember any such case. The juryman then asked was it not strange, in these unprecedented circumstances, that none of them had made any search for Carey. Lowell admitted that they might have been too ready to take things for granted, and said he was not trying to justify their action, but simply stating what had taken place.

Once again Parry felt a little surprised by Lowell's manner. He still seemed self-conscious and uneasy, not to say apprehensive. These manifestations were slight, and Parry did not think that a stranger to Lowell would have noticed anything amiss. But to him there did certainly seem to be something unusual on Lowell's mind.

Pole was then examined. He briefly confirmed Lowell's general statement, saying that he had left the office about five minutes after Lowell and gone straight to 'Serque'. Carey had not returned to the office when he left it.

The next witness was Bragg. After answering a few questions as to the good relations which had obtained between the contractors' and railway staffs, he described Carey's visit to his office, referred to by the previous witnesses. It was about blasting at the tunnel. Carey had gone about five minutes to six. Bragg had then left, Parry remaining behind.

Parry was then called. Asked several general questions, he confirmed what Lowell, Pole and Bragg had said. Then Mr Latimer took him to the night of the tragedy.

'After Mr Bragg left your office, what did you do?'

'During the day I had overlooked sending a plan to Inspector Holford, our Permanent Way inspector. As he wanted it the next morning it had to go out that night. I turned up the plan and wrote on it some special memoranda which the inspector required.'

'Then you left the office.'

'Yes.'

'At that time the tradesmen's work was normally over for the day and the yard was closed?'

'That is so.'

'I understand there is a watchman on duty at night? Did you see him on your way out?'

'Yes, he opened the gate for me.'

'Now, Mr Parry, between the time you left your office and the time you met the watchman, did you see anyone else in the yard?'

'I did,' said Parry, and he told his story about the silhouetted figure.

Interest in the proceedings, which had waned slightly, waxed once more. But only for a moment. Parry reiterated his former statement that he could not say who the man was, and Mr Latimer did not press him. Parry was the last witness and when he stood down the coroner began his address to the jury.

After a word of introduction Mr Latimer reviewed the evidence, and Parry was struck, as he had been struck on the previous occasion, with the fair way the facts were presented. Then in a sort of charge the coroner went on to give his own views, repeating a good deal of what he had said in the Ackerley case. Three possibilities were to be considered: accident, suicide or murder. Fortunately for the jury, he did not think they would have much difficulty in deciding to which of these categories the present case belonged. Accident, he suggested, might be dismissed at once. He did not see with what object, other than self-destruction, the deceased could have tied the rope to the roof principal, even if he might have accidentally got it round his neck and fallen off the stool. The jury would, of course, consider these possibilities, but if they rejected them, they would proceed to consider the alternatives of suicide and murder.

For murder, he suggested, there was no evidence whatever. Murder by hanging in circumstances such as this was practically unknown, and for a very good reason: its extreme difficulty. In fact, except in the case of a particularly weak and puny victim, it might be taken as impossible. Here the victim was anything but weak or puny.

'It is true,' went on Mr Latimer, 'that many murdered persons are found hanging. But they are almost invariably murdered beforehand by some other method, and swung up with the object of misleading the police. Now, in the present case the doctor has told you, not only that the state of the remains was consistent with hanging, but that there was no other wound upon the body.

'You have also to remember, though this is neither so important nor so conclusive, that no possible motive has been suggested by which anyone might have desired the deceased's death. On the other hand, all the evidence we have tends to show that he had no serious enemies.

'If then, members of the jury, you conclude that a murder verdict is inadmissable, you will turn your thoughts to suicide.

'In this theory you will, I think, find a completely

satisfactory explanation of the death. Hanging is a method frequently adopted by suicides, and the more you consider the actual details in this case, the more, I think, you will see that every one of them is consistent with this hypothesis. The deed done in the man's own office after everyone had left. The rope, taken from a place deceased knew of, namely, from round a bundle of large pegs. The use of the office stool, lying where it would lie if it had been kicked aside. In short, had suicide been committed, you would naturally expect to find just what was found.

'There is just one remark which I still wish to make in connection with the man who was seen to enter the hut with a key. I do not think you need let this matter weigh with you. Unless you are satisfied that murder was committed, it is of little importance to you who this individual was. Your duty is confined to three questions: first, what was the cause of death? second, was the death due to accident, suicide, or murder? and third, if murder, you can, if you like, add an expression of your opinion as to the guilty party. Now, members of the jury, will you please withdraw and consider your verdict.'

In five minutes the jury returned. The verdict was a foregone conclusion to everyone present. It was that Michael John Carey had committed suicide while temporarily insane by hanging himself in his office on the evening or night of Tuesday, the 24th of November.

Two days later Carey's funeral took place. It was supposed to be private, but in the end was largely attended. Though he hadn't been particularly popular, the dead man had performed many a kindness and these were now remembered. Parry and Bragg went as a matter of course, as did also most of the men in the yard. To everyone's surprise, Mr Spence, the partner who had given evidence at the inquest, came down from London in order to be present.

Not entirely to be present, however. It was afterwards found that Mr Spence had another and a more pleasant motive in making the journey. When the funeral was over, so Parry heard later, he called Lowell into the private office, and after a long conversation about the Widening, told him that the firm was satisfied with the way in which he had done his work up to the present, and proposed to offer him Carey's position, subject on account of his youth to more frequent inspections from headquarters.

It was, as a matter of fact, a wise move of the partners. Not only was Lowell thoroughly competent from a professional point of view, but he also had enough character to carry his decisions through. Moreover, he had made himself popular with all concerned.

Parry was really glad at the promotion and said so in no uncertain terms, as also did Bragg. As Bragg pointed out, they might have got some crooked old fellow from town who would have stood on his dignity and given them no end of trouble. Bragg in fact was delighted.

When Parry returned to the office on the Monday morning after the funeral and greeted Lowell in his new position, it seemed to him as if a page of his life had somehow been turned. This terrible period of tragedies was surely over. It could not go on for ever. He felt brighter and more hopeful than at any period since the death of Ackerley.

Yet on that very day was to be enacted the first scene of a fresh drama, in one sense less dreadful than those which had preceded it, but which still was to take its toll in perplexity and suffering, not only from Parry, but from many another, both within and without the Widening.

10

The Torn Print

Parry began work that morning in the usual way, with the correspondence. He was alone in the office. Ashe had been sent to an outlying station to make a survey and would not be back for two or three days. Bragg would be down later, but in the morning he had some engagement in Lydmouth. At the moment work in the Widening office was slack, but in four or five days measuring up for the next certificate would begin.

There was not much in the letter-box and Parry soon passed on to his next job; looking over his engagements and arranging his programme for the day. In the afternoon Bragg and he were going to walk over the Widening. He had no special interviews for the morning and he need not, therefore, go out at present. He decided that he would spend his time till Bragg arrived in finishing a small supplementary plan of certain modifications to a culvert wingwall, which, though it was not required at present, soon would be.

He set to work, therefore, at his drawing-board.

Practically all the office drawings were done in pencil on paper, then were traced in ink on linen, using a standard sized sheet, of which there were a number of different sizes. The pencil drawing was then destroyed and the linen became the original and was kept in the drawing-office files. The drawings actually in use on the various jobs were photo prints, taken from these linen tracings. As the linen original was never allowed out of the office, it was possible at any time to obtain as many fresh and identical copies as might be required.

Parry had finished the pencil drawing and was unrolling the cloth for the tracing when the door was pushed open and Lowell came in.

'Hullo, Parry. By yourself?'

'Yes, Bragg won't be down till the 12.55.'

'We're going to start concreting at Arch III tomorrow,' Lowell went on. 'Do you want to O.K. the reinforcement before we do so?'

'It's all right,' said Parry. 'Bragg and I were over it three or four days ago.'

'Right.'

The two men discussed a number of other items connected with the work. Then Lowell held up a sheet of paper.

'I must congratulate you people on your tidiness and care,' he announced. 'See what I've just found kicking about our office.'

Parry took the paper. It was triangular shaped, a corner torn off a larger sheet. A photo print, it was ruled in squares and bore one or two coloured cross sections showing cutting. It was dusty and crumpled.

'Good Lord!' said Parry, 'that's out of our book of sections.

See, there's one of Ackerley's notes on it.' He pointed to a faintly written pencil note that Bridge 986 was 15 ft. 9 in. east of Section 48. 'Where was it?' he went on.

'Among a lot of other papers in one of Carey's drawers. I've been turning them out.'

Parry nodded. He got up and went to the cupboard in the inner office. 'Here's our copy,' he said, slamming down a book on the desk.

This was the book which Bragg had produced when French was inquiring into his alibi. It consisted of a stout Manilla binder containing some seventy or eighty sheets of photo print paper. The sheets were about 18ins. by 12ins. in size, their working area being squared with 1/10in. squares. Each sheet bore from one to six cross sections, depending on the depth of the cut or fill. These cross sections had been taken every hundred feet along the whole line and were numbered from 0 to 188. They were doubly coloured on the prints, firstly, with a faint wash of red or blue to show the total area of cutting or filling to be done, and secondly, with various other stronger colours, to indicate the amount of such cutting or filling which had been completed up to various given dates.

The torn sheet showed Sections 48 and 49. Parry turned to the sheet in question.

The page in the book was complete.

Parry laughed. 'Why, you cuckoo,' he said, 'it's your own copy that's torn.'

'No, it's not, Parry,' Lowell rejoined. 'I looked it up first thing. Our page is complete, too.'

Parry shrugged. 'Well, it's simple enough, isn't it? A third copy must have been sent down which we didn't know about; that's all.'

'I never heard of it.'

'Nor I.'

Lowell seemed dissatisfied. 'But look here, Parry,' he went on; 'did Ackerley write his note twice?'

'Eh? His note? What do you mean?'

'That pencil note about the position of Bridge 986.'

Parry's expression changed. He seized the torn sheet and laid it beside the one in the book. 'By Jove!' he said.

There on both pages was the note, written in the same hand and at precisely the same place; in fact, the two notes were identical, as if they had been traced.

'I say,' said Parry presently, 'look at this.'

Near the centre of the book sheet was a note in Bragg's upright and rather crabbed handwriting: 'Field drain at 48.56 to be piped to watertable.' The tear on the other sheet had gone through the place where the word 'table' was written, and the fragment bore in pencil the identically shaped letters '-ble'!

'Did Ackerley write his note twice?' Lowell repeated.

'He might have,' said Parry, 'if they were changing the sheet. But it's strange that the two notes should be so exactly similar. I say, Lowell, I don't understand this a little bit. Somebody has made a duplicate, but for what?'

The plans indeed looked identical, with one exception. Both were coloured with the original faint red, the conventional indication of cutting. But whereas the copy in the book also had the later colours, showing the amount done on various dates, these colours had not been added to the torn copy.

Suddenly Parry gave an exclamation. 'See,' he pointed, 'they're not the same. They're not even printed from the same tracing. Look at the original ground level.'

It was true. There was a difference of a foot between the two copies. The original ground level shown on Section 48 was 52.74 on the fragment and in the book 53.74, while the similar figures for Section 49 were 50.26 and 51.26 respectively.

'Let's check them over in detail,' Lowell suggested.

They did so. Lowell read from the fragment, Parry following in the book. Then they looked at each other with mystified faces.

Every figure on the sheets was identical on both copies except that which they had already observed: the reduced level of the original ground at the centre line. On both sections the original ground was shown one foot lower on the fragment than in the book. Moreover, in the drawings, the corresponding lines representing the original surface varied similarly.

'What on earth does it mean?' said Lowell.

'Blessed if I know.'

Silence fell as the two men pondered. Then Parry asked: 'Which figure is given on your copy?'

'I don't know,' Lowell answered. 'I'll slip over and see.'

He was back in a few moments with the book. 'This is the same as your book,' he reported.

'It's very strange,' Parry said presently, 'but I'm hanged if I see that it matters.'

'It wouldn't worry me one iota,' Lowell declared, 'if it wasn't for the pencil notes. I must say I don't like the look of that.'

'Nothing in it,' said Parry. 'I bet you I know what has happened. A sheet of these sections was made and found to be wrong, and a new sheet was made to replace it. The old print, instead of being destroyed, got lying about and was stuffed into Carey's drawer. Someone then amused himself by copying on the notes, sort of absent-mindedly, as one sometimes makes nonsense sketches on one's blotting paper.'

Lowell looked relieved. 'I suppose that's it,' he answered slowly, and then more happily, 'Of course, that must be it. Funny that the incorrect sheet should have got down here all the same.'

'Well,' Parry went on, 'it's not so funny after all. We supplied you with a book, didn't we? Very well; what's to prevent the old incorrect sheet getting into that book before we sent it out? That would account for the whole thing.'

'That must be it,' Lowell agreed again. 'I thought it funny at the time, but of course it's all right. I say, Parry,' he went on nervously, 'do you know—er—that is, you didn't hear that—eh—Brenda and I— We've fixed it up.'

Parry sprang to his feet. 'Splendid, old man,' he cried warmly, holding out his hand. 'Best congrats and all that. She's one of the very best. I'm frightfully glad. Look here,' he went again to the cupboard, 'we must celebrate. Say when.'

He produced the bottle of whisky and two tumblers, and they solemnly drank to the success of Lowell's new contract. Though he never took too much, Parry was fond of celebrating. When callers came to the office his idea of doing the honours was to produce the bottle, and experience had shown that it usually made its appeal.

'I'd better go,' Lowell said when the ceremony was complete. 'I don't want to be party to your being found blind on the floor.'

Parry began the tracing of his pencil drawing. It was easy mechanical work and left his thoughts free to rove where they would. For a time they lingered on Lowell and Brenda. Presently they returned to the matter of the torn sheet.

On this problem they lingered for some time. Then Parry turned to the telephone, got through to the Lydmouth office, and asked for Bragg.

'I say, Bragg,' he went on when he heard the other's voice, 'I want you to do something before you come down. Lowell has raised the question of the levels of the original ground on the centre line at Pegs 48 and 49. Apparently there's some mistake about them on our prints. Will you look up the figures on the originals—on the tracing, please, not on a print? And if a revised section was made, will you note what is the correct figure? Have you got that? . . . Ha, ha, you're right there . . . What? . . . Yes, it's a mystery here, too. Too long to explain over the 'phone. I'll tell you when you come . . . Right-ho.'

Parry finished his tracing, lunched, and got ready a small file of papers to be taken over the Widening. Then, as it wasn't worth while starting anything till Bragg turned up, he lit his pipe, put his feet on the stove, and settled to read the paper.

Presently Bragg came in.

'Hullo, young Parry. Busy as usual? You know, if you're not careful you'll crack up from overwork.'

Parry got up slowly.

'Curse you, Bragg, for interrupting me. I was in the middle of the serial. The heroine had just found another body.'

'You can tell me about it as we walk. Have you got those papers about Nelson's right of way?'

'Yep. And about that man of Mellon's stopping the 3.45,

and from the post office about those three poles that are sliding down the bank at Cannan's Cutting, and—oh, two or three other small things. I have them in order and I'll bring them up as we walk.'

'Right. Then let's get on.'

'Did you look up those levels?'

'Oh, yes, by the way, what's the excitement?'

'What are they, Bragg?'

Bragg took his notebook from his pocket and began turning over the leaves.

'You're darned mysterious about it, I will admit. Here you are. Original ground level; Section 48, 52.74 and Section 49, 50.26. That what you want?'

These were the figures given on the torn sheet, not those in the book. For answer Parry silently put the book down before Bragg.

'Well, what about it?' Bragg returned irritably. Then as Parry still did not answer, he looked more carefully, referred again to his notebook, then whistled softly.

'Found a mistake, have you?' he said. 'Well, what about it again? I guess you'll find a darned sight more before this job is through.'

'There's more in it than that, Bragg,' Parry insisted. 'Look here; what tracing was that printed off?'

'What tracing? Good Lord, how do I know? I suppose someone made a mistake and made a second tracing and you've got the wrong prints. Things like that have happened before now in railway offices.'

For answer Parry took out the torn print and laid it beside the other.

'What's that?' said Bragg. 'There you are. That's the correct print. Where did you get it?'

'Lowell found it in one of Carey's drawers.'

'Well, what if he did? It accidentally got into the book we sent them. I don't see what's worrying you about it, Parry. What's in your mind?'

'Those notes of Ackerley's,' Parry went on. 'Would he have written them twice?'

Bragg made a gesture of impatience. 'Of course he would. He had the note on the wrong sheet. The revised sheet was sent him. Naturally he would copy his note on before destroying the old sheet.'

'Did you write your note twice?'

'Eh? What do you mean?'

Parry pointed to the final '-ble,' appearing in Bragg's writing on the torn sheet.

Bragg for the first time looked impressed. He put the two sheets side by side and compared them carefully. 'It's a bit funny, that,' he admitted presently. 'Someone evidently wanted to keep the change dark, so he copied the notes. That accounts for my not having heard of the revised sheet being got out. Someone had made a mistake and wanted to correct it without giving himself away. Darned silly fool, if so. There's nothing wrong with making an occasional mistake, provided you own up to it and then correct it. I'll make inquiries about the thing when I go back. Not that it matters. An error of a foot in two sections on a job of this size is neither here nor there, as poor Carey would have said. Give me that torn sheet. Right. Now, if that's all, we'll get on.'

They walked through to Redchurch, inspecting progress, interviewing foremen and gangers, settling the hundred and one tiny problems which arose, literally from hour to hour, discussing grievances with adjoining farmers, and between times mixing their shop with a good deal of gossip.

At Redchurch they parted, Bragg going on to Lydmouth, while Parry returned with a sheaf of notes to Whitness. Most of these, however, he left over till the next day, attending only to such as were urgent.

Next morning Bragg rang him up. 'I say, young Parry, I want you to come up to the office and bring all those sections with you.'

'Now?'

'Yes.'

Parry glanced at his watch. 'I'll be there at 10.50.'

'Right.'

Parry, on reaching Lydmouth, turned into a doorway off No. 1 Platform and ascended a couple of flights of dark and steep stairs. These led to a corridor, imperfectly lighted by skylights and with doors at intervals at both sides. Through one of these he pushed his way.

It led into a fair-sized room with a continuous window along one side. In front of the window stretched a drawing-desk arranged for three draughtsmen. At two of the three spaces young men were working. A small fire burned in the grate and there was a smell of smoke in the air.

'Gosh!' said Parry. 'What an atmosphere! Don't you blokes ever open the windows?'

'Here,' returned the nearest draughtsman, 'who asked you to come in? The room's bad enough without that.'

'If I didn't look in occasionally, you'd never do anything at all. Is Bragg next door?'

'Yes, but old Horniman is with him,' answered the second man. 'What on earth brings you here? We thought we'd been lucky and got rid of you permanently.'

'A cheery crowd, you are,' Parry remarked as he hung up his coat. 'What's the great work now, Bolton,' he went on, moving to the nearest draughtsman and looking over his drawing.

'Nothing really; only a new footbridge for Lydwater.'

'The usual thing?'

'No. You see, these steps—' and Bolton launched out into a dissertation on his work, of which he was evidently extremely proud.

Parry was interested and they discussed the traffic requirements of Lydwater till Bragg put in his head and wanted to know if that was what Parry had come up for, as, if so, he might as well have saved himself the journey.

'Must do something while I'm waiting for you to get a move on,' Parry retorted as he followed Bragg into the other office.

Bragg shut the door behind them.

'I was thinking over those sections in bed last night,' he said, holding out his cigarette case, 'and I began to agree with you that the whole thing was a bit queer. I thought just for curiosity's sake we'd have a look over one or two other pages.'

Parry nodded. 'Right-ho. But what's the big idea? I understood you were satisfied enough yesterday that it was just some small mistake?'

'I was,' Bragg returned, 'and am still. All the same, seeing these sections are being worked to, I thought we'd better make sure there are no other errors.'

'Right-ho,' said Parry again. 'Shall we start with No. 1 and go through them?'

'Yes. Here's the office copy. We'll try the original levels

on the centre line first. You read, "Section So-and-so" and the reduced level off your copy and I'll check off these.'

After leaving Redchurch the line ran for some half-mile along level ground. For this stretch there were four and sometimes six sections to the sheet. Parry began at No. 0 and read steadily on. When he came to No. 24 he stopped.

'That's two dozen of them,' he pointed out, 'all correct and proper. Do you really think we must go on through the lot?'

'Do a few more at all events,' Bragg decided.

Parry continued. Now the ground rose and the railway began to get into cutting. Section 25 checked out right, as did 26, but at 27 Bragg called a halt.

'Read that again,' he said quietly.

'Twenty-seven; thirty-eight point two-nine.'

Bragg looked queerly at Parry.

'Twenty-seven; thirty-seven point two-nine, my copy says,' he declared. 'I say, Parry, I don't like this. There's another.' He seemed strangely moved. 'I was just a bit afraid of it, you know,' he continued. 'However, don't let's be too quick. Carry on and see if there are any more.'

Parry expressed his astonishment at this development, then continued reading.

'Twenty-eight: forty point one-seven.'

'Twenty-eight: thirty-nine point one-seven. There's another. Go on.'

As they continued, the affair did not get any simpler. In each one of the next six sections, 29 to 34 inclusive, there was an error of a foot. Bragg was now looking very grave.

'Go on,' he said as Parry stopped to give vent to his feelings.

'Thirty-five: fifty-three point two-one.'

Bragg gave a little gasp. 'Good Lord,' he said in awe-struck tones. 'Thirty-five: fifty-one point two-one. Two feet of an error.' He looked blankly at Parry.

Parry stared equally helplessly.

'But bless me, it couldn't be,' he objected. 'Let's see.' He examined Bragg's copy for himself. 'Fifty-one it is. What on earth does it mean, Bragg?'

Bragg shook his head. 'I'm afraid it means trouble,' and there was still that suggestion of awe in his voice. 'It looks as if what occurred to me last night was true.'

'And what was that?'

'Wait till we've finished and I'll tell you. Go on through the lot.'

They checked through the remainder of the sections and then settled down to collate their results. And very strange results they were.

Out of the 188 cross sections, 89 had an error of one foot and 42 an error of two. There was no greater error than two feet in any section.

'Now,' said Bragg, 'if my theory is correct, these errors will occur only in cutting of definite depths. Let's try that now.'

This took a considerable time, as to get the depth of the cut at each section, the reduced level of the new formation had to be deducted from that of the old surface. These depths of cutting had then to be filled into one of three columns, corresponding to correct sections and errors of one and two feet respectively.

But at last it was done. The results were at least interesting. All the cutting of a less depth than 15 ft. 0 ins. was shown correctly. Cuttings between 15 ft. 0 ins. and 30 ft. 0 ins. deep were shown with one foot of error, and cuttings over 30 ft. 0 ins. with two feet.

'But what does it all mean?' Parry repeated for the *n*th time. 'What's your theory, Bragg?'

Bragg again shook his head.

'Just that we've tumbled to a fraud, young Parry,' he said grimly, 'and a damned serious fraud at that. This'll be a matter for Marlowe, and I expect after him, for the police.'

11

Fraud!

Parry stared as if Bragg had taken leave of his senses.

'Good Lord, Bragg,' he questioned, 'what on earth are you talking about? A matter for the police?'

Bragg was in no humour for answering questions. 'Look here, Parry,' he said, 'you keep your mouth shut about this. See? Now, we've got to report to Marlowe. You go and catch him in case he should go out. I'll follow when I get one or two of the tracings. Here, take your book of sections.'

When Bragg was in this state of mind Parry knew that it was best to do what he wanted without comment. He rolled up his book, went down the passage, and after tapping at another door, opened it and passed through.

It led into a small room furnished in a rather better style than the drawing-offices. At a typewriting desk sat a good looking young woman with a pearl necklace and gold bangles.

'Hullo, Miss Amberley! Chief in?' Parry grinned at her.

'I'll find out.'

She disappeared through a door in the side wall, leaving Parry standing before her desk. He was keenly interested in this cross section affair and glad that Bragg had not taken it entirely out of his hands. It would have been rather like Bragg to do so. He was inclined to get particulars about things from others and then shove them in to Marlowe himself. Not unfairly exactly: he gave credit where it was due. All the same—

'Mr Marlowe can see you now.'

The girl held the door open and Parry passed through. The chief was writing at his desk. He looked up. 'Well, Parry, how's the Widening?'

Marlowe was generally reputed to be somewhat unapproachable, but Parry had always found him easy enough to get on with. He had been particularly friendly when appointing Parry to his present job. Since then Parry had been with him on different occasions in connection with the work, always leaving with the same pleasant recollections of the interview.

'All right, sir,' Parry answered; 'everything's going on as usual. Bragg sent me in to see you about a rather curious thing that's happened. He's following when he gets a tracing.'

Marlowe sat back in his chair. 'Well,' he said, 'that's not a bad beginning for a story. What's the epoch making event?'

'We've found, sir, that a lot of our cross sections are wrong.'

'Oh?' Marlowe's manner at once grew sharp. 'What do you mean?'

Parry explained in detail. Marlowe nodded, but made no comment. 'We'll wait for Bragg,' he said.

At that moment Bragg entered.

'Bring over chairs, you two,' Marlowe went on. 'Now, Bragg, what's all this about?'

They settled themselves round the table desk, the cross sections upon which the inquisition was to be held lying between them.

'Parry has explained what we've discovered?' Bragg asked.

Marlowe nodded.

'Then I'll tell you, sir, what occurred to me when I was thinking over the thing last night. So that you'll understand, I shall have to remind you of just what I knew when I went home. Firstly, we had found that there was a sheet in Parry's book of cross sections which differed from the linen originals by just one figure in each of two sections. Secondly, that part of a torn sheet of the same sections had been found which was identical with the original, and therefore, of course, different from Parry's. Thirdly, that exactly similar pencil notes written by both Ackerley and myself, appeared on each of the sheets. I was aware also, of course, that so far as was officially known, no mistake had been made in getting out these sections and no revised linen originals had been traced. Further, I was perfectly sure in my own mind that I had not written the note about the piping of the field drain twice.'

Marlowe nodded again. He was listening with close attention.

'It was obvious, therefore,' went on Bragg, 'that someone had *secretly* copied this sheet, and I asked myself why had this been done? At first sight I supposed that one of the boys had made a mistake in his levels and hadn't wished to give himself away. But as I thought over the thing further, this seemed to grow less and less likely. If any of the boys in the office had done so, he would have destroyed the original linen tracing and replaced it with his own new one. Do you agree with me so far, sir?'

'Yes, I think so,' Marlowe answered. 'And there is surely another consideration which points the same way. None of the boys would have made a new tracing. He would simply have rubbed out the incorrect portions he wouldn't have done even this off his own bat. He would have spoken to you, said he had made a mistake, and consulted with you as to the easiest way of dealing with it.'

'I quite agree,' said Bragg. 'I thought of those points, too. I may say also that when I examined that one original tracing yesterday in response to Parry's request, I saw no discoloration at the figure. If the figures had been altered there would have been discoloration. I've brought in one or two of the tracings and you can see for yourself that they've not been altered.'

'Quite,' Marlow returned.

'I thought over all these points,' Bragg repeated, 'and the more I did so, the more they seemed to involve a very serious conclusion; so serious that for a long time I hesitated to accept it.'

'I don't follow that,' Marlowe interrupted.

Bragg moved uneasily. 'Well, it seemed to me to follow that this new sheet was made by someone outside the office.'

'Oh.' For some moments Marlowe sat whistling absently beneath his breath. ''Pon my soul, Bragg, it looks like it. Very nasty that. Well?'

'I went over the premises again and again, but I just felt

more strongly forced to this conclusion. So I accepted it provisionally, and I asked myself the question, Who outside the office could have done it?'

Bragg paused in his turn. Marlowe seemed a good deal upset, while Parry found himself filled with excitement.

'I hate to go on,' Bragg said at last, 'but you must see for yourself that only one answer was possible. If none of our men made this alteration, it must have been done by the contractors. Very unwillingly I asked myself why.'

'Ah,' repeated Marlowe, 'why? Were you able to answer that question?'

'Not at first. For a long time I puzzled over it. Then I began to consider the precise change which had been made, and suddenly I saw its significance.'

Marlowe made a gesture of impatience. 'I'm hanged, Bragg, if I can see it even now. Go ahead and explain.'

Bragg took a sheet of paper from his pocket and laid it on the desk.

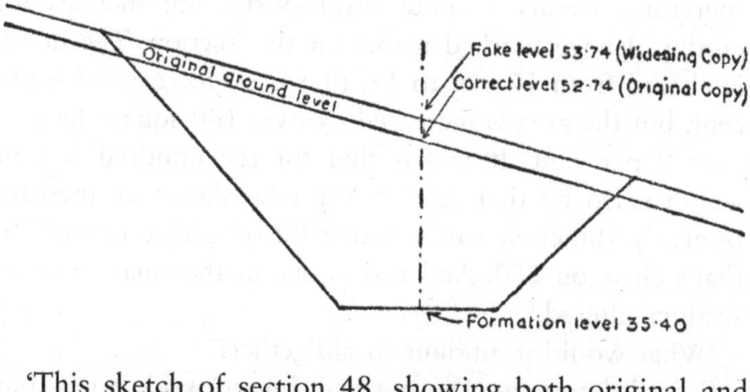

'This sketch of section 48, showing both original and faked levels on one sheet, will I think, clear it up. Just see the result of the alteration. The level of the bottom of the cutting is shown the same on both copies as 35.40. But on the Widening copy the original ground level is shown one foot higher than the office copy. Now, sir, I think we may take the office copy as correct and the Widening one as a fake. The result of the fake will, therefore, be that the cutting is shown one foot deeper than it really is, 18 feet instead of 17 feet.'

'And you take your quantities for the certificate off these sections?'

Bragg nodded. 'That's it, sir.'

Marlowe was frowning angrily. 'Then these infernal scoundrels are being paid for doing more excavating than they really have done? Is that what you mean?'

'That's the only conclusion I could come to,' Bragg answered. For a moment there was silence, then Bragg continued. 'There are two more things to consider. First, as of course you know, that foot involves a good deal more than appears at first sight. Owing to the flat slope of the sides the cut at the top is very wide, and that last foot, therefore, means a quite disproportionate increase of cutting. I have worked it out for this section. The depth is altered from 17 feet to 18, that is an increase of 6 per cent, but the area is increased by over 100 square feet, or over 9 per cent. It means that for the hundred feet of length ruled by that section, the fake shows an increase of nearly 400 cubic yards, and at the scheduled rate of 2/6 that's close on £50. And this is one of the smallest cross sections altered.'

'What would it amount to altogether?'

'I don't know, sir; I've not had time to work it out. But I should say off-hand that the total would be at least three hundred times as great. That would be £15,000. Say from

£12,000 to £18,000. That's as much as they would dare exceed the earthwork estimate, or more, without having the whole thing gone into from A to Z.'

Marlowe thought for some moments.

'Are the faked sections altered; I mean the drawings? Are they shown deeper than the originals?'

'Oh, yes, it's not confined to the reduced levels. The actual drawings are altered to suit.'

'Then there should be no difficulty in proving the drawings wrong?'

'Oh, none. It only means relevelling the ground at the top of the cuttings.'

'Very well; let's have the things checked. We must be absolutely sure of our ground before we raise any question.'

Once again silence descended on the little group, broken again by Marlowe.

'I'll tell you another thing; we'll have to check the other plans as well. For example, what about the concrete cube in the bridges? A very small alteration in overall dimensions would make a hell of a lot of difference in the money.'

'I don't think, sir,' said Parry speaking for the first time, 'that there could be much error in the bridges. All the concrete work has been checked again and again.'

'I know,' Marlowe said impatiently, 'but was it checked off correct plans?'

To this Parry could make no reply. He shook his head in silence. Marlowe turned to Bragg.

'Tell me, Bragg, who is responsible for all this? Who actually carried it out?'

It was now Bragg's turn to shake his head. That was what he had himself been wondering. He had considered everyone whom he had thought possible, and had dismissed each from his mind. Marlowe looked at him keenly.

'You naturally don't like to put it into words,' he said, 'but the idea must have occurred to you. Is there,' he dropped his voice instinctively, 'is there any connection between this affair and the recent tragedy?'

Parry felt his heart beat faster. This suggestion surely offered a solution of the whole terrible affair? If Carey had done this thing and in some way learnt that discovery was imminent . . .

'That idea, of course, occurred to me,' Bragg said slowly, 'but I didn't see that there could be anything in it. Any money the scheme would bring in would go to the contractors; I mean to the firm. Carey wouldn't have got any of it.'

'Unless they were paying him to do this.'

Bragg shrugged. 'They're a reputable firm. I can scarcely see them committing a criminal fraud.'

'So I should have said,' Marlowe answered, 'but we must remember that times are pretty tight at present. A few thousand might even stave off a bankruptcy. Another point, Bragg. Have you considered how these faked prints could have been produced?'

'Only, so far as I can see, by making a new set of tracings from the book we sent down. The sections and levels would be altered as the tracing was done, then two new sets of prints would be got. Any existing notes would be copied on to the new prints and these would be put into our covers.'

'Yes, I dare say you're right. But—'

Marlowe's desk telephone rang stridently.

'Marlowe speaking,' he answered. 'Oh, very well, Miss

Hunt. Any time he comes down.' He replaced the receiver. 'That's the chairman. "He's down here today and wants to be taken round the yard. You two'll have to clear out. Now remember, both of you, not a word of all this to anyone. You come in and see me again, Bragg, say about four. Graham's not here today, is he?"

'No, sir. He's gone to meet the Ministry of Transport Inspector about that Lydminster derailment.'

'Of course. Parry, you'd better get back to Whitness. There's no need to have everyone wondering what's up. That'll do.'

'If you scoot, you'll catch the 12.55,' said Bragg as they reached the passage. 'Better leave your book with me.'

Parry nodded. He had three minutes and he had to run. He stepped into the train as the guard waved his flag.

Parry sat motionless in his corner seat, his mind full of this strange affair which had just come to light, an affair, as far as he knew, without parallel in the annals of railway contracting. Would it, he wondered, really come to a police prosecution? If so, against whom would the prosecution be brought? He tried to look at it from a detached point of view, to estimate how Bragg's theory would appeal to outsiders such as the jury in a court of law.

Contractors, he reflected—it was the professional outlook—were often very tricky people, given to sailing close to the wind and not always above a lapse into actual sharp practice. But they were not swindlers or forgers. It was one thing to put a strained interpretation on a specification clause, but quite another to falsify figures. Parry agreed with Bragg; unless in the face of overwhelming evidence no jury would hold that the firm, as a firm, had stood for the fraud. All the same he could imagine the

Railway Company proceeding against the firm to recover their loss, on the ground that though the principals might not have been involved, their agents were. Whether, however, this position could be maintained, he did not know.

The next two days he and Bragg spent in comparing the Widening office prints with the originals from headquarters. It was a tedious job, for beside the viaduct there were several smaller bridges, not to speak of culverts and other less important works. But nowhere could they find any other discrepancies. The fraud seemed to be limited to the excavation.

The checking of the cross sections on the ground was simultaneously done by Ashe and a couple of other juniors. They found, as was expected, that the head office copy was correct and the Widening copies wrong.

Parry naturally badgered Bragg to know what was going to be done. Nothing, Bragg told him, not till all the facts were known. He had made an estimate of the amount the scheme would have netted for the contractors, and it amounted to £16,750. Marlowe, however, was going to make no move till all possible investigations had been made. Then he proposed to get the contractor partners down, put the facts before them, and ask them what about it?

Five days later this meeting was held, very secretly. Parry indeed did not hear of it till it was over. Marlowe, Graham and Bragg were present on the Company's side, while the contractors were represented by the partners, the Mr Spence who had been present at the inquest and his cousin, Mr Elmer Spence, together with their accountant, a man named Portman.

It was from Bragg that Parry heard what had taken place. Marlowe had opened the proceedings by apologising for calling such busy men down to Lydmouth in so urgent a manner, and by expressing his regret at the unpleasant nature of the communication he had to make. Then he said he proposed to put the whole of his cards on the table, and he called on Bragg to explain what had taken place.

Bragg told the whole story, beginning with Lowell's discovery of the torn print and giving details of the inquiries this had given rise to, right down to his estimate that, had the affair not been discovered, the contractors would have received between £16,000 and £17,000 to which they were not entitled.

Marlowe then took up the tale again. He said his visitors were not to misunderstand his attitude: he was very far indeed from suggesting any fraudulent intention on the part of the firm. All the same, as they would see for themselves, the facts required explanation. He was sure the partners would be even more ready to give this to him, than he was to ask for it.

Mr Elmer Spence, the senior partner, who showed signs of emotion, then got up and said that, speaking for himself, he felt appalled and overwhelmed by what he had just heard. He need scarcely assure Mr Marlowe that the facts had come to him as a complete surprise and a devastating blow, and he could not at such short notice make any kind of detailed reply. For the present he must, therefore, content himself with a couple of remarks. First, he wished to express his heartfelt regret that anything had happened which called in question the honour of his firm. Next, he would like to say how much he appreciated the direct and considerate way in which Mr Marlowe had acted, in calling himself and his partner there and telling them privately exactly what appeared to be wrong. He could assure Mr Marlowe that he would be equally straight with him. He would hold an immediate and searching investigation into the affair. If anyone were found to be guilty he would be prosecuted without respect to his position or influence, and finally, if it were found that his firm had received any monies to which they were not strictly entitled, every penny would be at once refunded.

To this Marlowe replied that he thanked Mr Spence for taking up the attitude he had, which was just the attitude which he, Marlowe, had believed the head of a firm with so high a reputation would take up. They on the Company's side would await with interest the result of Mr Spence's inquiry. In the meantime, before parting, could they not settle the date of their next meeting, at which they would hear this report? After discussion a further meeting was arranged for that week, and the protagonists parted on outwardly amicable terms.

Mr Spence was as good as his word. The very next day a searching inquiry into the whole affair was begun in the contractors' office at Whitness. Parry and Bragg were politely asked to give evidence, but were not invited to remain when their respective hearings were over. Every endeavour was made to keep the details secret, and while the staff knew that a big row was on, no one who was not actually concerned had any idea of what it was all about.

Before the end of the week Messrs Spence sent Marlowe a confidential report of their findings. They began by saying that they had made a formal investigation into the matters brought to their notice by the Company and that the weight of evidence—of which a *précis* was given in appendix A—had led them to the following general conclusions:

1. That the affair did in point of fact constitute a deliberate fraud, perpetrated with the object of obtaining money upon false pretences from the Railway Company.
2. That the directors and officials of Messrs John Spence & Co. were, as a whole, entirely innocent of participation in the fraud, and were indeed quite ignorant of its existence until receiving the Railway Company's communication thereon.
3. That the fraud owed its inception to, and was carried out by, their late chief resident engineer, Mr Michael John Carey.
4. That no other person in the employment of the firm, or connected with it in any way, was party to, or was aware of, the fraud.

The report then went on to say that the partners, though personally not in any way to blame for the affair, had unhesitatingly decided to make themselves responsible for their late engineer's actions, and were prepared to refund whatever sum the Company had lost as a result thereof. They, therefore, proposed the setting up of a small joint committee to go still further into the matter and ascertain the amount of this sum.

'I say, Bragg,' Parry observed when Bragg showed him the document, 'all that's rather a triumph for you. If you hadn't stayed awake at night thinking about it, the Company would have lost their sixteen thousand.'

'As far as a triumph for me is concerned,' Bragg returned,

'you have as much to say to it as I. I may tell you that Marlowe is pleased with you about it.'

Parry grinned crookedly. 'I did nothing,' he said, 'but if Marlowe thinks I did, for goodness' sake don't disabuse his mind.'

Presently Parry asked a question. 'There's one thing I don't understand, and that is how Carey could have got the cash. D'you remember, you said yourself that one of the reasons he could scarcely have been guilty was that the cash would go to the firm and not to him?'

'Ah,' said Bragg, 'we had a job to find that out. But Marlowe handled them well and they had to tell. They were giving Carey a huge commission on both extras and excess profits. No less than twenty per cent net. He would have made about three thousand out of the fraud, and I should be inclined to bet the whole three that no question about the savings would have been asked.'

'Still,' Parry persisted, 'I don't quite understand how it was done.'

'Well, it's simple enough. Each certificate showed so many yards excavated at so much per yard, totalling such a sum. Suppose it showed 8000 yards at half a crown. That would mean that the contractors were due £1000, and £1000 they were paid. Now, suppose their excavation costs for the period came to, say, £600: that was £400 profit on 8000 yards. But the normal profit they had reckoned on for those 8000 yards was, say, £200. Carey had, therefore, made an excess profit of £200, and of this they paid him twenty per cent, or £40. Follow it now?'

'Yes, I see that,' said Parry; 'jolly cute.' He paused in thought, then went on slowly: 'But surely, Bragg, when these enormous profits began to come in, the Spences must have known there was something wrong. They must have known they couldn't have been earned.'

Bragg shrugged. 'You may hold what opinion you like about that,' he answered. 'Marlowe put it to them in the neatest possible way. Naturally they weren't admitting anything. They said the profits, even with the fraud, were not by any means abnormal, and that they put them down, partly to Carey's organising ability, and partly to the use of those new Benbolt shovels with the direct delivery on to the conveyors. Of course, there was nothing to be said to that.'

'No,' Parry admitted, 'but it's damned fishy all the same.'

Some days later Parry found himself nominated with Bragg and Mayers, of the clerical staff of the office, to represent the Company on the small committee which was to ascertain the amount of the contractors' refund. In the end the sum was unanimously fixed at £11,465.

It was about this time that a faint rumour began first to be whispered. In the extraordinary way that rumours have of coming into being without ascertainable cause or source, this rumour was born, took on shape and grew to maturity.

Immediately that news of the fraud had leaked out it had become connected in the public mind with the suicide of Carey, it being believed that in some way that unhappy man had seen that discovery was inevitable, and being unable to face the consequences, he had taken the easiest way out. But this new rumour went farther.

It began with the suggestion that a fraud of the magnitude of that which had just occurred, could not possibly have been carried out by one man. It was argued that a confederate on the Company's side would have been absolutely essential. From this it required but a slight effort of the imagination to suggest that Ackerley had been the confederate in question. Finally it was hinted that not only was Ackerley's death suicide, due to the fear that the affair was coming out, but that the railway officers knew this to be the case.

Parry's furious denunciations, when at last these suggestions were put to him, did little to discount them. It was immediately remembered that not only had Parry been a special friend of Ackerley's, but that he was intimate with, if not actually in love with Ackerley's sister. His view, it was assumed, would be biased.

When matters were in this stage substance was given to the rumour by an altogether unexpected development. Mayers, the clerical member of the staff who had sat on the small committee with Bragg and Parry, came forward with an unpleasantly suggestive story.

It appeared that some three or four days before his death, Ackerley had paid a visit to the Lydmouth office on business connected with the Widening. When there he saw Mayers. They were speaking of costs and quantities when Ackerley accidentally disclosed the fact that he was worried about the excavation. The question had arisen out of a discussion with one of the gangers as to the amount of clay held by a small ballast wagon, he and the ganger differing on the point. For his own information he had made a test. From the ballasting returns he had taken out the number of wagon loads carried from a certain cutting. The cube removed from this place was known from the cross sections, and from these two figures he was able to calculate the average wagon load. This came out higher than either Ackerley or the ganger had estimated. Ackerley had followed up the matter by selecting a dozen loaded wagons at random, and sending them into Redchurch to be run over the wagon weigh-bridge. To his surprise he found that the ganger's lower figure was right after all.

The calculated and actual weights were therefore different. Ackerley evidently had not considered the matter serious, but he had said he was going to make some further experiments. He had never had an opportunity to do so. Mayers had also considered the matter unimportant and had said nothing about it. But it was now seen that had Ackerley pursued his inquiries, he must have come on the fraud.

Parry was able to remind Mayers that part of his recollection was inaccurate, for on that very day Mayers had repeated the story to him. Apparently, however, neither Parry nor Mayers had told it to anyone else.

Now, however, when the matter was made public, Parry hotly argued that the story was in itself a proof of Ackerley's innocence. Had he been involved, Parry pointed out, he would never have carried out those tests nor spoken of them to Mayers. But against this it was argued that even at this time Ackerley saw that the fraud was about to come out, and that he was preparing the way for a 'discovery' by himself. It was further suggested that he had seen the same danger as Carey, but that Carey had been able at that time to divert suspicion, though later this had passed beyond his power also.

When, as eventually happened, the rumour reached Mr Ackerley's ears, the old man's distress was pitiable. Parry's repeated assurances that no one in authority believed the story did little to comfort him. A slur had been cast on his son's name, and he could not and would not rest till it was removed. But in the end he saw that he could do nothing. The suggestion was not printed in any paper nor had anyone made any direct statement about it before witnesses. No action at law was possible. Even, however, had it been, Mr Ackerley recognised that no such action would clear away the stain. At most it would show that Ronnie's guilt could not be proved; under no circumstances could it establish his innocence.

And then, as the days began to pass on, the police suddenly took drastic and unexpected action, causing a fresh shock to the workers on the Widening and extending public interest in the affair from a local to a national basis.

12

French on the Fraud

While the Southern Railway Company and Messrs John Spence & Sons were composing their differences as to the true price of earthwork on the Whitness Widening, Inspector French had not been idle.

He had gone to London on the Monday of Carey's death to interview that unhappy man's employers in the hope of picking up some hint of a possible motive for the murder of Ackerley. He had gone, not because he hoped for much result from the visit, but because he had worked out, or was in process of working out, every other vein which he had thought might contain ore. His prognostication had been justified. He had called at the firm's offices in Victoria Street and seen Mr Hugh Spence, the junior partner. He had put to him all the questions he could think of relative to Carey and Carey's relations with the other men on the Widening; he had received as complete answers to his questions as he could have wished; and in them all there was not a single iota of information bearing on his quest. Why Carey should have desired Ackerley's death, if he really had done so, remained to French an impenetrable mystery.

Disappointed, though scarcely surprised, French took advantage of being in town to call next morning at the Yard to make a general report of his progress. Being human, he made the most of the portion which he had solved—that Ackerley had been murdered—minimising the question of who was guilty, upon which, he pointed out, he was still working.

It was while discussing the affair with Chief Inspector Mitchell that he received a telephone call from Rhode, telling him of Carey's suicide and asking him to return in time to attend the inquest.

This message filled French with chagrin. He believed he understood what had occurred, and it looked bad for him. He had been guilty of the unpardonable sin! He had let his man slip through his fingers. Carey had murdered Ackerley. Carey had seen the net slowly closing. Carey had come to expect arrest, and before it was too late he had taken the only way out!

Though French was careful not to put this view into words, he was uncomfortably satisfied as to its truth. He blamed himself wholly. He had been far too open in his interrogation of Carey. He should not have let the man know that he was suspected. It would have been quite easy to have obtained his information and still kept that essential fact a secret.

French was not in the habit of crying over spilt milk, but this *dénouement* really worried him. It worried him more than mere failure in the case would have done. This was worse than failure. This was nothing more nor less than inefficiency. Well, it was a warning. He had been inclined latterly to be too pleased with himself. This was the result. He wondered whether or not this suicide of Carey's would end his case. Was there any use in proceeding with his inquiries? Did Carey's guilt or innocence now matter? The man was beyond the reach of the law. Suppose French proved him guilty: how would anyone be the better?

Rhode, however, with whom he talked the affair over on arrival, was of a different opinion. Rhode apparently had kept a more open mind and did not accept the guilt of Carey as demonstrated.

'If you don't prove it,' he pointed out, 'we'll always have it on our minds that it may have been someone else. I think you'll have to go on, inspector. Are you quite up against it?'

'By no means,' French returned bravely. 'All my conclusions so far were merely tentative.' He paused, then went on: 'It's true I've not got formal proof of Carey's guilt, as you say. But don't you think his suicide in itself is proof?'

Rhode shrugged. 'I think his guilt is likely,' he admitted. 'But likely is not enough. I'd be better pleased if there was something more definite.'

French smiled crookedly. 'Not better pleased than I,' he declared. 'I'm perfectly aware that until we can put up a decent motive, the thing remains unsatisfactory.'

Rhode nodded his large head. 'That's it, inspector. That's just what I feel. Suppose you look into it again.'

French thereupon went down to Whitness and attended the inquest on the body of Carey. He took no part in it, simply making sure afterwards from Sergeant Emery that no facts had come out, other than those mentioned at the inquiry.

French, feeling really rather baffled, settled down to try to push a little farther the lines of investigation he had already explored. On the pretext that the boy Langton was his nephew, down for a holiday after measles, he brought him round the Widening, introducing him in turn to Bragg, Parry, Lowell, Pole, and Templeton. He was, however, unable to surprise a flicker of recognition in the eyes of anyone concerned. Next he got Peabody, as a prospective purchaser of a dozen old sleepers, to ring up each of his suspects in turn, in the hope that the man might recognise the voice which had ordered the bicycle: again without result. He made an intensive but fruitless search at Lydmouth railway station for anyone who might have noticed a patron use the telephone box at the time the message to Peabody was put through. He tried unsuccessfully to find someone who might have seen a man with a bicycle going to the cliff beneath which Mr Ewing had taken his walk, or a man without a bicycle returning from it. He chatted with anyone he could find who had known either of the deceased men, in the hope that some word, accidentally dropped, would indicate a fresh line of research, but no such word fell from the lips of any of these persons. In fact, for several days French worked hard and had nothing to show for it.

Then Parry told him of the fraud.

Parry did not volunteer the information. Parry, indeed, was obviously reluctant to give it. But a phrase he used suggested to French that there was here something of which he had not heard. The mere hint of such a possibility was enough for French. Soon he had wormed out all the particulars, so far as Parry knew them.

To French the information was like the rolling away of

a fog and the revealing of a landscape, till then invisible, but now clear and sharp in its every detail. Here at last was the key for which he had been searching! This fraud would supply all the motives he wanted to complete his case.

Suppose Carey had learned that Ackerley was making those inquiries into the loading of the ballast wagons which must inevitably lead him to the discovery of the fraud. Such a discovery would mean for Carey disgrace and imprisonment; in fact, utter and complete ruin. Suppose, rather than face such an end, Carey had decided on a bold throw: that Ackerley should meet with a fatal accident. Suppose, the murder consummated, Carey found that in spite of his precautions the fraud, or the murder, or perhaps both, were about to come out. Suppose, indeed, that he believed that French was already on his track. What more likely, then, that he would have recourse to suicide as the only thing left him?

The more French considered this theory, the more adequate it seemed. It certainly covered the facts. True, it had not been proved, but with the information he now possessed its formal proof should not be difficult. Full of these ideas, he went in to have a consultation with Rhode. The superintendent's first remark took a lot of the wind out of French's sails.

'I was just going to ring you up and ask you to come in and talk about it,' he said. 'Curious that we should both have heard about it at the same time. Old Mr Ackerley got on to the chief constable about it and Major Duke reacted on me. The rumour appears to be that so large a fraud couldn't have been carried out by one man; that there must have been an accomplice on the railway side, and that that accomplice was Ackerley. The story has hit the father badly. He was almost in tears to the major, asking him to push on inquiries to clear his son's name. I don't blame the old man either; I would do so myself in his place.'

'Reasonable enough,' French agreed.

'From the old man's point of view, yes; but not from ours, I say. However, Major Duke was sorry for old Ackerley and said that if it would not cost us very much he would like to have a shot at clearing the boy's name. Another reason, inspector, for your going on and straightening things out.'

French made a gesture of impatience. 'Surely the fact that Ackerley was murdered clears him?' he protested. 'If it had been suicide he might have been guilty all right, but I'm hanged if I can see how his murder and his guilt square up.'

'I agree with you, but the rumour meets this difficulty. It is suggested that Ackerley *must* have been party to the fraud because Carey couldn't have worked it alone. It is next suggested that Ackerley saw it was coming out and to save himself decided to "discover" it himself. Most unlikely, I agree. Still, we'd better have it settled.'

It was in a much more hopeful frame of mind that French withdrew to his room at the hotel to think things over. This business of the fraud was going to make all the difference. It was the hinge on which his entire case turned. Instead of consisting of a couple of isolated acts, the drama was now a complete entity, properly motivated and bound together into a logical whole.

As he began to consider his next step, French saw that he must first settle the question of whether Ackerley was or was not party to the fraud. He did not himself believe in the young man's guilt, but the matter was fundamental and no progress could be made till it was set at rest. What was the suggestion founded on? Nothing connected with Ackerley himself. It depended wholly on the question of whether Carey could or could not have carried through the fraud alone. If Carey could have done so, there was not the slightest particle of evidence for suspecting Ackerley.

How was he to settle this point? Clearly by getting still more information about the fraud. French decided he would make more detailed inquiries, first from the Railway Company and then from the contractors.

Next morning, therefore, he took an early train to Lydmouth and asked to see Bragg. French had already questioned Bragg on the general situation, and he now turned at once to the fraud. He listened while Bragg explained its details. 'Of course,' Bragg ended up, 'a good deal of it we don't fully understand. We were not present at the contractors' inquiry except while giving evidence. But if it's essential to your case I have no doubt that you could get further information from Messrs Spence.'

'I shall do so,' French agreed. 'Now, Mr Bragg, I want your opinion upon another matter. It has been suggested, as you know, that Mr Ackerley was party to the fraud. What is your view on that?'

Bragg had mentioned many things with an air of doubt, but this time he seemed convinced.

'I don't believe it for a moment,' he declared emphatically, 'and everyone who knew Ackerley would say the same.'

French hitched himself a little closer to the desk.

'But surely,' he went on more confidentially, 'a fraud

like that did really require a confederate on the railway side? This, of course, has been suggested and it seems reasonable to me.'

'It doesn't to me,' Bragg retorted.

'It doesn't? You think one man could have done it all?'

Bragg passed his cigarette case to French.

'I think so,' he said slowly. 'But don't take my opinion for it. Let's follow the thing through and you can form your own. Now, first, you must understand exactly what plans were in existence. There were the original tracings of these cross sections, filed here in our plan-room, and there were five copies—identical photo prints. Two of these copies were signed and formed part of the contract documents, one being held by our secretary and one by the contractors at their headquarters. One was kept for reference in the office here and the remaining two were on the job, one in our office hut and the other in the contractors'. Of these five sets, only the two on the job were really used. As I have explained, they became progress charts on which the work done was periodically shown, and from which the certificates for payment were made. I tell you all this to show you that only the two sets at Whitness required to be faked, and you will understand that those two would never in the ordinary course be compared with the others. Have you followed me so far?'

'Yes, sir.'

'Very well, suppose somebody wanted to carry out the fraud; Carey, for argument's sake. How would he do it? He would begin, I think, by making a new set of linen tracings of the sections, putting in the alterations he required as he went along. Then he—'

'Excuse me, but how long would that take? Would it be a big job?'

'It would be a fair-sized job, yes, but not overwhelmingly big. The trouble would, of course, be to get the necessary time. He would probably work at night and on Sundays. You understand that he could take a few sheets at a time out of the cover: they're just held by a Stolzenburg loose-leaf binding.'

'He could take them home?'

'He could take them wherever he wanted to.'

'And out of his own cover, of course? I mean, the contractors' copy.'

'Of course. Well, the tracings made, he would require to get two sets of prints on the same paper that we use. "Arcoba, X35" is its trade name. It's a ferrogallic paper and it's made by Messrs Redpath & Halliday. Then he would trim these sheets and—'

'Excuse me again, but where would he get the prints made?'

'Ah,' said Bragg with a little shrug, 'now you're talking. It would require an apparatus. We have one here and the contractors doubtless have one at their headquarters, but I happen to know there is none at Whitness. You've asked a question that I can't answer.'

'Are those prints ever done by outside firms?'

'Frequently, indeed usually. It is only large offices that do their own.'

'Then I might be able to trace its having been done?'

Bragg shrugged again. His manner suggested that this was not his business, but on French's direct question he admitted he thought it might prove a profitable line of investigation.

'Another point,' said French. 'Suppose he had access to a printing apparatus, but wanted to get the paper. How much would he have to get?'

'I can't tell you definitely, because obviously it depends on the size of the roll, but if he used the size we get, which I think is the usual size,' Bragg made a short calculation, 'it would take two rolls. And then there is the tracing cloth.'

'Ah, true,' said French, 'I should have thought of that. By the way, is the cloth the same as the linen you spoke about?'

'Yes. Some people call it linen and some cloth.'

'Then I suppose he would want two rolls of tracing linen also?'

'No. You see, he would only want one tracing for every two prints. Besides the rolls of cloth are longer. One roll would be ample.'

'Thank you,' said French. 'Now we suppose he receives the prints. What does he do next?'

'His next step would be more difficult,' went on Bragg. 'He would somehow have to obtain access to our set down at Whitness. He would have to borrow it, which obviously he wouldn't wish to do, or he would have to get a key and go into our office at night, or something of that kind. Then he would have to copy on to his prints all the notes or colourings which had been added since the book was made up. There wouldn't be many, because the essence of his scheme would be to get the fraud going before much earthwork had been done. Simultaneously he'd have to forge his own people's notes on to his second set. Then he'd simply change the new sets for the old in both the covers and the thing would be done. The fraud would follow automatically as soon as the certificates were made from the faked plans.'

French was considerably impressed by all this. If Carey had not required assistance from a member of the railway staff, the argument advanced for believing Ackerley a party to the fraud had no foundation. As a result of this interview with Bragg, French felt his opinion of Ackerley's innocence confirmed.

This view was considerably strengthened by a talk which he had with Mayers, of the clerical staff of the office. It was Mayers' story of Ackerley's dissatisfaction with the earthwork quantities that had been considered the strongest argument for Ackerley's guilt. But as French listened to the details of the interview, he saw, as had Parry and others, that they would also bear a very different interpretation. Ackerley had not introduced the subject. The two men had been talking generally about the financial side of the job, and Mayers had remarked that, judging by the money paid, the work must be getting on well. It was in reply to this remark that Ackerley had said that he was satisfied with everything but the earthwork quantities, and told his story about the loading of the wagons. Mayers declared that Ackerley was genuinely puzzled, and scouted the idea that the young man could have been party to the fraud.

Mayers stated also that he had no idea that his report of this conversation had been taken as an indication of Ackerley's guilt, and declared that nothing was farther from his mind in mentioning it. He had simply hoped it might clear up something about the fraud.

Retiring to the waiting-room, French summarised what he had learnt.

Firstly, the fraud could have been carried out without Ackerley's help.

Secondly, so far as was known, Ackerley was keen on his job, ambitious and anxious to make a name for himself. He was not financially embarrassed, there being a reasonable sum to his credit in the bank. His bank-book gave no indication that he had been in receipt of more than his salary, of which, indeed, he was not spending the whole. He was not engaged to be married, nor had he any entanglement with a girl. He was not gambling. His life was healthy and normal.

Prior to his death his manner had also been normal. He had shown no signs of worry or excitement or embarrassment.

If the young man had been in such financial straits as to have adopted so desperate a remedy as the fraud, French did not believe he could have hidden the fact. Nor did he believe that under such circumstances his manner could have been anywhere near normal. French, in fact, came to the definite conclusion that Ackerley had had nothing to do with the frauds. He therefore put this problem out of his mind and went on to consider his next move in the case.

If Ackerley were innocent and were about to discover the fraud, as was now certain, and if Carey were guilty of the fraud, which according to Spence was also certain, it followed that the theory that Carey was the murderer of Ackerley was entirely reasonable and satisfactory. French was convinced of its truth, though here again he could not supply formal proof. For the *n*th time he wondered how this proof might be obtained.

For the moment he could not think of any direct way.

He therefore turned to the line of inquiry suggested by Bragg's statement: the obtaining of the prints. He drafted a notice addressed to all firms who made photo prints of engineering drawings, describing the Widening cross sections and asking for information as to the sale of one or more sets. This notice he sent to the Yard for insertion in all the technical journals to which such firms might have access.

At the same time he wrote to Messrs Redpath & Halliday, the manufacturers of the special paper which had been used, explaining what he wanted and asking if they had sold one or two rolls about the date of the beginning of the work on the Widening to Carey or anyone not a known customer, or indeed to any private individual in the neighbourhood of Lydmouth or Whitness.

Two days later there was an answer to this last letter. Messrs Redpath & Halliday wrote that on the 28th of January previously they had received through the post an order for two rolls of 'Arcoba X35' ferrogallic photo printing paper and one roll of 30-inch tracing cloth from a person whose name had not been previously on their books. He was a Mr John Salvington, of 16 King Street West, Drychester. The money, postal orders for the correct sum including postage, had been enclosed. They had duly forwarded the goods, which, so far as they were concerned, had closed the transaction.

Drychester was situated at the apex of a triangle of which the line Lydmouth-Redchurch formed the base. It was about twelve miles from Redchurch, and though rail connection was via Lydmouth, there was a direct service of 'buses. An hour after receiving the letter, French turned into King Street West.

French had expected to find that Mr John Salvington was an engineer or architect who had decided to do his prints himself, or perhaps a stationer who proposed to add photo printing to his other activities. When, therefore, he saw John Salvington's name above a small tobacconist's shop, he rubbed his hands. An accommodation address!

Mr Salvington was a wizened old man with a gray goatee beard and a whining voice. When French looked at him he immediately thought that the majesty of the law would be his best suit. With a serious air he produced his credentials and said that he was a police officer from Scotland Yard engaged on a murder case, and that he had reason to believe Mr Salvington could give him some important information on the matter.

Salvington, duly impressed, said he didn't know nothing of no murder case and that the officer had been misdirected.

'I don't think so, Mr Salvington,' French returned ponderously. 'We generally know what we're after. I don't suggest that you were personally concerned in the crime. I suggest you unwittingly had dealings with the murderer. Tell me, did you,' he produced and looked up his notebook with the usual overawing effect, 'on the 29th or 30th of January of this year, receive a parcel from Messrs Redpath & Halliday, Engineering and Optical Instrument Makers, of High Holborn?'

Mr Salvington, who had been showing uneasiness, made a gesture as if a light had broken on him. 'Was that a wrong 'un?' he exclaimed eagerly. 'You wouldn't never 'ave thought it. 'E was a quiet, civil-spoken man, not noways like a murderer.'

'That's the man I mean,' said French. 'Tell me what you can about him.'

Salvington spoke willingly enough. It appeared that three or four days before the date mentioned by the inspector, a man had entered the shop and said he wanted Salvington to do him a small service, for which he would pay the usual fee. His name, he said, was Roberts, and he was setting up in Drychester as an architect. He had not yet got rooms, and he wanted Mr Salvington to receive one or two letters and parcels for him. Salvington was not in the habit of giving an accommodation address, but he saw no reason why he should not do so, especially as it would mean sixpence a parcel. Roberts then said he was expecting some stuff from Redpath & Halliday, and would Salvington keep it till he called?

Three or four days later a parcel came, not addressed to Roberts but to Salvington himself. He was about to open it, but seeing the legend 'Engineering and Optical Instrument Makers' on the label, he did not do so. It was a long, thin parcel and might easily have been three rolls of paper.

Next day Roberts called. He claimed the parcel, saying that he had made a mistake in ordering the stuff, as he had given his, Salvington's name to the firm instead of his own. He paid his sixpence and took the parcel away.

So far the affair had not struck Salvington as being out of the ordinary, but he was surprised when the days passed and no letters or other parcels for Roberts arrived. In fact, this was the only transaction in which Roberts had figured, and Salvington had never seen him again.

French, very pleased at this story, now asked his critical question. He took from his pocket a number of photographs which he had managed to pick up, in one or other of which all the engineers employed on the Widening appeared. Handing these over, he asked Salvington if he could recognise Roberts.

Even to so old a hand as French a moment like this was always exciting. He watched the old man with a but slightly veiled eagerness as he slowly turned over the cards, peering short-sightedly at one after another. Then Salvington held up one of the photographs.

'That's 'im,' he exclaimed, pointing with a dirty thumb to a figure in one of the groups.

It was Carey; a good photograph, showing the features clearly.

Here, then, was valuable confirmation of the Spences' report on their chief resident engineer. This purchase of the printing paper proved that Carey was guilty of the fraud, apart from anything his employers had discovered. It did not, of course, prove that no one else was involved. French, however, felt that his investigation was getting on satisfactorily and that some other line of inquiry would give him that.

As he sat in the 'bus on his way back to Redchurch it occurred to him that he might obtain this remaining piece of information from studying the profits of the fraud. How were these paid? To whom were they paid? Did anyone but Carey participate in them?

This would involve another visit to Messrs Spence's headquarters. French decided that he would ring them up in the morning and make another appointment.

In the meantime a further line of research presented itself to him. If Carey had obtained the photo paper, how and where had he made the prints?

French was not certain what the process involved, though he believed its principal ingredients were printing in a frame like that used for photographs and washing with water in a bath. Whether a dark room was necessary, and whether chemicals were used, he did not know. He noted to inquire on these points from Bragg, then try to find out if Carey had access to, or could have improvised, the apparatus.

Next day, however, if the Spences could see him, he would go to town.

13

The Drawn Blinds

After dinner that night French settled down in his room at the hotel to bring his notes up to date and to take stock of his position. He always found that the careful revision of his conclusions in the quiet of his office or bedroom, was worth while. Frequently a flaw which he had overlooked in the hurry of the day's work, or an additional clue or deduction, would then occur to him, perhaps saving him from falling into some serious error or from wasting time in unprofitable inquiry. Even more valuable was the writing down in sequential order of the various points of the case. An argument set out on paper, the logic of which was intrinsically sound and each premise of which had been carefully checked and re-checked, was much more powerful than if it were merely carried in the mind. Moreover, it represented an invaluable preliminary to that concise and convincing report which it was always French's object to achieve.

His notes of the present case were already growing pretty voluminous, and to them he had added copies of everything that had been put in writing by the police at both Redchurch and Whitness, as well as the depositions of the witnesses at the inquests. Experience had taught him that these apparently irrelative documents were worth studying as a source of fresh ideas. Many a clarifying flash of insight had come to him in just that way.

He finished writing and arranging his notes and then began to read through the other papers. He skimmed the various police reports and the papers relating to the inquest on Ackerley. Finally he took up the records of the Carey inquest, intending when he had run through them to put the case out of his mind and turn to a novel.

Suddenly he stopped reading, and wrinkling his brow, sat gazing in front of him into vacancy. Here was something rather curious.

He was going over the depositions of the witnesses, recalling to himself their appearance and even the tones of their voices. He had reached the evidence of Albert Bradstreet, the assistant storesman, and it was a statement of his which had attracted his attention. This Bradstreet was the man who had found Carey's body. He had stated that when he had gone into the office the blinds were down as they always were; that he raised them to obtain light to set the fires; and that when he had done so he had seen Carey hanging from the roof.

French put down the papers and lay back in his chair, thinking intently. This certainly was a very surprising statement. How was it possible that no one had noticed its strangeness? How had he missed it himself? The more he now considered it, he more puzzled he became. With some faint dawning of actual excitement, he picked up the *dossier* again to refresh his memory as to the position in which the body had been found.

Carey was hanging by a rope from one of the beams of the roof, and the office stool, on which he had evidently stood to fix the rope round his neck, was lying kicked aside on the ground at his feet. French pictured the entire scene, then once again he pushed away the papers and sat rapt in profound thought.

Here was something which he certainly ought to have noticed before. Though every moment it seemed to grow more and more important, the whimsical idea shot through French's mind that it was the kind of point which would have appealed to Sherlock Holmes, as it would have enabled him without leaving his sofa to surprise Watson with a new and startling theory of the crime.

If Bradstreet had raised the blinds in order to obtain light to set the fire, it followed that the electric light was off. French now saw that he should have known this, as, had it been on, the fact would have been mentioned. But, and this was what was giving him so furiously to think, if the electric light was off, how had Carey seen to make those last terrible arrangements with the rope and stool?

Could he have done it in the dark?

Upon this question French pondered. For Carey, the getting of all the details right would have been of the very first importance. He could not afford any bungling. He could not risk merely hurting himself. If he were going to commit suicide, nothing mattered but the encompassing of his death. It was obvious that without light the rope could not have been taken off the bundle of pegs, nor could it have been tied to the beam and the noose made and adjusted to the proper height. It would not have been possible without light to have moved the stool to the exact place required. But would the dreadful final scene have been possible? Would Carey have attempted in the dark to climb the stool, adjust the rope round his neck, and kick away the stool?

French doubted it. He believed that had the extinguishing of the light been vitally important, Carey might have risked it. But in this case there was no object in turning out the light. One or other of the engineers frequently worked late, and a light in the office windows would have attracted no attention; at least, not till hours after Carey's terrible purpose would have been fulfilled. Nor would a light in the windows have attracted anyone who might not otherwise have gone to the office. No one would see it except the watchman or some person who was going there in any case.

The more French considered it, the more satisfied he became that Carey would never have turned out the light before taking his dreadful step.

But when French thought of the consequences of this conclusion, he became absolutely aghast. If he were right it followed that Carey had not committed suicide, but had been murdered!

He rose and began to pace the room. Carey murdered! Was it possible?

Then it occurred to him that if Carey had been murdered, the turning out of the light by the murderer before leaving the hut would have been a profoundly natural action. A mistaken one, no doubt, but none the less natural for that.

French grew more and more excited. Was this not too revolutionary an idea? Carey's death had been unhesitatingly accepted as suicide by everyone connected with the case, and this assumption worked in reasonably and naturally with all the other details. The theory of murder would upset everything. It really did seem out of the question.

Then French saw that if it were true it would affect the possibilities in the case of Ackerley's murder also. If Carey had been murdered it might well turn out that his alibi was good and that some unknown had killed both men.

French whistled softly. If there really were anything in this new idea the entire case that he had so laboriously built up would crash to the ground. All his deductions would be thrown once more into the melting pot and he would have to start again at the very beginning.

Then he pulled himself up sharp. He had been overlooking the fact that murder by hanging was practically unknown except in two cases; firstly, when the odds were several to one, as in the case of lynchings, and second, when the victim had been rendered helpless by sandbagging or drugging or in some other way. For this, of course, there was an excellent reason: it was too difficult. The victim would not submit without a struggle, and in the face of a struggle the physical strength required to carry out the deed would be greater than any ordinary man possessed.

French had brought a copy of *Taylor* in his suitcase and now he looked it up. His recollection was correct. The thing was put clearly on page 706. It read:

> '10. *Difficulties in Homicidal Hangings*.—It has been truly observed that of all the forms of committing murder hanging is one of the most difficult, and it is, therefore, but seldom resorted to. In most cases, when a person has been hanged by others, it has been after

death, in order to avert a suspicion of homicide. Hence the discovery of a body hanging affords *primâ facie* evidence of suicide, supposing it to be certain that death has taken place from this cause. We must, however, admit that a man may be murdered by hanging, and that the appearances about his body will not afford evidence of the fact. The circumstances which will justify a medical jurist in making this admission are the following:—1st. When the person hanged is feeble and the assailant a strong, healthy man. Thus a child, a youth, a woman, or a person at any period of life worn out and exhausted by disease or infirmity, may be destroyed by hanging. 2nd. When the person hanged, although usually strong and vigorous, is at the time in a state of intoxication, stupefied by narcotics, or exhausted by his attempts to defend himself. 3rd. In all cases murder may be committed by hanging when many are combined against one person, (*e.g.*, lynching). With these exceptions, then, a practitioner will be correct in deciding, in a suspected case, in favour of the presumption of suicide. Unless the person laboured under stupefaction, intoxication, or great bodily weakness, we must expect to find, in homicidal hanging, marks of violence about the body; for there are few who would allow themselves to be murdered without offering some resistance . . .'

According to *Taylor*, then, death by hanging might be taken as suicide, except in one of certain cases. French, having reminded himself that according to the medical evidence death was definitely due to hanging, went through these exceptions one by one. Carey was not feeble nor worn out nor exhausted by disease or infirmity. He was not in a state of intoxication, as had there been evidence of drink, it would have been commented on at the inquest. Nor was he exhausted by his attempts to defend himself, for the simple reason that he had made no such attempts; there were no marks of violence upon the body. Finally, the idea that he had been lynched by a number of persons was too unlikely to be seriously entertained.

There remained then just one possibility that the death had been murder: If Carey had been stupefied by narcotics. So far as the medical evidence was concerned, this might have been the case, as nothing but a post-mortem could demonstrate it, and a post-mortem had not been considered necessary.

As French thought over this possibility he saw that it offered him a definite solution of his problem, one way or another. From *Taylor's Principles*, Carey could not have been murdered unless he had first been drugged. French thought he might safely assume the converse also: that if he had been drugged he could not have committed suicide and, therefore, must have been murdered. What it came to then was that if Carey had been drugged, the case was murder, and if he had not been drugged, it was suicide.

French, having grown absorbed in this new possibility, forgot the havoc it might make with his case and became filled with satisfaction. An exhumation and a post-mortem should settle the question. Then it occurred to him that exhumations were not easy to arrange, and he wondered if before applying for one, he could produce some stronger evidence for murder than the point about the turning out of the light.

His mind full of repressed excitement, he went down next morning to Whitness to investigate the scene of the tragedy. There he found Lowell alone in the technical office, Pole and Templeton having gone out along the Widening.

'In the making up of my report on these tragedies, Mr Lowell,' he explained, 'I've got as far as Mr Carey's suicide. I hope you won't object to my having a look over the office in that connection?'

'Of course not,' Lowell returned. 'As a matter of fact, I'm just going down to the viaduct, so you can have the place to yourself. You don't want me?'

'Not at present at all events, sir. If I find anything that I don't understand I may want to ask a question or two.'

'Well, I'll be back in an hour and if you want me before that I'll be at Pier IV.'

This was just what French wanted, but had scarcely dared to hope for. He began by checking over the statements in the *dossier*, and Lowell presently took his leave.

An examination of the office confirmed French's idea of the previous evening. The preparations for the deed certainly could not have been done without light, and he felt his opinion strengthened that neither could the actual deed itself.

In the first place, the stool was not at all easy to climb upon. It was high and its base was small and the effort of mounting tended to overturn it. French indeed made three attempts before succeeding. In the dark he did not believe he could have done it.

Then the noose on the rope was all important. There must be no risk of its tangling or being improperly adjusted.

Here again light seemed essential. Nor was there any way in which, after Carey had reached the top of the stool and adjusted the rope, he could have turned off the light. The switch was out of reach, and had he tried to use some cord or other apparatus, this would have been found and commented on.

Systematically French continued his researches, examining the stool, the switch and other objects in the room on the chance of finding something helpful. But nowhere did he see anything. Finally, as a last resource he thought he would have a look at the beam to which the rope had been fastened. Piling some books on the stool, with a good deal of difficulty he climbed up.

At once he became keenly interested. As he flashed his electric torch on the top of the beam, he felt he had obtained the proof he required.

The tie beam, part of a small kingpost truss, was planed smooth and was thick with dust, and it was the marks in this dust which had attracted his attention. It was at once evident that the rope had not simply been thrown over the beam and made secure. It had been drawn over it while supporting a weight, and while thus being drawn, had slid sideways along the beam for over a foot. That the pressure had been very great was shown by the fact that the wood itself was marked.

So far as French could see, there was only one way in which that marking could have been made. Suppose Carey had been drugged and rendered unconscious. The murderer must then have lifted the inanimate body beneath the beam, fixed the rope round its neck, and raising the body with one arm, pulled down the rope with the other. It was the easiest, if indeed not the only way in which the deed could have been done. And it would have produced just those marks on the beam. The stool would, of course, have been afterwards laid on the floor as a blind.

On the other hand a suicide would have tied the rope to the beam in the first instance, and that mark of heavy dragging would not be there.

French was overwhelmed with delight. Neat, very neat, this demonstration of his! It was certainly a score off these local men. He would have bet a tidy sum that Emery had never looked at that beam, or if he had, he had missed its lesson. And both he and Rhode and the chief constable knew about the light, but none of them had had the wit to see its significance. No imagination, that what was wrong with these local police! It was no wonder they had to send for help to the Yard.

All the same French realised that he must not make the mistake of building too much on his own cleverness and neglecting detailed work. He must continue his search of the office in the hope of finding some further clue. It was surprising how often murderers dropped some small object or in some way impressed their personality on the scene of their crime. French looked very thoroughly everywhere, without, however, finding anything which pointed to the criminal.

He did not wait for Lowell's return, but made his way back to Redchurch. This was a matter of such importance that Rhode must be told of it forthwith. Besides an exhumation was now obviously necessary and Rhode was the man to make the arrangements.

Rhode, however, was from home and could not see him till the evening. Then he listened to French's story in his accustomed silence, though as the details revealed themselves amazement struggled with dismay on his heavy features. Only when French had finished did he speak. His comment took the form of a somewhat lurid oath.

'That's the second time we've been and gone and done it,' he observed bitterly. 'We let the Ackerley inquest go through with its suicide verdict, and it was murder. Then we let the Carey inquest go through the same way, and again we're wrong. I should congratulate you and all that, inspector, but that doesn't help us.'

'I'm afraid, sir, I'm in the same boat as your men,' French said tactfully. 'I was present at the second inquest and it wasn't till last night that the point about the light occurred to me.'

Rhode made a gesture as if dismissing compliments. 'What do you propose now?' he asked.

'There's another point to be considered,' French answered. 'I suggest that we say nothing about this till it's been gone into. It's this,' and he repeated the argument about the dope, which with the aid of Taylor's *Principles and Practice of Medical Jurisprudence* he had elaborated. Rhode immediately grew less sympathetic.

'I suppose all that means you want an autopsy?' he grumbled.

'Well, what do you think, sir?'

'Have you seen the doctor about it?' Rhode went on after a pause.

'No, but I question if he can help us much. He didn't notice dope or he'd have said so. And, of course, if he wasn't asked to make a post-mortem, you can't blame him. There was nothing to suggest murder.'

'I'm not so sure about not blaming the doctor. However, only a fool is wise after the event.'

French, having satisfactorily interpreted this somewhat cryptic utterance, tactfully agreed.

'I'll have a word with the chief constable,' Rhode said at length. 'If he agrees, we'll apply for an order to exhume the body.' He sat silently, staring before him. 'This is going to mean an upset for your theory, inspector?'

French nodded. 'Complete. I've got to start from the beginning again.'

'Is it as bad as all that?'

'I think so, sir, though I've not considered it enough to say definitely. This murder of Carey makes it unlikely that he killed Ackerley, and if he didn't kill Ackerley, the whole of my theory goes west.'

'Well you know, French,' the superintendent leaned forward confidentially over his desk, 'I was never very satisfied about that alibi of Carey's being a fake. You realised the difficulties?'

'I think so, sir. What do you include?'

'Just that if Carey wrote that letter he showed himself a bigger fool than one would have expected. In the first place, if the man was really in love with this girl, Brenda Vane, and I take it there's no doubt about that, would he have chosen the particular reason for the meeting given in the letter: that the girl was in trouble through one of his assistants? I scarcely see him doing that. Then for the same reason he wouldn't want to bring her into court, even to testify on his behalf. Besides, if they were believed to be in love, he would know that her evidence would be discredited. It would be argued that she was lying to save him. You thought of these points?'

'Yes, I thought of them.'

'And considered them unimportant?'

French shook his head. 'No, I shouldn't say that. I thought them important enough. But on the balance I thought they weighed less than the arguments for Carey's guilt.'

'You may be right,' Rhode admitted. 'Carey may have murdered Ackerley and someone else may have murdered Carey. But it isn't likely.'

'No, sir, it isn't likely. Someone has done both jobs. Probably there was someone in the fraud with Carey and they've had a row. That for a guess at all events.'

'I should say you were on to it, French. What are you going to do next?'

'I've not decided yet, sir. I'll go and get some dinner and then have another look over the thing and fix up a programme.'

The fixing up of the programme turned out more difficult than French had anticipated. Indeed he was surprised to find that the more he thought over the case, the more puzzled he grew. He had imagined that his new discoveries would clear the affair up, but they did not after all do so. On the contrary, they seemed to have left things in a worse tangle. They certainly offered no suggestion as to the identity of the guilty man. Feeling a trifle up against it, French turned back to his earlier solace, the *dossier*, and began to consider from the new viewpoint what he read.

First as to what had actually taken place, or was alleged to have taken place, on the night of Carey's death. Just before the usual closing time, 5.30, all the members of the staff happened to be in the office. About 5.30 Carey left. He said he was going over to the railway hut and that no one need wait for his return. The other three men then left, Templeton about 5.40, Lowell about 5.45, and Pole about 5.50. The clerical staff having already gone,

Pole turned out the lights and locked up. None of these persons, either clerical or technical, had returned to the office that night.

Carey, after leaving his own office at 5.30, had visited that of the railway engineers' and had waited there to see Bragg. He had left about 5.55, and where he had gone was not known. No one appeared to have seen him either leave or return to the yard, if indeed he had done so. He might, of course, have used the engineers' gate. He frequently entered and left by this route, walking across the railway to the sea front. At all events he had presumably returned to his office by 6.15, when Parry saw the light in the window.

The doctor had given it as his opinion that Carey had been dead for many hours when found. Probably, therefore, the murder had been committed on the previous evening, perhaps comparatively early.

All these circumstances, French saw, gave a new value to the episode of the silhouetted man. It certainly looked as if this man might be the murderer. French read up the details of Parry's statement. On his way from his own office he had passed within some forty yards of the contractors' hut. As he did so he saw a figure approaching the hut. It passed between him and the lighted windows of Carey's office, and he saw the silhouette of a man's head and soft hat. The man had knocked at the door, but as it was not opened to him, he had presently opened it himself with a key.

Parry had been unable to suggest the identity of this man or indeed to describe him otherwise than as tall. He was sure, however, about the knocking at the door, the waiting for a moment and entering with a key. These points struck French as important. They were certainly unusual actions. If one has a key for a door one doesn't knock, or at all events one only gives a short knock as a warning of one's approach. One opens the door and walks in. But this man knocked and waited. It was only when he found that the door was not going to be opened for him that he opened it for himself.

For some minutes French puzzled over the point, then suddenly he saw a possible explanation. This man whom Parry had seen was the murderer. At the time of his visit Carey had already been doped, either by this man himself or by some confederate. On reaching the hut the murderer did not know whether or not the dope had taken effect. He perhaps did not want Carey to recognise him, lest Carey might have realised his danger and called for help. He therefore knocked. If Carey had been able to open the door, the murderer, on hearing his footsteps, would have slipped away and returned later. As Carey did not open, the murderer assumed he was helpless from the drug, and entered.

This, French saw, was pure speculation, but it did at least cover the facts. It also indicated a necessary item for French's programme, the finding of this mysterious visitor.

Temporarily dismissing this particular problem, French took a clean sheet of paper and began to work on another line. A complete list of all the persons who might be guilty, so far as he could make it, would probably be useful.

There were in the case as a whole, three separate episodes: the fraud, the murder of Ackerley and the murder of Carey. It was not definitely known that these were connected, but the probability of their being so was very great. Assume they were and see where it led.

First then the fraud.

Here the questions he had to answer were two in number: (a) Who would have gained by the fraud? and (b) Who could have changed the sections?

French saw that in order to answer the first question he must interview the contractors, as he had already intended. This had now become a vital matter and he noted to ring them up in the morning and fix up a meeting. In the meantime he could only assume that Carey alone had benefited. Carey, however, might have passed on part of his illicit gains to some other person.

As to the changing of the sections, he realised that practically anyone could have done it. Carey, Lowell, Pole, Bragg, Ackerley, Parry and Templeton: anyone of them could be guilty. In fact, anyone, whether he could have changed the sections or not, might have been Carey's accomplice.

Secondly, Ackerley's murder.

Into this French had already gone, though he was not sure that he would not have to reopen the question. His preliminary inquiries had led him to the conclusion that only Carey could have been guilty. He had reached this conclusion because every other possible—so far as he knew who were possibles—either had an alibi or failed to comply with the boy, Langton's, description.

There remained the third episode, the murder of Carey. The problem here was simple. Who of the possibles had no alibi for the period in question?

French had to admit that he had not sufficient information to enable him to reach a conclusion. Whether Lowell, Pole and Templeton had alibis, he didn't know. Parry and Bragg had each a tentative alibi—one was supposed to be busy at a plan and the other to have gone to Drychester—but it was, of course, possible that investigation might break these down.

French was becoming rather appalled at the amount of work which was stretching out before him as he added these items to his programme. However, it was at least good to have a programme, and somewhat more hopeful than when he began his review, French had a drink and went up to bed.

14

The Payment in Notes

Next morning French put through an early call to Messrs Spence, fixing up an appointment with Mr Hugh Spence for that afternoon. He followed his message up to town and at three o'clock presented himself at the firm's offices in Victoria Street.

'Well, inspector,' Mr Spence greeted him. 'What's the new trouble? I gathered from your telephone that something serious had happened.'

'I'm afraid you're right, sir,' French returned, 'at least, in a way. It's not that anything fresh has occurred, but that we've found that we were mistaken in the views we held about what did happen. That's not very clear perhaps, but I'll explain. It's about those two deaths. It was assumed that Mr Ackerley was accidentally killed and that Mr Carey committed suicide. I'm afraid, sir, neither of these assumptions was correct. I regret to tell you that both were murdered.'

That French had justified his call in Spence's eyes, there could be no doubt. The junior partner made no attempt to hide his amazement and horror. 'Good heavens, inspector! You're not serious?' he gasped. 'Carey *murdered*! I can scarcely believe it.'

'There's unhappily no doubt about it, sir,' French went on. 'Both the crimes were carried out exceedingly skilfully, one to suggest accident, the other suicide. It was quite by chance that the true facts were discovered.'

Mr Spence seemed quite upset. 'I must call my partner,' he declared. 'He should know of this and he would like to hear the story at first hand.'

He disappeared and French was left alone in the elaborately furnished office. At least, he thought, he would not be faced with any difficulty in obtaining information from the firm. In Mr Hugh Spence's present frame of mind he would certainly give all the help he could. And when in a moment the cousin, Mr Elmer Spence, appeared, French felt he might say the same about him.

Elmer was a much older man than his cousin. He looked more responsible and a good deal sterner, and French believed he was now in the presence of the real head of the firm. But in spite of his obvious strength of mind he was showing the same evidences of agitation as Hugh.

'This is terrible news, inspector,' he began at once. 'I can scarcely believe it. You say that both Carey and Ackerley were murdered? I suppose there can be no mistake about it? You really are quite sure?'

'Quite, sir,' French assured him. 'As I told your partner, we discovered it almost by chance, but there is no doubt of the facts.'

The partners subsided into chairs. 'Terrible, terrible,' Mr Elmer murmured; 'and so utterly surprising. It's just about the last thing I should have expected to hear. Tell me, have you—er—any idea of who could have done it?'

French contrived to look mysterious. 'We've not quite made up our minds as yet,' he answered, 'but, of course, we're making inquiries. Hence my presence here today.'

The partners exchanged glances. 'I'm afraid we've already told you everything that we know,' Hugh declared, 'but, of course, we'll be glad to help in any way we can.'

'Yes, yes,' Elmer added, 'of course. The inspector knows that. But really, with the best will in the world, I don't think there is anything that we can tell you. We know absolutely nothing about this terrible affair.'

French nodded. 'I'm sure of that, sir,' he declared tactfully. 'But you can tell me something that may help me to find the motive. The obvious suggestion is that the tragedy was connected with the recent fraud. Now, gentlemen, you inquired into that and I want you to tell me what you learned.'

In spite of the partners' cordiality, they were evidently far from pleased at this. French wondered if he knew why.

'Of course, you understand, gentlemen,' he added, 'that anything you tell me will be considered strictly confidential unless it proves to be material evidence. Otherwise we do not wish to pry into your or anyone else's business.'

'Yes, yes,' returned Spence senior, 'we understand that. But we have nothing to tell you beyond what was contained in our report to the Railway Company. You've seen that, of course?'

'Yes, sir; Mr Bragg showed it to me.'

'Well, what more do you want?'

'I want this, sir,' said French. 'I want to know, firstly, what sums by way of bonus or percentage were paid to

Mr Carey as a result of the fraud, and secondly, whether any similar sums were paid to any other person or persons, and if so, how much?'

The partners hesitated and exchanged glances. Finally old Mr Spence replied.

'That, of course, is strictly confidential information, inspector, which under normal circumstances we should not dream of giving. We cannot and will not stand in the way of justice, but I'm afraid you'll have to convince us that it really is necessary before we give it.'

Beneath his breath French swore; outwardly he nodded gravely and said he admitted fully the reasonableness of Mr Spence's position, but that he thought he would have little difficulty in supplying the necessary proof. 'It's a matter of motives,' he went on. 'I must know who got that money and how much it was, if I am to know whether its receipt was or was not connected with the crimes.'

'It all went to Carey. You might have known that from our report to the Company.'

'I imagined it did, but Mr Carey may have passed it on. I must know how much went to him and the dates on which it went, to enable me to ascertain whether anyone else benefited.'

Messrs Spence were so unwilling to say more that presently French pointed out very politely that if they couldn't see their way to give him the information in private, he would obtain an order for recovery of documents and their books would be taken into open court. A good deal more argument ensued, but at last the cousins gave way. Then they gave way handsomely. Not only did they produce the figures, but they showed French their books and explained how these had been made up. The bonus sums had been paid by separate cheques from those representing Carey's salary, as they became due every four weeks, whereas the salary was paid monthly.

It seemed that as a result of the fraud Carey had received allowances totalling to some £2025. Payments had been going on practically since the start of the job twelve months earlier, and the amounts per period had varied between £75 and £300. French made a detailed note of the figures.

'Thank you, gentlemen, that will be a help. Now, one or two more questions and I have finished. Can you tell me anything of Mr Carey's family or to whom his property goes?'

Messrs Spence were unable to do so. His parents they knew were dead, and so far as they were aware he was not married nor had he other relatives.

'Now this,' French went on, 'is a more difficult question because it is a general one. Can you tell me anything, of any kind whatsoever, which might throw light on these tragedies, or which might suggest a line of inquiry into them?'

The Spences immediately replied that they could not. French, however, was not satisfied and plied them with further questions. He obtained, however, nothing of the slightest value.

'My last question.' French was interested to see a flicker of relief pass over the partners' faces. 'You know, of course, the fraud involved the tracing of all the cross sections and the making of two complete sets of photo prints. Now, I can prove that Carey secretly bought enough tracing linen and photo print paper for this purpose. But I've—'

'We didn't know that, inspector.'

'No, sir, I forgot to mention it when I was telling you

of the case. I was going to say that I've not yet discovered where the prints were made. I understand you have an apparatus and what I want to know is, could they have been secretly made here?'

This was a new and evidently a disconcerting idea to the Spences. 'I see what you're getting at,' Elmer Spence said unhappily. 'You think Carey had an accomplice here in the office?'

'Not necessarily. Could Carey, for instance, have come up here on a Saturday, worked all night and returned to Whitness on Sunday? He had a key for the office?'

Spence looked doubtful. 'Oh, yes, all the technical staff have keys,' he said, then paused, glancing at his cousin. 'I suppose what the inspector suggests is possible, Hugh?'

Hugh agreed that it was theoretically possible, but neither of the cousins believed for a moment that anything of the kind had been done.

'All the same I should like to ask a question or two of your staff,' French persisted. 'Someone may have noticed something which might help me.'

To this the partners made no objection, and calling their chief technical assistant, gave him instructions that French was to be given every facility for making his inquiries.

This was a long shot and French did not wish to spend much time on it. All the same he made a reasonably complete investigation. In the end he had to conclude that the Spence cousins were correct, and that while it was just possible that the faked prints had been made in Victoria Street, it was most unlikely.

As that evening French sat in the train on his way back to Redchurch, he felt that his day had not been wasted. He had got what he went up for; the amounts the fraud had brought in to Carey, and the knowledge that it had not brought in anything to anyone else. The matter of the printing of the sections was secondary, and he had not hoped to obtain any information about it. There now remained the question of whether Carey had passed on any of his ill-gotten gains to any other person. That French would tackle in the morning.

Accordingly next day he laid another course of the structure he was so carefully erecting. Soon after the Whitness Branch of Lloyd's Bank opened he called and asked to see the manager.

'I saw, sir,' he began when he had stated the business which had brought him to Dorset, 'from papers in the late Mr Carey's desk that he banked with you and it is about his finances that I have called.' He went on to explain in confidence his belief that Carey had been murdered, and added that so far as was known the deceased had been alone in the world and had made no will. 'I know, sir,' he went on, 'that a gentleman in your position will not without special authority give the police information about his client's affairs, but I put it to you that this case is quite exceptional.'

He enlarged so movingly on the reasons why he thought he should get his information that to his own surprise he finally convinced the manager.

Carey, it appeared, had been in the habit of paying into his account all the cheques he received from the contractors, issuing his own cheques to pay his bills or if he wanted cash. All his salary cheques were thus lodged in full, but when French came to examine the bonus cheques he found a surprising exception to the rule.

From the first bonus cheque up to that for the

four-weekly period ending on the 3rd October, only half the bonus amounts had been lodged. In every case Carey had taken the other half in notes. But in the case of the last two cheques, that for the period ending 31st October and 28th November, he had received no cash, the entire sums going to his account.

French next obtained from the manager the actual figures of income and outgo which made up Carey's account, looking at once to see if any cheques had been issued to cover the half amounts of the last two bonus payments. But there were none.

He left the bank, and going to one of the railway waiting rooms, sat down to think the thing out. Carey had received the entire profits of the fraud. But it looked very like as if he had not kept the whole of the money. What about those half payments in notes?

Well, French could suggest an obvious explanation for that, though he would be very much surprised if it proved true. Did these facts not look as if in the early stages Carey had had a partner in the fraud, a confederate who received half the profits? And did they not further suggest that in October the partner had dropped out, leaving the entire proceeds to Carey?

If so, who could the confederate have been? Here the answer was equally obvious. One person had left the work during the month in question, and one person only. Ackerley! Did these facts mean that Carey and Ackerley had formed a guilty partnership to defraud the Railway Company, which partnership had been dissolved on Ackerley's death?

For a couple of hours French sat smoking in the waiting-room while he considered the question from every angle, and the more he thought of it, the more convinced he became that no other explanation would meet the facts.

He saw clearly enough that this theory contradicted his previous conclusion that these two men were innocent and that some third person had murdered them both. Well, if some third person had done so, he had missed the reward. The money had gone to Carey. Except for those early half payments, the money had remained in Carey's account. If a third person had committed the murders, it was impossible to imagine his motive.

French swore. The thing was confoundedly puzzling. He had been getting on quite well and now here was a snag. He would have to reconsider his conclusions.

Rhode had asked him to call that evening to let him know the result of his visit to London. French had still some hours to spare and he thought he could not better employ the time than by trying to follow up the matter of the printing of the cross sections.

Accordingly he took the first train to Lydmouth, and calling on Marlowe, asked if he could help him with the inquiry. It appeared, fortunately, as French thought, that Bragg and Parry were out of the office. Marlowe, therefore, rang for the junior, Bolton, with whom Parry had discussed the footbridge for Lydwater, and told him to assist the inspector in every way he could.

Bolton proved communicative. He showed French where and how the prints were made, and went into the possibilities of the work being done secretly. The result was the same as so many previous results in this exasperating case. It seemed possible that anyone who had a key of the office could, with care, have developed prints without leaving traces. That anyone had done so, however, there was not the slightest particle of evidence.

When French got back to Redchurch Rhode was expecting him. He heard the tale of French's adventures without comment.

'So there it is,' French ended up. 'That one bit of evidence about Carey getting half those payments in notes during Ackerley's lifetime, and not after Ackerley's death, suggests that Ackerley was a partner in the fraud. On the other hand all the remaining evidence suggests he wasn't. It's a bit puzzling.'

Rhode was impressed about the payment in notes. 'I think we may take that as quite definite proof that Carey had a confederate with whom he was dividing fifty-fifty,' he remarked. 'I'm not so sure of the Ackerley part of it.'

'Nor am I,' French agreed, 'but I don't see how else to explain Carey's keeping the whole of the payments since Ackerley's death.'

Rhode whistled tunelessly below his breath. 'Suppose,' he said presently, 'Carey had an accomplice, not Ackerley; and suppose they had a row and Carey refused to pay any more cash. Wouldn't that account for the whole thing? As a result of the refusal mightn't the accomplice have murdered him?'

'A bit of a coincidence that the row should occur just at the time of Ackerley's death.'

'No doubt, but coincidences do happen.'

French thought over this. 'There's another difficulty, sir. If what you suggest were so, how would the accomplice get his money: I mean after Carey's death? The money was paid to Carey and to Carey only.'

'That's a fact.' Rhode paused, then went on: 'It looks

like Ackerley right enough, and yet as you say yourself, there's a lot of evidence as to Ackerley's innocence.'

'It's been what's puzzling me,' French admitted. 'I would jump at the idea of some confederate other than Ackerley, but I can't see who it might be.' He paused and a sudden eager look came into his eyes. 'I tell you, sir; it has just occurred to me this moment. There is one person to whom the difficulty of losing the money wouldn't apply.'

Rhode glanced at him keenly. 'Get on with it,' he growled. 'Think I'm a thought reader?'

'Carey's successor.'

Rhode nodded slowly. 'It's an idea,' he agreed. 'Yes, it's an idea. If his successor had been going halves with him, Carey's removal would leave the entire proceeds to the successor. Instead of getting nothing, he'd get all. That's more hopeful, French. Go ahead to the next stage.'

'The next stage is that Lowell is the successor. But the question is, did he know that during Carey's lifetime?'

'He'd have a pretty good idea. These appointments usually hinge on whether there's anyone else for the job, and he'd know that. It seems to me, French, that there's another line for you: Lowell.'

'I agree, sir. I'll go into it at once. All the same we mustn't forget that Lowell had an alibi for the Saturday night before Ackerley was killed.'

Rhode shrugged. 'I shouldn't build too much on that,' he advised. 'You know as well as I do that alibis can be faked. See what this Lowell idea gives you, and if necessary you can go into the alibi again later.'

'I'll do so.' French got up. 'I suppose that's all we can do now?'

'No, sit down again. We exhumed that body last night.'

'Oh,' said French in some surprise. He had expected to have been asked to be present.

'Yes. You were in town when we got the order and I thought it wasn't worth while waiting for you.'

'I came back last night, sir.'

'I didn't know that or I should have advised you. However, it doesn't matter. What I wanted to say is that I'm expecting to hear from the analyst every moment. You better wait till his report comes through.'

French was so certain of the correctness of his conclusions as to Carey's death that he had lost a good deal of his original interest in the analyst's report. Evidence of drugging would, of course, be useful when the case came into court, but French did not think it would materially assist his present inquiry. He said as much to Rhode and the two men drifted into a desultory conversation on drugging as an asset to crimes of violence.

'You might be able to trace the purchase of the drug, you know,' Rhode said presently. 'That would be something that you couldn't afford to sneeze at.'

French had not overlooked the possibility, and while they discussed the steps which might prove desirable in this connection, the analyst's report arrived.

It was as French had believed. Carey had been heavily drugged with butyl-chloral hydrate and the analyst estimated that the dose must have amounted to about 60 grains.

'There you are,' Rhode said somewhat grimly. 'Does that satisfy you?'

French agreed that, so far as it went, it was right enough. 'Butyl-chloral hydrate,' he went on; 'if I don't mistake, that's not a poison under the act. Anyone could get it by making up some plausible story and signing the poison book. Not so easy to trace the sale, but of course, I'll have a shot at it.'

That night French wrote confidentially to Hugh Spence, asking him to let him know what had been the arguments for and against appointing Lowell as successor to Carey, and also saying how far these arguments might reasonably have presented themselves to Lowell. Then he drafted a circular for insertion in the various chemists' and druggists' journals, requesting information as to the purchase of butyl-chloral hydrate by persons unknown to the salesmen.

French felt that he need not wait for a reply from Spence before testing his suspicions of Lowell. No matter what the reply, Lowell was a suspect and his actions on the night of Carey's death must be gone into. Next day then he would take up this line of research.

He trusted it would be the last in a very puzzling and troublesome case.

15

Elimination

On the following morning French went down once again to the contractor's office. There he was lucky enough to find Lowell, as well as Pole and Templeton. The news of the exhumation had leaked out, and all three seemed just as keen to get information from French as he was to learn from them.

'Yes,' he said in answer to a question from Lowell, 'there is reason to suspect that it may have been murder, and that will excuse my having to put to each of you gentlemen some purely formal, but I am afraid, rather unpleasant questions,' and he went on with his little tale about these being a mere matter of routine.

French was interested by the reaction each of his hearers displayed. All three at once told him to go ahead, but whereas Parry and Templeton were obviously merely interested, Lowell betrayed undoubted signs of uneasiness. However, he answered as readily as the others.

'I want, in a word,' French went on, 'to know just how you gentlemen spent your time that evening. I think it might be more convenient if you would tell me one by one, and if you will let me have the use of the inner office, perhaps one of you would come in?'

'Of course, inspector,' Lowell answered. 'I'll come with you, and when you have finished with me the others can go in turn.'

They sat down in the private room, closing the door.

'Now, if you please, Mr Lowell. Give me all the detail you possibly can, so as to save my having to ask questions.'

'It isn't so frightfully easy to remember everything one did on an occasion of this kind,' Lowell began. 'Now, I could tell you about next day. Everything is fixed in my mind by Carey's death. But the evening before there was nothing to fix things on my mind. However, I'll do my best.'

French replied with non-committal encouragement. If Lowell were innocent, what he said was perfectly true: if guilty, it was the thing he naturally would say.

'That afternoon we were all in the office. I was rather slack and was finishing up some unimportant routine work. As I was sitting there it suddenly occurred to me that concreting was to begin on the arch of Bridge 982 first thing in the morning. That's a small bridge at the far end of Cannan's Cutting, a mile or more from here. I remembered that I hadn't inspected the reinforcing steel work. I had intended to do so that day and had forgotten. It's my job, you understand, to see all reinforcement before it's covered, and if anything should afterwards be found wrong, I should get it in the neck.

'I thought for a while that I needn't trouble about the thing and that it would be all right. Then I saw that it would be too serious for me to risk a possible mistake, and I decided I'd go out then and there and have a look over the work. Carey and Templeton had gone and I didn't say anything to Pole about it, simply because I didn't want to be chipped for my forgetfulness.'

Again Lowell paused, but French making no comment he presently continued: 'It was closing time in any case, so I put my torch into my pocket and went out. It was pretty dark, but I knew the way well and managed all right. I went over the bridge carefully with my torch; it didn't take very long. Then I went straight to "Serque". I got in before dinner, which, as Carey didn't come in, I had with Pole. After dinner I didn't feel like going out again and I lay on the sofa and read a novel till bedtime. Pole didn't go out either, so he can bear witness to that part of it.'

French made a mildly deprecatory gesture.

'That's all very clear, Mr Lowell. Now, I wonder could you put times on to it all? I like things set out in the form of a railway timetable. First, can you say what time you left the office?'

Lowell considered. 'About quarter to six, I should think: I'm not quite sure.'

'Good enough. And when did you arrive at "Serque"?'

'Let's see. It would have taken, say, twenty minutes to walk out, twenty to inspect the steelwork and twenty-five to walk back—it's a little farther to "Serque." I must have arrived at "Serque" about ten minutes to seven. That would be about right, too. We have dinner at seven and I had just comfortable time to change.'

'Good enough again.' French moved a little forward and became more confidential. 'Now, Mr Lowell, our instructions are always to get as much confirmation as possible when we take statements.

'With regard to the time you spent in the office before going out to the bridge, and at "Serque" after returning, we needn't worry: there'll be plenty of corroboration for that. That leaves the hour from 5.45 to 6.45. What confirmation can you give me about that?'

Lowell shrugged. 'None, I'm afraid,' he answered shortly.

'Did no one see you walking out or in?'

'Not that I know of. You see, it was dark and the men had gone home.'

'The watchman?'

'He didn't see me. I went out by the small gate near the offices.'

French slowly rubbed his chin. 'I wish you would try and think of some confirmation for that part of your statement,' he persisted. 'You know, we believe that it was during that hour that Mr Carey was murdered, and it would, therefore, be better for everyone concerned to be able to prove where he was at that time.'

There was now no question of Lowell's anxiety. He went some shades paler and nervousness showed in his jerky movements. He shook his head helplessly.

'Well, if you can't, you can't,' French said presently, moving back in his chair. 'But if you think of anything, let me know. Thank you, Mr Lowell. May I see Mr Pole?'

Lowell got up, walked to the door, hesitated, and came back.

'I've just remembered a little incident,' he said. 'I'm afraid it doesn't exactly prove my story, but at least it tends towards corroboration.'

'Good,' said French. 'Let's have it.'

Lowell once more sat down. 'It's a very small thing,' he said; 'only that while I was checking up the reinforcement

I lost my rule. I laid it down to consult the plan and forgot it. As a matter of fact I afterwards learned that it had slipped down to the springing and got hidden behind some rodding. It wasn't till the second day that it was discovered.'

'Yes?' French encouraged.

'That's all, I'm afraid. I thought perhaps the rule having been found there would be evidence of my going out.'

'Can you prove all that?' French asked doubtfully.

'I think so. I had my rule that day before Carey's death. I was using it that afternoon at the viaduct. Pole was with me and saw it. From then I was in the office all the time till quarter to six, so I couldn't have dropped it before that.' Lowell's manner became more eager and he seemed to be warming to his subject. 'I believe this is going to help after all, inspector. Next day, that was the day after Carey's death, I was about the yard all the time. Someone must have noticed me. I missed my rule that day and asked if anyone in the office had seen it. Then next morning it was found at the bridge. I hadn't been out a second time when it was found.'

'That would seem quite useful, Mr Lowell.'

French's manner was non-committal. This was not quite the kind of alibi he liked. There was rather too much of a coincidence about losing the rule at the very time and place at which its recovery would provide the required evidence. However, it might be right enough. It would be his duty to test it and he would do so carefully.

That being all Lowell could tell, French asked him to send in Pole.

Pole said that on the afternoon of the day before that on which Carey's death was discovered Carey was the first to leave the office. Templeton followed a few minutes later, and after him Lowell. Lowell went out about quarter to six. He, Pole, left very soon after, shortly before six, shutting up the office. He went straight to 'Serque', where he changed and sat about reading the paper till dinner. After dinner Lowell and he spent the evening with novels.

Pole did not know whether he could get any confirmation of his whereabouts during the hour 5.45 to 6.45. The watchman had seen him leave the yard, but whether the man would remember this, he couldn't tell. He had reached 'Serque' a few minutes after six, but he had let himself in and he could not tell whether anyone had seen him arriving. French took a note to make inquiries on the point.

French next turned to Lowell's alibi. Yes, Pole had seen Lowell using his rule at the viaduct that same afternoon. In fact, he had used it himself and he knew it was Lowell's because he had noticed his initials on it. Next day Lowell complained that he had lost it. He mentioned it in the office and asked whether anyone had seen it. That was on the day of the discovery of Carey's death. On the day following it was found. It had slipped down under the reinforcement of a bridge near Cannan's Cutting. Lowell then said that he had gone out to check the reinforcement on the evening before Carey's death, having forgotten to do so earlier in the day. Yes, Lowell was in the office all that day on which the tragedy was discovered and could not possibly have gone out to the bridge. Oh, yes, the finding of the rule showed that Lowell was there all right, at least it did so in his, Pole's, opinion.

French did not really suspect Pole. He thought he was too junior to have carried through these terrible operations. However, if proof were available that he reached 'Serque' a little after six, it would set the matter at rest.

Templeton followed Pole. He explained that he had lodgings in another quarter of the town and that when he left the office he went straight to them. He did not know whether anyone there had seen him enter, but he had had supper at seven and his presence at the meal could be vouched for. After supper he had gone to the same billiard rooms as on the night of Ackerley's death, and the proprietor would doubtless remember his being there.

French next immersed himself in the rather uninteresting work of checking the statements of these three men. In the cases of Pole and Templeton he made little of it. On calling at 'Serque' and at Templeton's lodgings he learned that both men had had their evening meals at seven, that both were believed to have come in some time before that hour, but that no one knew how long. Templeton's statement that he had spent the evening playing billiards proved true.

So far as French could learn, then, either Pole or Templeton might have committed the murder. But he did not believe either of them had. This admittedly was merely his, French's, private opinion, and he still noted the two men as possibles, though improbables.

With regard to Lowell French did not feel so sure. That alibi about visiting the bridge and losing the rule had a very artificial sound. It was the kind of alibi that might be invented by a not very brilliant schemer, a man, French judged, with mental powers similar to Lowell's. A really finished rogue always eliminated the element of coincidence from his alibis, but here a most improbable coincidence was the foundation of the whole thing.

So thought French as he tramped out along the line to the bridge in question. It was an unpleasant day, dull and cold and gray, with a keen easterly wind which flecked the lead-coloured sea with white. French was interested in the work along the Widening, and on two occasions he could not help stopping to watch what was going on. Then he reminded himself that he had something else to do than stand and watch other people working, and that he was no better than a child on his way to school.

At French's request the foreman at Bridge 982 brought up the workman who had found the rule. This man described the place where it had been lying, though he could not actually point it out, as it was now filled with concrete.

'It was on Thursday morning that you found it, was it not?' French asked.

'Yes, I was 'aving a bit of a look round an' I sees it lying under the steel.'

'Quite. And you began concreting on the Wednesday, the previous day?'

'That's right, mister.'

'Did you have a similar look round on the Wednesday?'

'Oh, yes. I 'ad a look round. An' a good one, too.'

'Then how did you come to miss seeing the rule on Wednesday?'

The man was slightly aggrieved at the question. Instead of criticising his having missed it on the first day, he evidently thought he was entitled to praise for finding it on the second.

As satisfied as he expected to be, French turned back to Whitness. He felt that the presence of the rule really did prove the visit of Lowell to the bridge. If the man were guilty he would never have trusted any other person to plant it for him. The only doubtful question was the time at which the visit had been made.

On this point there could only be the evidence of Lowell's associates. As French turned their statements over in his mind, he saw that this was more complete than he had at first realised.

Pole had been with Lowell at the viaduct after lunch on the Tuesday. While there, Pole had seen Lowell using his rule and putting it away in his pocket. Pole had accompanied Lowell back to the office, and the latter had not left the office again before 5.45. Pole was with Lowell that evening from seven o'clock till bedtime, and again through the entire next day and evening. Unless, therefore, Pole was lying, it really would have been impossible for Lowell to go out and plant the rule at any time other than that at which he had said.

This, however, was another way of saying that Lowell was innocent of the murder. French, though still not absolutely convinced in his own mind, noted Lowell as 'provisionally' found innocent.

French's thoughts turned to Parry. Could Parry, by any chance, be his man?

French had considered the possibility on many occasions, and each time had rejected it. All the routine inquiries he had made had led him to this view. In the first place, it was most unlikely that such a very junior man should have been selected by Carey as his accomplice. Moreover, French had found nothing to suggest that the young man had ever received a penny more than his salary. With regard to the murder of Ackerley, Parry would not have had time to check the pitching and follow Ackerley to Downey's Point; but even if he could have managed this, he did not answer Langton's description of the man who had obtained the bicycle.

French believed that if Parry were innocent of the fraud and of Ackerley's murder, it followed automatically that he was innocent of the death of Carey. But as a matter of fact another piece of evidence had already brought French to this latter conclusion. From 6.0 o'clock, when Bragg left the office, till 6.15, when Parry followed to get his train, Parry had been working at a plan. There could be no fake about this, because Bragg had seen just before he started that the work had not been done, but when the stationmaster at Whitness received it just before the departure of the 6.25 goods, it was complete.

When, however, French came to the next name on his list, that of Bragg, he saw that more consideration was necessary.

In some ways Bragg was even more likely than Lowell to have been a confederate of Carey's. It was Bragg who, with Carey, agreed on the figures for the certificate and he, better than anyone else, could have connived at the fraud. Here again the acid test remained to be made: Where was Bragg at the time of Carey's murder?

French felt no doubt that Bragg could have helped Carey to carry out the frauds. He had access to the Lydmouth office and could have, again perhaps better than anyone else, made the photo prints.

But Bragg, French felt equally sure, could not have murdered Ackerley. His alibi was obviously watertight. There could be no doubt that he was working at the certificate at the time of the crime.

Did, then, innocence of Ackerley's murder involve innocence of Carey's. French did not think so. Innocence of both the fraud and Ackerley's murder would, he believed, do so, but not innocence of Ackerley's murder alone.

Suppose then Bragg were mixed up in the fraud. He might undoubtedly be innocent of Ackerley's murder and yet guilty of Carey's. An interview was the next item on the programme.

Bragg was not at Whitness and French telephoned to Lydmouth, making an appointment for the following morning. 'Well, inspector, how's the inquiry?' Bragg asked when French knocked at his door next day.

'Plenty of work in it, if there's nothing else,' French rejoined. 'I suppose you know, sir, that we have discovered that Mr Carey was murdered?'

'I heard so,' said Bragg with a look of interest. 'How did you find it out?'

'We found that he had been drugged, and of course if he was drugged he couldn't have committed suicide.'

Bragg smiled. 'That scarcely answers my question,' he pointed out, 'but I suppose it's not intended to. Well, admittedly it's your business to get information, not to give it. What can I do for you, inspector?'

'It's the same routine question as I asked you before,' French explained. 'As I told you in the case of Mr Ackerley's death, in a murder case we have to ask everyone concerned where he or she was at the time of the crime. Would you kindly account for your movements on the night of Mr Carey's death?'

Bragg nodded. 'I'm beginning to know what to expect,' he declared. 'I'll do my best to answer.'

He sat thinking for some moments, then resumed.

'That was the night I went to Drychester, which is fortunate for both of us: for you, because the unusual surroundings led me to remark my actions in a way I shouldn't otherwise have done; for me, because a lot of people can prove I was in Drychester and not here murdering Carey. That's what you really want, I suppose?'

'Yes, sir,' French answered so directly that Bragg obviously lost some of his confidence.

'Well,' he said, 'I'll tell you as best I can. I was here or about the Widening till six, or a few minutes past. Carey had been in to see me and he stayed till about five minutes to six. When he left I had some talk with Parry, then I followed.

'At this time a company was playing at Drychester in the farce, "Ethel Aldehyde": I'm sure you know it. The name part was taken by my cousin, Miss Lois Lawless on the stage and Mrs John Barlow in private life. I had promised to go over to see her and we had fixed up that night. When I left the office I took out my car and drove over. I reached the Drychester Arms Hotel a few minutes before seven. My cousin was there and we dined together. At least,' Bragg gave a crooked smile, 'it wasn't much of a dinner. She only takes a snack before going on. But of course you're not interested in that. All you want is the fact that I went to Drychester. After dinner we went to the theatre, and I saw the play through and had supper with my cousin and one or two other members of the company. I then drove home to Lydmouth, arriving about two in the morning. Is that what you want?'

'That's it, sir,' and French passed on into his second little formula about the need for confirmation.

'I dare say,' Bragg returned. 'That's all very well, but unless you know beforehand that you're going to be asked questions of this kind, you don't go about fixing up confirmatory evidence of all your movements. I don't know that I can offer you any confirmation, inspector; not real confirmation, I mean. Parry knows I left the office, and the porter and waiters at the Drychester Arms, not to speak of my cousin, can testify to my arrival there. I take it, however, that what you want is the hours of these things, and it's just there that I don't know that I can help myself.'

'How many miles is it from here to Drychester, Mr Bragg?'

'About twenty.'

'And you took an hour to go?'

'No, I didn't take an hour. I believe it was after six when I left the office and it was certainly before seven when I arrived: say fifty minutes. Then I had to get the car out, a matter of five minutes. I was only about forty-five minutes on the road. That would work out at nearly thirty miles an hour, which is good enough travelling.'

'And you didn't meet anyone on the road or stop for petrol or anything of that sort?'

Bragg shook his head.

French changed his position, turned over a page in his notebook and bent forward. 'Now, sir, let's see what that amounts to. Up till six o'clock the question does not arise, because Mr Carey was alive till then. From seven o'clock on scarcely worries me. You can no doubt get plenty of confirmation as to your presence at Drychester. But between six and seven I should like more details. Admittedly we can't prove the exact time of the murder, but it was probably early in the evening, certainly before midnight. Now, sir, can you not get the hours of your departure and arrival settled a little more accurately?'

Bragg would have been glad to do so, but didn't see how he could.

'Well,' said French, 'in that case I'll ask you to do the

same as you did before: come down and make the run while I time. Have you any objection?'

Bragg hadn't the slightest.

'Then could you come down to Whitness and let us leave the yard there at six?'

Bragg agreed.

'Good,' said French. 'Now, sir, there's another point. In addition to asking these questions of all concerned, I am making inquiries into their finances. I may tell you straight what I'd like. I'd like a note to your bank manager authorising him to answer my questions in so far as your account is concerned. Admittedy, Mr Bragg, you would be quite within your rights to refuse, but I put it to you that it is in your own interest to help me to satisfy myself of your innocence.'

For the first time Bragg showed annoyance. 'What next, inspector?' he asked indignantly. 'It's surely not your duty to rake up all my private affairs because I happen to be employed on a job on which a murder has taken place?'

'I have to be satisfied about everyone concerned,' French returned doggedly. 'You can refuse if you want to, and if necessary I can get powers to obtain the information. If you have anything to hide, you'll hide it. If not, sir, you can not only help my work, but perhaps save yourself from annoyance, if you'll give your consent.'

Bragg was very resentful, but after some further discussion he unwillingly gave way. Having arranged a meeting for the evening, French went up to town to Bragg's bank.

In making these inquiries at the various banks French of course realised their limitations. The fact that the half bonus payments had not been paid directly into the account of any given suspect, did not prove that that suspect had not received them. But French believed that had any suspect obtained the monies, it would, nevertheless, have affected his balance. Some bills would certainly have been settled with these ill-gotten gains, thus reducing the average withdrawals.

The result of his inquiries in the present instance was far from satisfactory. Directly, there was no evidence that Bragg might be guilty, indirectly, there was.

So far as the engineer's transactions with the bank were concerned, there was no direct record of his having come in for a penny whose source was not regular and well known. His income was confined to his salary and a very small additional sum from investments. French took the trouble to check these up and found them all correct.

On the other hand, an episode in Bragg's financial life gave French food for thought. About a year previously the man's account was, for its size, rather seriously overdrawn. French spent a considerable time in going into the history of that time of stringency as it was revealed by the various cheques lodged or drawn during the period. Heavy payments to dressmakers suggested the cause of the shortage, and a falling off of the same showed how the crisis had been met. All through there was no indication that Bragg had recovered himself in any way other than by economy and better conserving of his railway salary.

At the same time the thing was suspicious. Here was evidence that Bragg had been in financial difficulties, and at that very time Carey must have been planning his fraud. Bragg recovered himself, but during the period of that recovery Carey was apparently paying away a large sum every fourth week. Was there any connection? French did not know. The whole thing might have been perfectly innocent on Bragg's part: or again it mightn't.

French took a note that if that evening's inquiry into Bragg's alibi did not prove conclusive, he would have to go much more closely into the man's finances, particularly finding out if payments of debts amounted to more than was shown in the bank account.

French turned up that evening at the railway hut at Whitness before Parry had gone.

'I want, Mr Parry, to know as exactly as you can tell me, the hour at which Mr Bragg left the office on the night of Mr Carey's death. You told me before, but I want you now to think more carefully and see if you can come nearer to it than then.'

Parry really didn't see how he could go any closer to it than he had already done. He repeated that Bragg had said he wanted to leave at six, and he thought he had done so. 'He asked me,' Parry went on, 'if I was going by the 6.10. I had intended to do so, but had remembered that the plan of the shed was not finished; I told you about it. I remember looking at my watch and thinking that only for the darned plan I could have just caught the 6.10. That shows it must then have been six or a minute or two earlier, because it takes about ten minutes to walk to the station—we always allow ten minutes. I actually did leave at 6.15, after finishing the work.'

'Yes,' French agreed, 'that's what you told me.'

'Now I remember something more,' said Parry. 'There was a point about the plan about which I was not clear, and I asked Bragg. He sketched in the answer, heavily, I remember, for I couldn't quite rub the marks out. That must have delayed him two or three minutes.'

'All that, then, Mr Parry, boils down to the fact that he must have left at two or three minutes past six?'

'Yes.'

'I suppose you haven't got the plan you completed?'

'Yes, it's here. Holford returned it when he had got the foundations in.'

As he spoke Parry took a small photo print from a drawer. 'That's what I did,' he explained, pointing to certain ink lines and dimensions. 'And there's Bragg's sketch still showing through, in spite of all my rubbing out.'

French could see the impression of pencil lines moulded in the paper, though they were rubbed clean.

'Now, Mr Parry, will you do as you did before for me? Do that job again and let me see how long it takes.'

Parry readily agreed. He stretched a piece of tracing paper over the drawing and began scaling distances and marking on dimensions. French, watching him, felt that he was working fairly. Indeed, French did not believe he could have done the job more quickly. It occupied just thirteen minutes.

If then Parry had left the office at 6.15, this test pretty well confirmed his previous statement. Bragg must have left not later than about two minutes past six.

Presently Bragg arrived. 'Here you are, inspector,' he said. 'Shall we start now or do you want to wait till six?'

'It's only a few minutes,' French answered. 'I suggest we wait.'

On inquiry Bragg confirmed the statement Parry had just made on all points. He produced the plan, recognised his pencil marks, and agreed as to the time Parry's work should have taken. Then at two minutes past six o'clock precisely, the two men left the office.

'I went to the hut here,' Bragg said, suiting the action to the word, 'opened it up, started my car, backed out and locked the shed, just as I am doing now.'

They ran out of the yard, the watchman opening the large gates, and turned along the Drychester road. Bragg drove reasonably fast, neither at a breakneck pace nor a crawl. The road was narrow and winding, and a really high speed was out of the question. The men sat in silence, each occupied with his own thoughts. Mile quickly followed mile till presently they came to the outskirts of Drychester.

As they drew up before the Drychester Arms, French looked at his watch. It was exactly twelve minutes to seven.

Bragg, who though outwardly polite was evidently fuming internally, asked shortly if that was all French wanted, as he was anxious to get home. French, who had been doubtful as to whether he should have suggested a drink, was glad to have the question solved for him. He thanked Bragg and said he had quite finished, and Bragg with a curt nod drove off.

French thereupon settled down for an evening's investigation. First he talked to the hall porter, then while dining to the waiter, afterwards to the head waiter, and finally to the manager. All of these persons remembered Bragg's visit, and all were willing to tell him what they knew.

As a result Bragg's statement was very fully confirmed. Indeed, French established more than he expected. That Bragg had arrived at the hotel on the evening in question and dined with Miss Lois Lawless was certain, as also it was certain that he returned with her and a couple of others to supper, leaving the hotel about one o'clock. Moreover, the hotel manager had seen Bragg at the theatre:

all just as Bragg had said. But in addition French obtained information on the crucial point of the alibi; the exact hour at which Bragg had arrived. It was 6.53. Bragg had, indeed, himself called attention to it in conversation with the head waiter. He had looked at the clock and asked if Miss Lawless had arrived, and had made a joke about the probability of a lady being seven minutes before her time. It was this joke and also the two sevens occuring together—seven minutes to seven—which had fixed the time in the head waiter's mind.

It Bragg's story were true, he had taken five minutes longer to drive over from Whitness on the first occasion than on the second. French, however, thought this was not unreasonable. He had undoubtedly come faster than was necessary on the test run. If he had known he had plenty of time he would easily have taken another five minutes.

On the other hand, suppose Bragg was guilty. He would then have taken his car out of the yard and instead of starting out on the Drychester road, which led directly inland from Whitness station, he would have run round to the back of the engineering works and parked. Probably he would have turned before parking, so as to be ready to start away instantly. He would then have re-entered the yard through the small gate and gone to the contractors' office, knocking to find out whether or not Carey was conscious. That, if he had done it at all, must have taken place at 6.15, as the time at which Parry had seen the silhouetted man was well established. All preparations would doubtless have been made for the murder, but even so, French did not believe it could have been carried out in less than five or six minutes: say, seven minutes altogether from when he entered the hut until he regained his car.

That would bring it to 6.23. He had arrived at the hotel at 6.53, that left half an hour for the run.

French whistled softly as he considered the question of whether Bragg could have run that 20 miles in 30 minutes. At a fairly high speed it had that evening taken him 39 minutes, allowing for the time necessary to start up the car and get it out of the yard. Could that fast run of 39 minutes have been sufficiently speeded up to have been done in 30?

French did not think it was physically possible. An average speed of 40 miles an hour on that narrow, twisting road he believed was out of the question.

If so, Bragg was innocent. From this demonstration, innocent of Carey's murder; from that of the work at the certificate, innocent of Ackerley's. From both these results, innocent of the fraud. Yes, Bragg was definitely out of it.

Well, it was always good to get certainty on any point in a case. All the same, if Bragg were no longer a suspect, who was to take his place? So far as French could see, there was no one.

As he returned to his hotel French felt worried and dispirited. The case was not going as it ought. He had now been working at it for a long time, and his total result, as he put it to himself, was damn all. It was true that it was one of the most unsatisfactory cases he had ever handled. He had to admit it baffled him. There was plenty of evidence and yet, as again he put it to himself, he couldn't get his teeth in anywhere. Proof, where it existed, was negative. Everything hinged on probabilities. It had begun well. The first two or three points he had tackled had been nebulous when he started on them, and clear and proven when he had finished. But after that everything had remained vague.

What added to his despondency was the fact that an interview with Rhode was overdue. And if there was one thing French hated more than another, it was to have to report failure.

He was hanged if he would report anything of the kind! He would go over the case again. Dash it all, there *must* be some way to clear it up.

16

Light at Last

In the privacy of his room in the hotel, French once again sat down to consider his position.

He took out his list of possible suspects and went over the names, weighing carefully the evidence against each person. The operation did not make him feel any happier. The more he considered the case against each, the thinner it seemed. He found himself at last forced to admit that though the guilt of one of them appeared unquestionable, for the simple reason that any other hypothesis seemed absurd, the evidence stopped wholly short of indicating which of them it was.

But if he felt doubt as to the guilty man, there was something else of which he had no doubt at all, and that was that not one of his suspects could be taken into court. He did not believe that he could put up a case that would even pass the grand jury. And the worst of it was that he couldn't think of a single person outside his list against whom there was any suspicion whatever.

For some time he sat gazing vacantly at his gas fire,

feeling horribly up against it. Then he pulled himself together. This would never do. He dare not admit defeat. This was not the first occasion on which failure had stared him in the face; no, not by many! Again and again he had been in a precisely similar position, and again and again in the past light had come. The thing was difficult, but that was its glory. If it hadn't been difficult he wouldn't have been called in. He had been sent for because other people couldn't do the job. Very well; he would do it; he *must*. His jaw took on a more determined set and his hands involuntarily clenched. He decided he would go on thinking the thing over till he saw his way clear. He wouldn't leave it till he got some light; not if he sat in that confounded room every day for a month!

This very decision helped him. He felt brighter, more confident, more certain of ultimate success. But he was going to neglect no chances. Physical condition was an enormously important item. He rang, and ordered strong coffee.

For upwards of three hours he sat in his chair or paced his room, but the longed-for idea failed to materialise. Then, feeling himself stale, he went out for a six-mile tramp. He rested for an hour at the pictures, had dinner, and settled down once again to his problem.

It was an hour after his usual bedtime when a possibility which he had also frequently considered recurred to him with a new force. Could it be that he was wrong in one of the ideas which he had been holding as fundamental to the case, and that therefore all the reasoning built on it was false? From the moment at which he had learned of the death of Carey and of the existence of the fraud, he had assumed that these events were connected, not only with each other, but also with the murder of Ackerley. To this assumption he had clung with a tenacity which he now saw might be nothing more nor less than an obsession. Suppose he had been wrong. Suppose these three crimes were independent, or at least suppose that the two murders were independent. Where would that lead?

The only person known to gain by the fraud was Carey. Very well, why assume that anyone else was involved? Suppose that Carey, and Carey alone, had engineered it. Suppose further that Carey had learnt that Ackerley was about to find it out, and suppose that Carey had murdered Ackerley.

This part of the theory was, of course, not new. But in passing, French noted once again how convincingly it was supported by no less than five facts:

1. That Carey could have carried out the fraud alone, and that Messrs Spence's opinion, founded on inquiry, was that he had done so.

2. That Carey had received all the profits, whatever he might or might not have done with part of them.

3. That in his conversation with Mayers, Ackerley had shown that he was on the track of the fraud.

4. That Carey could have murdered Ackerley.

5. That Carey had (or might have) attempted a fraudulent alibi, by stating that he was at the Whirlpool Cave at the time of the murder. He had at least produced a forged letter as evidence for the statement.

French saw that every fact in the case up to Carey's murder was covered by this theory, with the one exception of Carey's cashing of those half bonus payments. Admittedly, however, this was not inconsistent with his sole guilt in respect of the fraud.

How, then, could Carey's murder be accounted for? Simply, French now thought, that Carey had been murdered for something quite unconnected with the fraud. Was there any such thing?

Of course there was! This was where French felt he had been so stupid. Of course there was! There was the rivalry about Brenda Vane. Could Lowell have murdered Carey to put him out of the running? This theory would do no violence to the probabilities. Such things were constantly happening.

This was the second line of reasoning which had led to Lowell. To substantiate the first, that Lowell had been Carey's partner in the fraud, no evidence could be found. French wondered if there was evidence for the second.

He had of course not forgotten Lowell's alibi, founded on the loss of the rule. But though on investigation French's reason had told him that the alibi was watertight, his instinct had bade him distrust it. The suspicion was inevitable that the rule had been planted for the purpose for which it had been used.

There was nothing for it but to try again. First he must estimate the strength of the passions evoked by the love of these two men for Brenda Vane. Then, if these proved really serious, he must re-test Lowell's alibi.

Much cheered by the prospect of productive work, French set off next morning for Whitness. His principal business would be at 'Serque', but he did not want to call there too early. He therefore went to the contractors' yard and began operations by interviewing Parry.

Parry was not communicative, principally because, French imagined, he had hearsay evidence of a disquieting nature, but knew nothing at first hand. He did, however, tell French something of importance: that Brenda and Lowell were engaged; moreover, that the engagement had taken place just after Carey's death.

Pole, however, knew more of the matter. Pole was most unwilling to speak, and it was only when French bluffed him with all the terrors of the law, that he answered his questions.

It was true, he said, that relations between Lowell and Carey had been strained. For several weeks they had scarcely been on speaking terms. It had been because of Brenda Vane. Both men were very much attached to her. On two occasions shortly before Carey's death their feelings had come to the surface. Once in the office and once at 'Serque' they had had a row. Pole had heard their voices, not much raised but, as it were, very intense and evil. No, on neither occasion had he heard the words; only their tones.

French had a shrewd suspicion that Pole knew more than he had stated, but the young man would make no further admissions, and French had left him and walked down to 'Serque'.

He was more pleased than otherwise to find that Brenda Vane was out. Though it might eventually prove to be his duty, he hated the idea of trying to get from her information which might hang her lover. Instead, he saw first her sister, and then her mother.

He did not learn much from either. They both 'believed' that there had been strained relations between Lowell and Carey, but neither knew anything from her own knowledge. They would have been glad to have helped the inspector, but as it was . . . The inspector would understand . . .

The inspector understood very well; and asked to see the servant.

Kate turned out to be a Cornish girl, deliberate and sensible-looking. French, rapidly sizing her up, made no attempt to bluff. In the quietest way he told her his business and pointed out that though she was not then bound to answer his questions, eventually she would have to do so, and it would save trouble all round if she would do it at once. She answered as quietly that she knew that, and what did he want to know?

She admitted readily that Carey and Lowell had scarcely spoken to one another during the six or eight weeks prior to the former's death. Everyone knew the cause; they were both in love with Miss Brenda. Miss Brenda had been a good deal upset about it, and Mrs Vane had wanted to get rid of them both. But Miss Brenda would not agree to that. Oh, yes, the men had had 'words' over the affair. She had unwittingly heard some of their remarks. Yes, each had threatened to kill the other. No, she couldn't remember Mr Lowell's exact words, but it was to the effect that Miss Brenda was his, and that if Mr Carey didn't keep off he'd do him in, if he swung for it.

The girl made her statement in a matter-of-fact, unemotional way which carried conviction. French saw at once that she would make an admirable witness. He knew the type. Under severe cross-examination she would probably smile good-humouredly, make no damaging admissions, and stick like a leech to her previous statements.

French's next job was to re-test the alibi of the rule. As he lunched in a Whitness restaurant he racked his brains over the question of how this was to be done.

Not very clear as to his ultimate proceedings, he walked out once again to Bridge 892 and asked to see the workman who had found the rule.

'Sorry to trouble you over this thing again,' he said pleasantly, 'but I think I must have made a mistake when I spoke to you before. I said, I think, that the rule had been lost on the night before you started concreting?'

'That's right, mister.'

'I meant the following night,' French lied. 'That would be the night before you found it, wouldn't it?'

The man reacted more satisfactorily than French could have hoped. He stood silent for some moments, evidently thinking in his slow way, then expressed the opinion for which French had been fishing. This explained what he had been quite unable to understand; how he had come to overlook the rule on that first day of concreting. He had gone over the entire reinforcement, and if the rule had been in the corner he would have seen it. He had only admitted that he had overlooked it because he had been assured that it was there, and he therefore supposed he must have done so. Now, however, the affair was cleared up. He had looked over the work on both days. When the rule was there he saw it, and when he didn't see it, it was because it wasn't there. That was clear at last.

French realised that the workman probably would say something of this kind in any case, to prove his alertness. But the man's satisfaction was so obviously genuine that French could not but accept his statement. The point, of course, was much more important than the man could imagine. If he were right, the rule had been placed under the bars on the night after, not before, Carey's murder. This meant two things: first, that Lowell need not have been at the bridge during the fateful hour and therefore could have killed Carey, and second, that the very fact that he had afterwards thought it necessary to fake an alibi, practically proved his guilt.

French wondered how he could find out when Lowell really had been at the bridge. Had anyone been along that stretch of line between 5.45 and 6.45 on the night in question, the hour for which Lowell had tried to account?

French stood for some time chatting with the foreman, and in a discussion of overtime managed to slip his question in. But it produced nothing. At five o'clock, the closing time, the men had left off work and assembled with the members of other gangs at Downey's Point. There a train had stopped for them and taken them into Whitness. After that train the line had been deserted.

French walked slowly back to Whitness, stopping at each gang and chatting to the ganger. Four of these men were unable to help him, but from the fifth he learned something which filled him with a sudden eagerness.

This fifth gang was working on the rocky shelf near the tunnel. The ganger stated that on the day in question a post office squad was engaged in carrying out some repairs to the telephone wires which here ran along the railway. The ganger knew the boss of this squad, a man named Downes, who lived in the same street in Redchurch as himself. The two men had a little talk and Downes told the other that he was on a hurry job and that they would have to work late to finish it. They evidently did so, as they had remained behind when the railwaymen left, and had not turned up again on the following morning.

Wondering if he had hit on anything valuable, French took the first train to Redchurch and at the post office asked the address of the district telephone engineer. Quarter of an hour later he was seated in his office.

'You want to see John Downes and his men?' the engineer repeated. 'That's easily done. Have you a car?'

'I can hire one.'

'Then hire one and drive out about three miles on the main Drychester road. You'll find them along the road there. You can't mistake them because they're the only squad in that neighbourhood.'

French had noticed a garage close by and he quickly obtained a car. Downes proved to be a reliable-looking man and he made no difficulty about answering French's questions.

On the afternoon in question some small repairs became necessary to the telephone wires near the tunnel, and he had been sent to carry out the work. He had been told to finish the job that night, if an hour or two's extra work would do it. He had started at half-past four and had gone on till after seven. They had worked with acetylene flares.

He knew Mr Lowell, as he had met him in connection with the alteration of the telephone wires on the Widening. He was positive that Mr Lowell had not passed along the railway while he was there.

French was impressed. 'Here was something vital at last! As Lowell could scarcely have reached the bridge without twice passing along that piece of line, he no longer felt any doubt as to his guilt. However, he must make things as sure as possible. Systematically he interviewed every man of the squad. None of them had seen Lowell, and about half were positive he had not passed.

Incidentally French noted that the mere fact that the squad had been there in itself strongly suggested that Lowell was lying. Lowell obviously realised the importance of establishing his alibi, and if he had known that these men were present he would have mentioned it to French. The fact that Lowell had said nothing about them seemed to French almost certain proof that he didn't know they were there.

As he returned to Redchurch, French was extraordinarily pleased. At last this long drawn out struggle showed signs of coming to an end. At last he was on to something tangible, something which should lead him to a satisfactory solution of his problem.

But he realised that he had not yet reached that solution. This evidence he had obtained was merely negative. Before he could take his case into court he must have positive proof. How could he get it?

It was obvious that the rule could not have been planted during the day, as, if so, the men who were concreting would have seen Lowell. Nor could it have been done on the Wednesday evening. There was ample testimony that Lowell spent the whole of that evening at 'Serque'. If, therefore, Lowell had faked the alibi, he must have gone out and planted the rule during the Wednesday night. French saw that if he could prove this his case would be practically complete.

He went down once more to 'Serque' and once again asked to be allowed a glance round Carey's room. It then seemed less unreasonable to beg for a glimpse of Lowell's and Pole's also. In Lowell's he crossed to the window to admire the view. Instantly he saw that without a rope no one could have entered or left by the window. Moreover, there was nothing in the room to which a rope could conveniently have been made fast.

Next he had a look at the front door. In the daytime

it was closed by a Yale lock, but at night a heavy finger-bolt was also shot. French tried them both. He was satisfied that with care they could be operated noiselessly.

Again he went upstairs. The house was solidly built and the stairs did not creak. He started a new inquiry: had anyone heard sounds of movement in the house on that Wednesday night?

Mrs Vane now remembered that she had. She had been so much disturbed that she had got up, opened her door, and listened for a few moments. But as everything remained still, she concluded she had been mistaken. That was about three in the morning. She had mentioned the matter next day, but none of the others had heard anything. It was because of this discussion that French was able to fix the date.

French's problem now took on another and very familiar form. Who could have been along any part of the route between 'Serque' and Bridge 982 in the small hours of that Thursday morning?

He settled down to it. He felt despondent about the inquiry, but it was his only chance. In vain he made the usual inquiries. None of the police or coastguards could help. The various doctors were approached, without result. The district nurse had not been out. There had not been, so far as could be learnt, any dance or late party. The night watchman at the contractors' yard had been in his hut during the period in question. Drivers and firemen of late trains had not seen anyone . . .

For a couple of days French worked on at the problem. At last in despair he called at every house overlooking the route. There were not a great number, only seventeen in all. At one after another he pursued his hopeless task, till at the very last, the seventeenth, he got more than he could have hoped for.

This seventeenth house was actually on the opposite or Whitness town side of 'Serque', but from its side windows there was a view of the entrance gate. It appeared that here a child was seriously ill. On that night its mother had sat up with it. The lady, sleepy and tired, had happened to go to the window in her room, throw open the lower sash, and stand for a few moments breathing in the fresh air. It was not very dark, and while standing there she had seen a man hurry up to the gate of 'Serque' from the direction of the tunnel, and pass quickly in. She was almost sure it was Lowell. He was walking stealthily, and had it been anyone else she would have assumed something was wrong. As it was, however, she remembered Lowell's job and supposed he had been working late on the Widening, as she knew often happened. The stealthy walk she thought natural enough; he would be anxious to move silently so as not to wake anyone in the house.

French pressed her as to whether she could swear that man was Lowell. She would not actually swear—there had not been light enough to be quite sure—but she had thought it was Lowell at the time.

French, jubilant, believed that this would do the trick. He rang up Superintendent Rhode and arranged an interview.

Rhode heard the story without comment and with a look of settled pessimism on his heavy face. French smiled inwardly as he watched him.

'So there, sir,' French ended up, 'that's what I've got to date, and the question is whether we should let it go at that and arrest Lowell, or whether there are any further lines that should be investigated before we show our hand.'

Rhode moved slowly.

'We've ample justification for bringing him in,' he answered, 'and, bar accidents, we've enough evidence for a conviction. We can prove motive; we can prove the accused threatened the life of the deceased; we can prove the accused had opportunity; we can prove he faked an alibi to account for his absence during the critical time. Why should he fake that alibi if he were innocent? I think, French, we're all right. What's your own idea?'

'I'd like to have found out who was getting those half bonus payments,' French said slowly.

Rhode shrugged. 'You can't get everything. Besides, what does it matter? If those payments were connected with the case at all, it was with the murder of Ackerley, not of Carey. Do you know what I think?' The super leant forward and demonstrated with his hands. 'I believe Ackerley and Carey were in the thing together. Ackerley saw that the fraud was going to come out, and he thought he would anticipate things and pretend to discover it so as to clear himself from suspicion. You say that Ackerley got no money out of it. That's no argument. You haven't found that anyone got that money. But someone must have. It might as well have been Ackerley as anyone else. I tell you, French, that would clear up the whole case.'

French was not entirely convinced. He had himself thought of this solution, and rejected it because it did not seem to fit in with Ackerley's personality. He was aware, however, that hearsay personality could be extremely misleading, and he saw that the superintendent might well be right.

'I'll have a word with the chief constable,' said Rhode, picking up the telephone.

He had a good many words, then turned to French. 'He's coming in. He'd like to have a chat over the thing. He'll be here in ten minutes.'

In fifteen Major Duke arrived. He heard French's statement and congratulated him on his work. Then he turned to the superintendent.

'It seems to me that this Lowell is our man. What do you think, Rhode?'

Rhode thought so too.

'And you, French?'

'He's the only person against whom we've any real evidence,' French agreed.

The chief constable stood up.

'Very well,' he said. 'We'll let it go at that. By all means get a warrant and make the arrest.'

Late that evening Henry Peterson Lowell was taken into custody on a charge of wilful murder.

17

Brenda Takes a Hand

While all this long drawn out police investigation was in progress, Parry carried on steadily at his job. For some time he had not been feeling well, and now the inquiry had got on his nerves. At intervals he heard of French's activities. These seemed to continue endlessly till at last French and French's doings ran like a *leit motif* through the whole texture of life on the Widening. He had been observed entering the police station at Whitness; he had called at the head office and had an interview with Marlowe; he had been out at Cannan's Cutting; he had spent an hour talking to various men in the contractors' yard; he had been seen at unexpected places along roads, discussing unknown subjects with strangers: mysteriously he moved about, apparently busy, though what exactly he was doing no one knew. Rumours naturally thrived in such an atmosphere and each fresh comer had a new tale to add to the general stock.

It would be safe, however, to say that no one anticipated the *dénouement* which was actually reached. The arrest of

Lowell came like a bomb to everyone concerned. Lowell was popular enough, and no one for a moment suspected him of murder. It was true the wiseacres at once began to shake their heads and to say that they had always felt that there was something, well, not just *quite*, you know, about him. But such tales were taken for what they were worth.

To Parry the worst feature of the arrest was its effect on Brenda. Poor Brenda! After a pretty hard life of it, she had scarcely begun to look forward to happiness when this terrible blow had fallen. When he heard of it, Parry at once put aside his work at the office and went down to see her.

He found her dressed and about to go out.

'Oh, Cliff,' she cried, 'I'm glad to see you. Come with me, will you? I hate going alone.'

'Of course, Brenda. Where to?'

'To the police station. He has no one to do anything for him. His people live in Italy; his mother's health is poor and she can't stand this climate. There's no one to act for him except me.'

'But, Brenda, what for? Tell me before we go. Perhaps I could do it for you.'

'Well, you see, he is to be brought before the magistrates at eleven and he must have a solicitor. I was going to find out if he wanted any special person and then go and ask him to act.'

'You'll do nothing of the kind,' said Parry. 'I'll do all that. Is he at the police station here?'

'Yes, I've just been speaking on the 'phone to the sergeant. He said something should be arranged about a solicitor.'

'Of course it should,' Parry declared firmly, though he had not thought of it till Brenda spoke. 'I'll see to it at once. I suppose you've no idea which solicitor he would like?'

'I don't expect he knows. But it seems to me it must be someone in Whitness: there's no time to get anyone else. And if so, I'm sure it must be Mr Horler. He has a good reputation. I know him pretty well and I'm sure he would do everything possible.'

'Right,' said Parry, 'I'll find out who Lowell wants, and unless he's got his mind fixed on someone else, I'll arrange with Horler. Don't come, Brenda. I'll fix it and I'll ring up at once if there's any hitch.'

The police station was not far away and in a few minutes Parry had explained his business to Sergeant Emery.

'I'll give Mr Lowell your message, sir,' the officer answered. 'Then whoever he agrees on can come and see him.'

'If I can't see him now,' Parry went on, 'tell him that all this has been arranged by Miss Brenda Vane, who is doing everything she can for him.'

'I'll tell him, sir.'

In a few moments the sergeant came back. Lowell sent messages of appreciation to Miss Vane, and he would like Mr Horler to defend him, if this could be arranged.

Parry reached Messrs Reid & Horler's office at the same moment as Mr Horler himself. He quickly introduced himself and stated his business.

Horler had not heard of the arrest, but said at once that he knew Lowell slightly and would be pleased to act for him. Upon this Parry insisted on ringing up Brenda to tell her the news. Horler knew little more of the case than had appeared in the papers, and he spent a few minutes in questioning Parry.

'There's really no hurry about it,' he said presently. 'The police would never have made an arrest unless they had ample evidence to justify a remand. I'm afraid you must make up your mind that Lowell will be remanded without bail.'

'I expected so,' Parry admitted.

'It's just ten: that gives me an hour. I'll go and see Lowell now and I'll appear for him when he is brought before the magistrates.'

Parry also attended the court. The proceedings lasted only a minute or two. Emery gave evidence of arrest and Lowell was remanded for a week. Then Parry went once more to 'Serque' to report to Brenda.

'We can't do anything for the present,' he concluded. 'Horler will see to things. Well, Brenda, I'll have to go, but I'll look in tomorrow night and if there's anything I can do in the meantime, ring me up.'

On the following afternoon Brenda did ring up, asking Parry to go to 'Serque' for dinner, as she wanted to see him as early as possible. When he arrived she told him she had had a telephone call from Horler, who had asked her to call up and have a chat about the case. She had asked if the evening would do as well, to which he had replied, 'Better.' Brenda had not wanted to go alone. Would Parry take her?

Parry felt complimented and said so.

'We're to go to Mr Horler's private house,' she said as they started off. 'It's out on the Drychester Road; about a mile. Do you mind the walk?'

'I'd love it,' said Parry.

Horler seemed pleased to see Parry. He greeted them both pleasantly and chatted about everything except the case while coffee was brought in. Then when cigarettes had been lit up he came to business.

'I knew your interest in this affair, Miss Vane, and I thought you'd like to hear just how it appears to me. I'm glad you've brought Parry with you, for three heads are better than two. I've seen the police and I've seen Lowell, and I've got a rough idea of what we're up against. Not in complete detail as yet; there hasn't been time; still a fairly good idea. Now, I want to tell you the truth, and I'm afraid I must begin by saying that we've got our work cut out for us.'

'They *can't* have anything serious against him,' Brenda objected.

'They've got something against him all right,' Horler returned, 'how serious I'm not going to say. But I will say that the young ass has gone and made a damned fool of himself. He's been too clever and he's made things a lot worse for himself than they need have been.'

Brenda had paled. 'Oh, Mr Horler, don't say that,' she implored. 'I *know* he's innocent and there *can't* be anything serious against him.'

'I believe he's innocent myself,' Horler declared with comforting assurance, 'and what's more I don't doubt that we'll be able to prove it. But I'm not going to pretend it can be done without an effort. Now, here's roughly the case the police have built up. I'm sorry, Miss Vane, extremely sorry that your name comes into it, but unfortunately it does.'

Brenda made a gesture of impatience. 'Oh, what does that matter?' she cried. 'Never mind me. We must think of him.'

'I thought you'd say that. But you're wrong. You matter

very much. However, that in a sense is an aside. Let us get on to the case itself.'

He leant forward, gesticulating slightly as he talked, and marking his points by prods of his right forefinger.

'The police say that both Lowell and Carey were very much in love with you, Miss Vane. They say that because of it feeling between the two men ran high. Apparently they can bring evidence to prove that on two separate occasions Lowell threatened to murder Carey. You see, I'm being perfectly straight and keeping nothing back.'

Brenda had gone whiter still and a terrible look of pain had appeared in her eyes. She nodded without speaking. Parry, who had heard something about the scenes, was surprised only by the rapidity with which the police had learnt of them.

'That,' resumed Horler, 'is what they are going to put up for motive. Now, as to opportunity. First of all, it is obvious that Lowell was so circumstanced that he could have committed the crime. By that I mean he had the necessary knowledge of the office and of Carey's movements. He had as good a chance as anyone of drugging Carey. He had a key for the office: all that sort of thing.

'Now, it is known that Lowell left the contractors' office about quarter to six on the evening of the murder and did not reach 'Serque' till just seven. The police suspect—though I don't think they can prove it—that the murder took place during that hour; at all events it might have done so. The question of how Lowell occupied his time during the hour was, therefore, raised. He was asked to account for his movements. And this is where the young ass made such an idiot of himself.

'He told the police that at quarter to six that night he

remembered that he had not inspected the steelwork of a bridge at which concreting was to begin on the following morning, and that feeling unhappy about it, he decided to go off then and there to see it. This was quite a reasonable decision, because the steelwork would have been covered by the concrete, so that if he didn't go to see it then, he wouldn't have seen it at all. He said nothing, however, to the other men in the office, simply because he didn't wish to admit his forgetfulness.

'The police then asked Lowell could he prove this story and he told them a long rigmarole about a rule which he had lost. He had had the rule on that Tuesday afternoon—Pole had seen him with it. He had had it at the bridge, because he was measuring with it. The next day, the day Carey's body was found, he discovered he had lost the rule. The day after that, Thursday, the rule was found at the bridge, and as Lowell had not been there a second time, he put forward that the finding of the rule proved his visit.

'Well, that seemed all right. The police went into the story. They found that it was true that Lowell had had the rule on the afternoon of the crime and that it was found at the bridge, and that all the remainder of Lowell's time was accounted for, and that he could not have gone out again. The alibi seemed to be perfectly established; then suddenly it went to bits.'

'Went to bits?' Parry repeated in amazement, while Brenda stared incredulously.

'Yes, the young fool had told them a string of lies. The police discovered that had the rule been dropped at the time Lowell stated—on the Tuesday evening—it almost certainly would have been found on Wednesday. The man who found it on Thursday had looked in that very place on Wednesday and it wasn't there. This made the police suspicious and they next found a gang of men—post office men, not railway men—who had been working on the railway during the hour in question. If Lowell had gone to the bridge he must have passed them, and they swore he hadn't. Then the police inquired further and found a young woman—that Mrs Dunn, who lives beside you, Miss Vane—who told them that about three o'clock on the Thursday morning she had been up with her sick child and had seen Lowell hurry up from the direction of the tunnel and creep stealthily into "Serque".

'From all this they naturally concluded that Lowell had not been at the bridge on Tuesday evening, but that he had gone out and planted the rule there in the small hours of Thursday morning, so as to bolster up a false alibi. They reasoned that he wouldn't have done that unless he was guilty, and they decided to arrest him.'

Brenda was terribly taken aback and even Parry had seldom felt so surprised. 'Oh,' Brenda moaned, 'there is some mistake; there must be. He didn't lie. He couldn't have.'

'Oh, but he did,' Horler returned. 'I put it to him in so many words and he admitted it. Admitting it was the one sensible thing he has done all through. The ass! Then he told me what I believe to be the truth. In a sort of way it explains his action, though it certainly doesn't excuse it.'

Brenda with a terrible eagerness was hanging on Horler's words.

'He got a letter that Tuesday; so he says and I believe it's true. A nasty letter which I'm afraid will hurt you. However, you'd better see it. Recognising that it might become important, he had hidden it in his office, and I got it before the police.' Horler passed over a sheet of paper and Parry, moving behind Brenda, read it over her shoulder.

It was typed on a sheet torn off one of those writing-blocks which are sold by the hundred thousand, and read:

> 'Tuesday
>
> 'Sir,
>
> 'Take warning. Brenda Vane is playing crooked with you. She is meeting Carey every other night. If you go to the Whirlpool Cave at 6.15 tonight you'll see for yourself. I only write because I don't like to see a decent young man fooled.
>
> 'Well Wisher.'

Instead of still further depressing Brenda, this epistle had a highly salutary effect. She became so furious that she could hardly speak. Her eyes flashed and bright red spots appeared in her cheeks. Parry thought he could read what was passing in her mind. It was not, he felt sure, the slight on herself which had so moved her. It was its effect on Lowell. It was the ugly means which had been used to get him into this trouble; for in some way this letter had evidently done so.

'Lowell tells me,' went on Horler when Brenda had somewhat cooled down, 'that this note upset him terribly. He swears he never for one moment believed it and his first reaction was to throw it into the fire. But as the day passed, he became more and more certain that he would have to go out to the Cave and see for himself. Not, he repeated again and again, and I think we can understand him, not that he doubted you, Miss Vane, but he felt that if he didn't see for himself that the thing was a lie, a little gnawing feeling would always rankle. He vacillated during the whole afternoon; then in the end he went.

'Needless to say, he saw neither you nor Carey, for this sort of letter represents a trick so old as to be threadbare. But he hadn't eased his mind. He now felt so ashamed of himself for having gone, that he could scarcely bring himself to speak to you. He was miserable all that evening.

'Next day came the discovery of Carey's death. Now Lowell, of course, knew of the doubt that Ackerley had really met with an accident. He himself had been unable to understand a man of Ackerley's experience being run over as he was supposed to have been. When Carey was found dead, Lowell, semi-instinctively, I suppose, connected it with Ackerley's death, and wondered if it was really just suicide. He explains that this was a mere idea and that he did not consider it seriously. But he happened to overhear some remarks made by the police, from which he gathered that it was supposed that Carey might have died between six and seven. Then suddenly he got a hideous idea. He believed he saw the purpose of the letter. Carey had been murdered and he was to be made the scapegoat. By sending him that letter the murderer had contrived to leave him without an alibi.

'Lowell realised clearly enough that if doubts of the suicide were raised he might be in a very serious position. He thought of the bad feeling between himself and Carey and remembered his threats. Moreover, he couldn't prove that he had gone to the cave; he had seen no one on the way. Even if he produced the letter it would do no good; the police could argue that he had typed it himself to back up his story.'

Horler paused, threw the stump of his cigarette into the fire, and took another. Then, as neither of the others spoke, he continued:

'So far all this story is reasonable enough, but it is just here that Lowell lost his head. What he should have done, of course, was to have gone to the police and told them about the letter. He says he didn't do so for two reasons. Firstly, he had no guarantee that he would be believed, and secondly, he thought the affair had been definitely taken as suicide and that no question of murder would ever arise. You can sympathise with that in a way, but you can't sympathise with Lowell's next step.

'He thought that if he were asked where he was at the time of the murder—if it proved to be murder—he must be able to give a convincing answer. Therefore, as he had no alibi, he proceeded to concoct one. It was clever, enough in its way, but I confess I can't get over his imagining he could hoodwink a body like the British police. The fact that the concreting of the bridge was started on the day Carey's body was found gave him his idea and he worked out the details to suit, slipping out of "Serque" in the middle of the night to plant the rule. He thought there would be no one along the route, either between six and seven on the Tuesday night or early on Thursday morning, so that no one would know whether he passed or not. But that's the sort of contingency on which these clever little arrangements are apt to trip one up. He knew there'd be no railwaymen on the line on that Tuesday evening, but he didn't know about the post office men. Nor did he know that Mrs Dunn would be up all Thursday night with her sick child and might look out of the window at an awkward time.

'So there you have the whole story. Personally I believe that if Lowell hadn't been such an ungodly ass as to give way to panic and fake that alibi, he would never have been arrested.'

Horler paused and the three sat smoking in silence for some moments. Then Parry moved uneasily.

'What do you think we should do?' he asked.

'Ah,' returned Horler, 'now you're talking. That's what we've got to consider. The first thing obviously is to try to prove Lowell was out at the Whirlpool Cave during the critical hour. That, of course, would clear him instantly.'

'He wasn't able to suggest how that might be done?'

'He wasn't. He was discouraging, in fact. He said he'd seen no one on his way either out or in. However, he may have been seen without his knowledge and we've got to make sure. Then failing that we must try to find out who wrote the letter. This might do as well. Indeed, it might do better; it might give us a line on the real murderer.'

'Not very easy,' Parry commented.

'Not very easy, I agree. But not impossible to a skilful man. But whether we can do anything ourselves is another matter.'

'How do you mean, Mr Horler?' Brenda asked.

Horler shrugged. 'Well, look at it this way. To find out these things is detective work, that is, it is work which can best be done by a specialist. I might say, indeed, can only be done by a specialist. Now, I'm a lawyer, Parry's an engineer, and you, Miss Vane, have your own duties. Is it likely that anyone of us should succeed at this specialised work?'

'Then what do you suggest?' Brenda persisted.

'I think we shall have to employ a specialist to do it for us.'

'A private detective?' said Parry. 'That would be rather an expensive item, wouldn't it?'

'I didn't necessarily mean a private detective. I fancy we might do better than that.'

Both the others looked their question.

'Tell me,' went on Horler. 'Both of you have seen this Inspector French who is in charge of the case. What sort of man is he?'

Parry and Brenda exchanged glances.

'All right, I think,' said Parry at last. 'Very civil and pleasant spoken and all that, but I dare say he could be as stiff as any of them.'

'Yes, I agree with that,' Brenda added, 'but I must admit that he struck me as both straight and kindly.'

'I know Sergeant Emery well,' Horler returned; 'have known him for years, and I'd say just the same about him. I believe him to be both straight and kindly. Now, my idea is this, though I should say it is a purely tentative idea and would require a lot of thinking over before being adopted; Why shouldn't we take these men into our confidence and ask them to make the necessary inquiries? With their organisation they could do it much better than anyone else. The only question is whether they would. Personally, I believe they would, but that's the point we shall have to consider.'

To this Brenda and Parry reacted differently. Brenda thought it an excellent idea, while Parry was dubious. He suggested that it was rather too much to expect the police to work energetically to break down the case to which they had committed themselves, and thought that they would probably make a superficial investigation and then report that they could obtain no results. 'Then,' Parry went on, 'our pitch would be queered. If we started an investigation we would be told: "Oh, the police have already gone into that. Go to the police about it."'

Horler concurred. 'I realise all that,' he answered, 'and, therefore, I say that we must carefully consider the thing before taking any step. However, in spite of the objection, I'm not at all sure that confiding in the police may not still prove our best policy. We won't decide for a day or two.'

'Could we try first ourselves,' Brenda suggested, 'and if we fail, then go to the police?'

'That's a good idea, Brenda,' Parry exclaimed. 'What do you think, Mr Horler?'

Horler was not enthusiastic. 'We have,' he explained, 'to remember another point. I must show this letter to the police. It would be most improper to hold it back now and then bring it forward at the trial. It wouldn't even pay us. The prosecution would say that it was a fraud, invented at the last moment to bolster up the defence. At least, if they didn't say so in so many words they'd manage to throw enough doubt on it to discredit it with the jury. The question then arises: Should the whole story not be told to the police at the same time? It mightn't be so easy to do it so convincingly afterwards. I'm not putting these questions to you in the expectation of an answer.' Horler gave a dry smile. 'I'm merely thinking aloud so that you may see just where we stand.'

For some time Horler continued to think aloud, while the others questioned and commented. Finally it was decided that for a day or two Horler would keep his own counsel, while he explored the possibilities of investigation apart from the police. Unless, however, he became speedily convinced that a private inquiry had a good chance of success, he would ask French to call and put the whole facts before him.

'There's one other thing, Mr Horler,' Brenda said when this decision had been reached. 'Can I see Harry?'

Horler shook his finger warningly.

'Now, Miss Vane,' he said, 'I want you to think of what is wise and politic as well as what is kind. The police case is that Lowell was profoundly in love with you. Don't strengthen that case unnecessarily. I'll see Lowell about it and I'll give him any message you like, but personally you keep out of the thing as far as you can. It's even a pity you approached the sergeant about getting a solicitor. That can't be helped, but don't do anything more of the kind.'

For some time longer they continued discussing the affair and then Brenda said it was getting late and that she must go home.

18

Brenda Learns the Truth

It was in a frame of mind, partly apprehensive, partly cheerful, that Brenda and Parry left Horler's. Both felt assured of Lowell's innocence, but with both a dreadful doubt lurked as to the outcome of the affair. Would the jury believe, as they believed, that Lowell really did receive the letter and go to the Whirlpool Cave? It seemed so reasonable, indeed, to them, so obviously true. Yet both had to admit that this tale of the letter was exactly the kind of story that would be put up if an explanation had to be found for Lowell's falsification of his alibi.

Just before lunch two days later Parry was called to the telephone. It was Brenda and he could tell from her voice that she was overwhelmed with excitement.

'Oh, Cliff,' she said eagerly, 'I've made such a discovery. I must tell you. Come down here to lunch, will you? I'm quite alone. Mother's in bed and Mollie's out. You'll come, won't you?'

'I've to go and pay a call,' Parry said to Ashe. 'I'll probably get lunch somewhere in town. Don't wait for me.'

He found Brenda quite as excited as her voice suggested.

'Do you know, Cliff,' she exclaimed, 'if anything comes of this it'll be largely due to my reading a detective story. I've forgotten its name, but it was about a typewritten letter and it said that typewriting was almost as distinctive as handwriting, and that a skilful observer could identify the machine upon which any given piece of work was done.'

Parry shook his head.

'You mean the make surely,' he objected. 'The types of the various makes are slightly different and an expert could pick them out. But surely no one could distinguish between two machines of the same make?'

'Oh, yes, they could; I mean both between the makes and the individual machines of any given make. But don't mind about that. Hear what I have to tell you.'

'Tell me, Brenda.'

'When I got home that night from Mr Horler's I was dreadfully bothered, wondering what you and I could do. I worried over it all that night and then I thought of something. I didn't really imagine it would lead to any result, but it would be something to do, and I felt if I hadn't something to do I should go mad. You do understand, don't you?'

'Of course, I understand. Very natural. What did you do?'

'I rang up Mr Horler and asked him for an enlarged photograph of the letter. I thought I would examine the type and see if there was anything about it which might be identifiable. Then I thought I would ask you to get samples from the different machines in the offices, so as to see if the letter had been done on any of them.'

For a moment Parry seemed dubious, but soon his face cleared. Neither of them knew that French had already made this investigation.

'My word, Brenda,' Parry said warmly, 'but you're the goods. A clinking notion, I call it. It might give the very proof we want.' His face changed again. 'But also it mightn't. Have you thought of that side of it? Suppose it turned out that it was done on the machine in Lowell's office? Wouldn't that—'

Brenda made a gesture of impatience.

'Don't be in such a hurry, Cliff. Wait and hear what I have to tell you. That's only what I thought we might do.'

'Sorry. Go ahead.'

'I rang up Mr Horler and he agreed my suggestion could do no harm, provided I didn't let anyone know what I was after. He got the photograph taken and I have just received it: just before I rang you up. Here it is. Do you see anything remarkable about it?'

The print was full plate size and showed the typescript nearly three times as big as the original. Parry read it over carefully.

'You wouldn't notice it,' Brenda went on, 'because you don't know what I know. And don't forget I am a trained typist.'

'I can type too,' said Parry.

'I know you can, but it's more than that. See here.' She took the card and pointed. 'Do you see that "r"? Do you see that it's considerably below alignment and also slightly bent to the side? It occurs twelve times in the letter and it has these defects every time. You see, it's quite unmistakable.'

Parry grew more interested. It was with something like eagerness that he waited for Brenda to go on.

'There are other defects which would confirm any conclusions we come to. This "t," for instance, has a little defect in its stem. It occurs thirteen times and the same defect shows always. The "n" also is slightly twisted. But all this is not the point. I only mention it to show that the machine on which it was done could be identified if we could find it.'

Parry moved impatiently. 'Then what is the point, Brenda?'

'This,' she said triumphantly. 'Do you remember that other letter, that one Mr Carey showed me in which I was supposed to have asked him to meet me at the Whirlpool Cave? It had the same crooked "r"!'

Parry whistled. 'What!' he cried. 'Written by the same person? By Jove, Brenda, that's a discovery and no mistake. Are you sure?'

'I'm as sure as that I'm alive. I noticed the "r" in the first letter. I didn't notice the "t" and the "n" because I wasn't looking for defects. Besides I had no enlargement.'

'We could ask Horler to get a photo of the first letter. The police are sure to have kept it. That would check the thing up.'

'We don't want to check it,' Brenda returned with some heat. 'I'm sure.'

'Of course,' Parry agreed hastily, 'but Horler will want to check it. Have you told him about it yet?'

'No. I wanted to see what you thought.'

'Well,' said Parry, 'I'll tell you. It's all important, I think, that we should find that machine and I suggest I should do what you thought of; get samples from all the machines about the railway and contractors' offices. But until that's done, Brenda, I shouldn't advise you to say anything to Horler.'

'Why not, Cliff? Surely he should know as soon as possible?'

Parry did not answer for some moments. 'You know, Brenda,' he said at last, 'I don't want to throw cold water on your discovery; it may save Lowell. At the same time you mustn't forget that it may cut both ways. Suppose it is proved that both letters were done on a machine to which Lowell had easy access. That might injure his case instead of helping it. You see, don't you, what I mean? Better say nothing till we know more.'

He could almost feel her disappointment. Obviously she had believed she held the keys of Lowell's prison in her hands, and it was a terrible blow to find that she might be only holding an additional bolt. But she admitted at once that Parry was right and the meeting was turned into a committee of ways and means as to how the necessary samples were to be obtained.

'By a stroke of luck I can do something this afternoon,' Parry declared. 'I have to attend a conference at Lydmouth at four o'clock. I'll take the opportunity to get samples from the machines there. I don't think I should have time to get them from our own offices before I start. I'm going on the 3.10.' He glanced at his watch. 'Indeed I must run now.'

'Then when shall I see you?'

'What about tomorrow night? I should have all the samples by then.'

'Splendid, Cliff. I'll expect you tomorrow night.'

Parry hurried back to the hut. Nothing of importance had come in and he went on to the station to get his train.

In due course he attended the conference, after which by various wiles he induced the typists to let him have samples from their machines. So far as he knew, he got something from every machine in the office, more than he had hoped to do. He was afraid Brenda would be a good deal disappointed with the result, for even he could see that none of these machines was that required. On the other hand he had thought out one or two suggestions for extending the range of the inquiry, which he believed would please her.

As he entered his lodgings his landlady shouted up from the kitchen. There had just been a caller to see him, a young lady, a Miss Brenda Vane. She had come only a few minutes before and had asked if he was in. Mrs Peake had told her she was expecting him every minute and the young lady had said, first, that she would leave a message and then, as he was not likely to be long, that she would come in and wait. She had done so. Mrs Peake had shown her up to Parry's room and she had remained there for some little time. Then she had come downstairs and said that she was sorry that she had an appointment, she could not wait any longer. She had hurried off, but without leaving any message.

'It's all right, Mrs Peake,' Parry said pleasantly. 'It was to remind me about some letters. I'm going down to see Miss Vane tomorrow and I'll take them with me.'

It just showed, Parry thought, Brenda's extreme eagerness. It was evident that she could not contain herself till he went to 'Serque'. She had wanted to get the samples and take them down with her. Well, she wouldn't have to wait much longer.

Parry was tired, really terribly tired. As he sat down to wait for dinner to be brought up, his bones ached. He thought he would turn in after dinner. He could read in bed for a couple of hours and he would be all right in the morning. This Lowell affair had got on his nerves. His mind remained full of it in spite of himself and it didn't help him with his work on the railway. The Widening was enough for all his energies, and he thought ruefully of no less than two matters which he had overlooked during the day, both of which would mean trouble among the men and unpleasant explanations to the office. He had meant to attend to them before lunch, but had been interrupted by Brenda's telephone, and after lunch he had forgotten. Curse it all, he'd better go back to the office after dinner and see if he couldn't get messages through before the men started work next morning.

Suddenly his eyes strayed to the chimney piece and he cursed again. Dash it, there was his letter to Pearl Ackerley! Parry had recently been seeing as much of Pearl as he could, and at last he was beginning to think that she was growing fond of him. She had been broadcasting and he had written on the previous night congratulating her on her performance. But because he hadn't a stamp he had left the letter there beside the clock so that he would see it in the morning. And with his mind full of Lowell's affairs, he had forgotten it. It was lucky that Pearl was such a sport. She would understand and wouldn't mind.

As Parry sat there before the fire a very unusual thing suddenly happened. He felt his heart give a flutter. His heart was strong, he knew, and except for occasional returns of his shell shock trouble, he was now physically fit. But now his heart faltered, as if about to stop, and immediately he got quite faint. For a moment he sat still, while a cold sweat came out on his forehead. Then fearing he would lose consciousness, he pulled himself out of his chair, staggered blindly across the room, and with shaking hands poured himself out a glass of whisky. He drank it neat.

It pulled him together. Still he felt strangely shaken. Such a thing as this had never before happened to him. For a moment the awful thought that death was approaching filled his mind, and he grew cold in sheer panic. Horror stricken, he took some more whisky. Slowly the crisis passed.

By the time that he had made a rather unsuccessful attempt to dine, the whisky had done its work. Once more his heart was beating normally and the sickly qualms had passed. He even felt better than before the attack came on; more rested, more energetic. He decided he would go at once to Whitness and fix up the matters he had overlooked. Also he would see Brenda about her call.

He sat for a few moments thinking, then became suddenly restless. He now could not stay quiet. He felt himself on pins and needles and consumed by a desire for movement. He wondered what Brenda had done. Had she gone back to Whitness? She did not like buses and usually travelled by train, but there had been no train at the time she had left his rooms. In fact, the next train had not yet gone. He wondered if he would have time to get to the station before it started. Scarcely, he thought.

Still far from normal, Parry left the house. He began to wonder had he taken too much whisky. No, there was no use in trying for the train; he would just miss it. In a sort of dream he began to walk. He came to a telephone box. He entered and rang up 'Serque' to say he was going down. He spent a long time fumbling with the telephone. He had certainly taken too much whisky. He came out. He saw a bus labelled 'Whitness'. He boarded it. It put him down close to 'Serque'. As he approached a girlish figure left it and hurried off in the opposite direction. He knocked at the door. Mollie Vane opened it. She seemed strangely upset.

'Oh, Clifford, is it you?' she cried. 'Brenda's just gone this very minute. You must have seen her.'

'Gone?' Parry echoed. 'Gone where?'

'Of course, you don't know,' Mollie answered excitedly, still standing in the hall. 'We've had such a quarter of an hour, mother and I. Brenda was out, you know. First there was your telephone, saying that you were coming down. You had scarcely rung off when there was a second message. Sergeant Emery wanted Brenda. He was speaking from the contractors' yard and he was with Inspector French, and they wanted Brenda to go up there at once. He said they had made a vital discovery which might clear Harry Lowell, and they wanted some information about Harry which they thought she could give. Well,' Mollie's eyes were starting from her head, 'as if that wasn't enough, Brenda herself came in a few minutes later, so excited that she could scarcely speak. She shouted out in a sort of triumph that she had just got proof of Harry Lowell's innocence. But she didn't tell us what it was. When she heard about Sergeant Emery's message she cried, "Oh, my God!" and hurried off. I wanted her to wait so that I could go with her. But, no, she wouldn't. She was beside herself with excitement and just dashed off.'

Parry seemed suddenly, as it were, sobered. His dreaminess dropped from him and he looked keen, efficient, and very grim.

'I don't like all that, Mollie,' he said quickly. 'I must telephone.'

He ran to the instrument and at once gave the word 'Police.' Then Mollie heard: 'Is Sergeant Emery there?' Then: 'Speaking? Good God, sergeant, I'm afraid there's something badly wrong! Miss Brenda Vane has just had a telephone purporting to be from you, saying you and French were in the contractors' yard and wanting her to go up there at once . . . Yes, she's gone. It seems she said she had found out something establishing Lowell's innocence. That may mean proving someone else's guilt. It looks bad to me, sergeant, as if someone had got to know about it.'

For some moments there was silence, then: 'Right, I'll follow her now and you'll send some help in case there's trouble. I'm frightened; for God's sake don't be long.'

Without a word to Mollie, Parry ran out of the house and disappeared in the direction Brenda had taken.

When Brenda received the message asking her to meet French and Emery in the contractors' yard, it never for one moment occurred to her to doubt its authenticity. Her mind was in a whirl from the discovery which she believed she had made, and which she hoped would establish Lowell's innocence. So excited was she that she was almost incapable of consecutive thought, much less the critical analysis which the situation really demanded. She hurried on, her one thought being to get as quickly as possible to her destination.

There were two routes by which she could go. The best was up through the town, across the railway by the overbridge at the station, then out through the suburbs by what was called the 'back' road to Redchurch. This road passed immediately behind the yard and joined the main road just after the latter had passed under the viaduct. The other was along the sea front and then up through the Whitness Public Park to a lane which passed over the railway just beside the yard gates. This latter route was dark and lonely, the park not being lit up at this time of year. This was the shorter way. Because it was shorter Brenda took it.

Though the lamps in the park were not lighted, it was not absolutely dark. There was no moon, but the night was clear and the stars were bright. A cold wind was blowing in from the sea, which moaned dismally among the trees and shrubs. There had been no rain for several days and Brenda's footsteps rang sharply on the hard ground.

It was very lonely in the park. As she hurried along the quality of her surroundings seemed to change. She could not explain it, but an unreasoning feeling of foreboding took possession of her. The moaning of the wind became eerie, the atmosphere grew dark and sinister, the shrubs seemed like crouching beasts menacing her passage.

Brenda shivered. She was not given to imaginative fears and she did not know what had gone wrong with her. Just this excitement, she supposed. Well, never mind. It was only natural that there should be a reaction. She was nearly through the park and then there would be only the short lane and the level crossing, and she would be with the police.

Suddenly she heard what sounded like steps, the steps of a running man: somewhere in the distance, she couldn't tell exactly where. Then as suddenly they stopped. She looked all round her. There was no one in sight.

Her path at this point was bounded by two long beds

of tall evergreen shrubs. For forty or fifty yards it was like a miniature railway cutting. The path here crossed a dip in the ground, and the city fathers in their wisdom had planted the shrubs to screen the path from the wind which usually blew up the tiny valley.

For a moment Brenda was downright frightened. Not that someone should be running, but about her own condition. What had happened to her? There was no one there. She had imagined the steps. It was this dreadful anxiety through which she was passing. It was affecting her mind. Or was it only her nerves that were getting unstrung? She really—

A sudden movement caught her eye. She stared, then stopped dead in her tracks, frozen stiff with horror. She had just reached the end of the beds of shrubs. Behind a thick bush crouched a man. As she saw him he sprang up and rushed at her. There was something in his hand, something that glinted dully as he raised his arm. Then she recognised his dreadful, distorted features. And in them she saw Death.

As he leaped she screamed, screamed as if her life depended on it. Power came back to her and like a hare she turned, and as if all Hell was after her, fled back the way she had come.

The man raced behind. He was gaining. His hand touched her arm. With a superhuman effort she jerked it away. She felt her sleeve tear. Again she screamed, despairingly. Then she tripped. The ground, as it were, flew up. It hit her in the face. She felt no pain. The man tripped over her. For a moment he staggered, then recovered himself. He swung back. He was standing over her. He raised his arm. She gave herself up for lost . . .

Then the miracle happened. The blow did not fall. There was a sudden rush of feet. Two dusky figures appeared. The man dropped his club and tried to bolt. The figures closed with him. They struggled on and on and on. But at last it ended. There was the sound of a snap.

Brenda slowly dragged herself to her feet. Grasped by two policemen, his face hideous and almost unrecognisable with hate and rage, stood Clifford Parry.

19

Conclusion

Two evenings later an unofficial and somewhat unconventional reunion took place at 'Serque'. In the seat of honour was Brenda, her head neatly bandaged and her left arm in a sling. She was pale, but the look of dreadful anxiety had gone from her face. Her features instead wore an expression of deep and quiet happiness, albeit tinged with sadness. The cause of her happiness could be seen by following the direction of her eyes. Beside her sat Harry Lowell, none the worse apparently for his nerve racking experiences. He seemed unable to take his eyes off Brenda and the expression she read in them made her smile dreamily.

In spite, however, of her obvious satisfaction, there was sadness also in her mind, for opposite sat Inspector French, and French's presence brought back almost too poignantly the unspeakable horror she had felt when first she had realised the truth about Clifford Parry. Even now she could scarcely refrain from shivering as she thought of that unhappy young man.

French at her invitation had just lit his pipe, and now he began to speak.

'I asked you to fix up this meeting, Miss Vane, firstly, because I thought it was due to you and Mr Lowell to know the truth, and secondly, because I was anxious to hear your experiences. I may say that this is an entirely unofficial meeting of which my superiors know nothing. But I think we may be quite open with one another for the simple reason that there will be no trial, at least, not in the ordinary sense. Parry has signed a full confession and will plead guilty. In the circumstances in which he was arrested he could scarcely do anything else. But besides that he said he had been trying to keep his secret for over a year till he had been almost out of his mind from fear and worry, that it had now got beyond him, and that all he wanted was to ease his mind by confession and then let the end come quickly.'

Brenda sighed. 'Poor man,' she said softly. 'In spite of everything I can't help feeling sorry for him; at least, now that things have come all right.'

'There can be no defence on the facts,' French resumed, 'though personally I think there might be a defence of unsound mind arising from shell shock. I feel sure he's not normal. However, thank heaven that's not my business.'

'Don't let's think of him,' Lowell interposed. 'We're both very much obliged to you, inspector, for coming down, and we're both very anxious to hear what you have to say. Suppose you tell us?'

'Yes, do, Mr French,' added Brenda.

'First, then, Mr Lowell, I think I should explain what made us believe in your guilt. You know, sir, it was your own fault: you have only yourself to thank. If you hadn't lost your head and faked that alibi, we should never have seriously suspected you. You see,' and French, starting at the beginning of his investigation, outlined the steps which had brought him to his conclusion. 'So you must admit,' he urged, 'that though we were wrong, we were justified on the facts.'

'We're not going to quarrel over that now,' Lowell answered. 'I don't suppose I'd have a claim for wrongful arrest in any case, but I'm not going to put one up. That's very interesting, inspector. Now, tell us what really did happen.'

'I'm going to, but I suggest that we take things in their proper order. Next, I think we should ask Miss Vane to explain how she came to suspect Parry, for it seems obvious that she must have. I think I know from his confession, but I should like to hear it from her own lips.'

'I agree,' said Lowell. 'Go ahead, Brenda.'

'There's very little to tell,' Brenda replied. 'The whole thing was so simple. You know that Mr Horler showed us the letter that you, Harry, received signed "Well Wisher"? You've seen that, Mr French?'

'Yes, I've seen it now. If I had seen it before the arrest there would probably have been no arrest made.'

'Well, I noticed that the "r" of the typescript was out of line and twisted both in that letter and in the one Mr Carey had received. I saw that both letters had been done on the same machine, therefore, presumably by the same person.'

'Good for you, Brenda!' exclaimed Lowell.

'Oh, no,' said Brenda, 'it was perfectly clear. Remember I'm a trained typist. Well, I settled up with Clifford Parry that he would get samples from all the typewriters in the railway and contractors' offices, in the hope of finding the machine with the twisted "r". He seemed so eager to help.' Brenda half choked.

'Of course he did,' said French. 'It was his best line. He admitted it in his confession. By pretending to help you he could keep in touch with the investigation and take any steps to safeguard himself that appeared necessary. His mistake was—I may as well mention it now while we're speaking of this point—his mistake was that he didn't know that the type of individual machines of the same make could be identified. He learned of his error from you at lunch on that Friday, two days ago, and that evening he intended to throw his machine into the sea and buy another. You were too quick for him. How was that, Miss Vane?'

'That was the merest accident. It was due to my impatience. He had gone to Lydmouth that afternoon and he said he would be able to get samples from the machines in that office. Next day he was going to get samples from those in the Whitness offices, and that evening he was going to bring them all down here. But I felt I just couldn't wait all that time. I was in Redchurch in any case, and I thought I'd call and see him for a moment on my way to the station. He hadn't arrived, but was expected at any moment. I went up to his room to wait. There I saw, standing beside the clock on the chimney piece, a letter. I couldn't help seeing the address—not that I meant to read it. But I did see it. I shall never forget it. It was typed, to Miss Ackerley, Hunter's Hotel, Strand, London, W.C. 2. I stared at it in stupefaction. In the address there were three "r's", and every one of them was out of line and twisted.'

Lowell gave vent to an oath while French nodded his head in satisfaction.

'Very remarkable and interesting case and very sharp of you, Miss Vane,' said French.

'There were two other defects in the type of Harry's letter, a "t" and an "n." I looked for these in the address. They were both there.

'For a moment I didn't see the significance of this. Then at last it came over me. Other things occurred to me, little things. I suddenly saw that this would explain everything. I saw it at once, in a flash. I think it was a sort of intuition rather than a reasoned conclusion. But I had no longer any doubt. Then all I wanted was to escape. I made some excuse to the landlady and hurried away.

'At first I was overwhelmed simply by the horror of my discovery. Then, waiting at the station I saw what it really involved about you, Harry. You won't believe it, but that didn't occur to me at first. I was wild with excitement when I got home. Then that message was waiting for me and I didn't stop to think, but just ran off. Then you know what happened.'

French nodded. 'That all works in exactly with the confession, Miss Vane. He guessed that you had seen the typing of the address and took his measures accordingly. But perhaps I'd better tell you in order from the beginning.'

Both his hearers signified that this was what they wanted, and as he slowly refilled his pipe, French went on:

'I don't know if you are familiar with Clifford Parry's history. In a sense I suppose it would be fair to say that all this trouble is due to the War. Parry served and left the army a wreck. During his service his father had died, and his mother was left hard up. Fortunately about that time they came in for a legacy of some £500. It was decided that this money should be spent in Parry's finishing the course in engineering which had been interrupted when he joined up. His health having somewhat improved, he qualified. Immediately afterwards his mother died. Her little income died with her and Parry was left alone and penniless. Worse almost than that, debts that he contracted had not been paid off.

'He passed through a very rough period. For a long time he couldn't get work. Then he got some jobs which just kept body and soul together, but were without prospects. I don't want to make excuses for him, but there can be no doubt that it was the cold shouldering he got and his sufferings during this period which hardened him against society and conventional morality and made him bitterly resolve to get his own back at any cost, if and when he could.

'At long last his luck changed. He visited Mr Marlowe for the second time. Mr Marlowe had known his parents and somewhat dubiously he arranged for him to be given a trial. Parry always had an exceptionally engaging manner, and partly owing to this, and partly to the fact that he really did his job well, the appointment was confirmed.

'Immediately all the old creditors were on his back. He was now getting a salary; very well, he could put aside part of it for them. He did so, but it left him very cramped and he had difficulty in living up to his position. His exasperation grew when he looked forward to years of this miserable existence. But he daren't refuse to pay. He feared his creditors would go to Mr Marlowe and that he might lose his job.

'Then the Widening started. Carey, who was a thorough paced scoundrel, intended to make a good thing out of the job, as he had done before on similar occasions. Carey looked round for a dupe, heard whispers as to Parry's position and felt that here was something too good to be missed. Very delicately he approached Parry. He wanted money? Well, there was a simple way in which he could get several hundreds, perhaps a thousand or two. Safe? Yes, as safe as houses; no one could ever know anything about it. Carey had tried it before; it had worked and it would work again. You can imagine the style of thing.'

French paused, but the others made no remark. This was a rather terrible tale they were hearing. Neither had realised that Parry's life had been so hard. Even Lowell was thinking of him less bitterly, and Brenda could scarcely refrain from weeping with the misery of it. Presently French resumed.

'Carey put up his scheme. They were to make the tracings jointly, then Parry was to do the photo prints in the Lydmouth office in the middle of the night. Carey would supply paper so that the railway stuff should not be missed.

'Carey knew that the dangerous point of the scheme was the getting of the prints, as these must be obtained in some way which could not be traced. This was to be Parry's job, and as the discovery would mean prison, it got him fairly committed. But Carey chiefly wanted Parry in the thing because he believed that in case of discovery he would be able to shift the entire responsibility on to him and so escape himself. Parry was to get half the profits.

'This was all carried out according to plan. The swindle was launched and no one suspected anything. For ten months it went on well and Parry, while still slowly paying off the debts, was living more comfortably and amassing cash, which he kept in a suitcase in his rooms. Then the first trouble arose.

'One day Mr Mayers told Parry that Mr Ackerley was investigating the earthwork quantities, which he thought were not coming out satisfactorily. Parry immediately became panic-stricken. He saw that discovery was inevitable.

'His first reaction was to go to Carey. Then he thought of a better way. Carey might be a swindler, but Parry did not believe he would stand for murder. Would it not be better if Mr Ackerley was simply to meet with an accident? Parry was very ingenious and he worked out a scheme which he felt sure no one would ever suspect.

'I think,' French continued, 'Mr Bragg would appreciate this perhaps more than you will do, owing to his knowing the details of what happened better. However, the scheme was something like this.

'Parry first discussed the excavation affair with Mr Ackerley and offered to help him in his investigations; the same trick as he adopted later with you, Miss Vane. In this way he got Mr Ackerley to put off telling anyone else what was in his mind. Then he fixed on the evening on which the certificate was to be completed as that on which the accident would happen.

'He had been told a day or two earlier to fix up an appointment between Mr Ackerley and an adjoining owner called Potts relative to a right of way, and it was this which gave him his idea. He fixed the meeting for 5.30 on the afternoon of the certificate. This, he felt sure, would involve Mr Ackerley's walking through from Whitness to Redchurch at the end of the day, as owing to the certificate Mr Ackerley would be at Whitness in the afternoon.

'He had now devised a plan for making Mr Ackerley walk along the railway at a time when it would be deserted. He had next to arrange for himself to be sent there at the same time.

'There was a piece of sea pitching at a convenient place, which he thought would help. It had been his duty to measure it up for the certificate, and he had done so, correctly. When Mr Bragg reached the Whitness office on that day, Parry put in his return, but he altered the figure, making it impossibly large. He knew Mr Bragg would question it and that he would probably be sent out to check it. He was not sure that the scheme would work, and if it failed he would have tried something else. But it worked perfectly. Mr Bragg noticed the erroneous figure and required it to be checked for the certificate. Parry made difficulties about going, so as to decrease the chance of suspicion, but at last he was able to arrange that he should walk out with Mr Ackerley when the latter was going to interview Potts.

'On the previous Saturday Parry had taken his worst risk. He had bought a second-hand bicycle,' and French explained the method. 'To cover his tracks he had made himself up to resemble Carey. He wore high internal heels in his shoes, padded himself out with clothes, spoke in a high-pitched voice and mimicked, so far as he was able, Carey's Irish accent. The disguise would not of course have taken in anyone who had seen Carey, but it was sufficient to obscure the issue.

'On that Saturday night Parry rode the machine to Downey's Point and hid it in the shrubbery at the side of the road. He had to take the risk of leaving it there over Sunday, but there was not a great deal of danger in this, as there was no occasion for anyone to enter the shrubbery. As a matter of fact no one did so, and the bicycle was not seen.

'He walked out with Mr Ackerley to where he had to measure up the pitching. It chanced that he there met Ganger Mutch going home along the railway. Parry had intended to make an excuse to walk on with Mr Ackerley to Downey's Point, but the presence of the ganger made it necessary for him to part from Mr Ackerley and go down the slope as if to begin the measuring of the pitching. It was not till afterwards that he realised that Mutch's evidence would be a valuable asset to him.

'As soon as Mutch had disappeared from sight, he ran after Mr Ackerley. He had not, of course, to measure up the pitching, as he already knew the correct figure. He took care to overtake Mr Ackerley at the place he had fixed on, and there, getting behind him, he struck him on the side of the head with a piece of lead pipe wrapped in a sock, which he had carried with him. He threw the pipe into the sea, arranged Mr Ackerley's body to look as if the unhappy young man had tripped in the drain and fallen across the rail, then he rushed up to the road, took out the bicycle and rode at full speed to Whitness. He hid the bicycle in the little spinney near the contractors' yard, and entering on foot through the small gate, turned up in the office as if he had just walked in along the line. His unavoidable excitement he would have explained by saying that he had to hurry back, but Mr Bragg did not appear to notice anything amiss.

'When the "accident" happened he had no longer any

need to act a part. His genuine horror and anxiety were taken as natural under the circumstances. No one suspected anything.

'By going back with Mr Ackerley to his house, Parry gave Mr Bragg time to go on to Lydmouth. He was thus left alone at Redchurch. He walked back to Whitness, recovered his bicycle from the spinney, rode it to a cliff near Lydmouth, dropped it over into what he thought was deep water, and walked back to his rooms.

'The inquest passed off as he had hoped, and he began to breathe more freely. He thought he was safe. But he was speedily undeceived. When the time came for the next payment from the fraud, Carey told him he was going to pay him no more, but intended to keep the whole of the profits for himself. When Parry began to bluster, Carey said: All right, did he want to be handed over to the police for the murder of Ackerley? Parry continued to bluster, then Carey made his position brutally clear to him.'

Lowell and Brenda were listening almost spellbound to this recital. Was this at last the connection between the two murders which had so long eluded everyone concerned? Without comment they waited while French resumed.

'I omitted to tell you one other thing that Parry had done. Should suspicion be aroused that Mr Ackerley's death was not really an accident, he wished to ensure that that suspicion should fall on someone other than himself. He chose Carey as the scapegoat, as he thought that Carey's removal would be the safest thing for himself. He therefore typed a note to Carey, the famous note which you, Miss Vane, know all about. That worked very well. Carey was taken in by it and went out to the Whirlpool Cave.

'This proved a tragic case of the biter being bit, of poetic justice, of digging a pit and falling into it oneself, or however you like to describe it. When Carey was returning to the office he unintentionally turned the tables on Parry. He was approaching the private gate when a bicycle arrived at a great speed, stopped, and was pushed into the spinney adjoining. Carey hid and saw Parry come out of the spinney and enter the yard. Knowing Parry had no bicycle, Carey became suspicious. He went into the spinney and took particulars of the machine. Next day he learned of Ackerley's death and also that the letter was a forgery. He began to put two and two together. He made inquiries and at last discovered the shop at which Parry had bought the machine. He made an excuse to call at Parry's rooms and found the typewriter with the crooked "r", though this he didn't tell Parry till later. What he did say was that if Parry didn't do exactly as he was told, he, Carey, would "discover" the fraud, pointing out that it must have been worked by Parry, and at the same time would tell about seeing the bicycle, the significance of which, he would say, had only then occurred to him.

'I may explain here,' went on French, 'that I also called at Parry's rooms on the lookout for the typewriter with the crooked "r". But by a piece of extraordinarily bad luck it happened that Miss Ackerley had borrowed it to do some Musical Society circulars, and I did not find it. Had I done so, not only would you both have been spared your anxieties, but Carey would not have lost his life.

'Parry, of course, had to knuckle under. The least breath of suspicion and he was lost. The old, miserable life then began again, with the dread of arrest added to it. Parry found his position intolerable. He had already by desperate means rid himself of one danger. It was practically inevitable that in this next emergency his thoughts should turn to the same expedient.

'He made four separate attempts to murder Carey: he has put it on record without the least evasion. The first three failed owing to small details not working out as he had hoped. The fourth succeeded.

'Mr Bragg had told him that he would be leaving the office for Drychester about six o'clock on a certain Tuesday evening. Parry decided to make this fourth attempt on that evening, provided Mr Ashe was not at Whitness. As it happened, Mr Ashe was otherwise engaged, and Parry went ahead with his attempt. His plan was to drug Carey and then get him alone in his own office. If he could get Carey to come in to see Mr Bragg shortly before six, and get Mr Bragg out of the way at the same time, he could manage the drugging. Parry had whisky of his own in the cupboard and Carey never could bring himself to refuse a drink. At this time Carey's office would probably be empty and if Carey went back there no one would know he had been drugged.

'Parry stated he obtained the drug from a London chemist, signing the poison book with the name and address of an Exeter resident which he selected from the telephone directory. He told the assistant he had been ordered the draughts by his doctor, giving the name of a well-known Exeter practitioner, and adding that he had unfortunately come away from home without them.' French's subsequent inquiries in London had confirmed Parry's statement.

'Parry had intended to see Carey and ask him to call at

the railway office, but it happened that that afternoon he met him at the viaduct. He was about to give his invitation when Carey played into his hands by saying he wanted to see Bragg about blasting at the tunnel. Parry arranged the interview for 5.30.'

French had laid his notebook on the table in front of him and every now and then he glanced at it to refresh his memory of names and hours. At the same time he surprised both his hearers by the completeness of his grip of the story.

'Parry had next to get Mr Bragg out of the way so that he could administer the drug. But he wanted Mr Bragg to see Carey in the office, so as to be able to back up his own future statement that Carey had left in perfect health. He did it by putting up a story to Mr Bragg that the contractors were mixing dust with the concrete. Mr Bragg fell for it, as Parry knew he would. When Carey arrived, Parry was alone. He brought out the whisky and Carey got his dope, Parry excusing the somewhat unusual indulgence by saying he was feeling cold after his wetting and wanted a drink and asking Carey to join him. Then Mr Bragg came in, but his leaving immediately for Drychester ensured that Carey would be out of the way before the effect of the drug began to show.

'When Mr Bragg left, Parry went over to the contractors' office. He knocked to make sure that everyone but Carey had gone, then let himself in with a key which he had made. He had obtained the impression by borrowing Mr Pole's keys to try to open a box, and taking a mould of the door key. Carey was alone and asleep. Parry then carried the murder through.'

French paused for a few moments. He certainly should

have been satisfied with the attention which his hearers were giving him. Breathlessly they hung on his words. They did not, however, speak, and presently he resumed.

'In spite of the warning as to the danger of safeguards which Parry had had, he this time took several precautions to turn aside from himself any suspicion which might afterwards be aroused. He knew that with this terrible affair before him, and indeed after it was past also, he could not preserve a normal manner. He therefore staged a deliberate fall into a pool to account for his agitation. Next, he wished to prove that he had been in his own office between the time Mr Bragg left it and the time he had himself to leave to catch the 6.25 goods. He did that by pretending he had to mark some information on a plan for Inspector Holford. He showed the unaltered plan to Mr Bragg as the latter was starting for Drychester, and the plan which he handed to the stationmaster at Whitness some twenty-five minutes later bore the extra information. He intended it to be argued—and it was argued—that he had done the work in the quarter of an hour before he left the office. In reality, however, he had made two identical plans, on one of which he had previously marked the additional details. All he had to do was to show the unaltered plan to Mr Bragg, then to copy on the other Mr Bragg's pencil marks, partially rub them out, and hand this second plan to the stationmaster. A further safeguard which he adopted was to tell an entirely false story of having seen the silhouette of a man approaching the contractors' office as he left to catch his train.

'To clinch the conclusion to which the details of Carey's murder were intended to lead, namely, that Carey had committed suicide, he took a further step. He planted a piece of one of the original cross sections where you, Mr Lowell, would find it, believing that you would remark upon it. He would then see that the matter was followed up, leading to the discovery of the fraud. This, he believed, would supply the required motive for Carey's suicide.

'But he also saw that some accident might reveal the fact that Carey had been murdered, and he faked another piece of evidence to safeguard himself in such a contingency. This was designed to throw suspicion on you, Mr Lowell. He determined to use the well-known bad feeling which existed between yourself and his victim. He wrote you that famous letter which led to his downfall. This was in order to prevent your having an alibi at the time of Carey's death. He trusted to your sense of chivalry not to reveal where you were and the reason you went there.

'When this part of his plan succeeded and you, sir, were arrested, he at once approached Miss Vane with offers of help. This, as I said, was to keep in touch with the progress of events, and perhaps supply further evidence if such became desirable. Thanks to your cleverness, Miss Vane, the truth came out.

'But only just,' French added, shaking his head at Brenda. 'Now that it's over I may tell you what you probably know, Miss Vane, and that is that you had a very close call yourself. Even in Parry's improvised attempt to murder you he showed great skill and ingenuity. He, of course, put through both telephone calls. Here at "Serque" he convinced your mother and sister that he was afraid that some other enemy was about to attack you, and his ringing up Sergeant Emery to test his pretended suspicions and to ask for help was nothing less than a stroke of genius. Fortunately for you, he over-reached himself. His anxiety seemed so genuine and his appeal sounded so urgent that Emery sent two of his men out in a car instead of allowing them to walk. Parry believed that by taking the short cut by the hotel stables he would have plenty of time to murder you before they arrived. He would then have thrown his bit of lead pipe away, run back in the direction he had come, and watched till the police found your body, when he would have rushed up and registered the necessary surprise and horror. As a matter of fact, if he had got his blow in when he met you, his plan would have succeeded. You saved your life by running back and so giving the police time to come up.

'I must add one other remark,' French continued, 'something to be said from my own point of view and that of the police. There was no fear at any time of a miscarriage of justice. I may say that I had made up my mind that if your alibi, Mr Lowell, stood, I should apply for warrants to search the houses and rooms of everyone on my list of possible suspects. I should then have discovered that Parry had a typewriter—a fact which does not seem to have been generally known—and, of course, I should at once have sampled the type and seen that he had written the Carey letter. As things turned out I am satisfied that your explanation of why you faked the alibi would have thrown sufficient doubt on your guilt to have ensured the making of that investigation. At the same time, Mr Lowell, I don't deny you ran a risk. It's never safe to play tricks in a murder case.

'That, I think, brings us to the end of our business. I may be allowed to add my regrets for the unhappy time through which both of you have passed, and my satisfaction that a happier period is now opening out before you.'

'No,' said Lowell, 'there's one thing more. You're a good fellow, inspector. We'll have a drink together to show there's no ill will.'

By the same author

Inspector French's Greatest Case

At the offices of the Hatton Garden diamond merchant *Duke & Peabody*, the body of old Mr Gething is discovered beside a now-empty safe. With multiple suspects, the robbery and murder is clearly the work of a master criminal, and requires a master detective to solve it. Meticulous as ever, Inspector Joseph French of Scotland Yard embarks on an investigation that takes him from the streets of London to Holland, France and Spain, and finally to a ship bound for South America . . .

'Because he is so austerely realistic, Freeman Wills Croft is deservedly a first favourite with all who want a real puzzle.'

TIMES LITERARY SUPPLEMENT

By the same author

Inspector French and the Cheyne Mystery

When young Maxwell Cheyne discovers that a series of mishaps are the result of unwelcome attention from a dangerous gang of criminals, he teams up with a young woman who is determined to help him outwit them. But when she disappears, he finally decides to go to Scotland Yard for help. Concerned by the developing situation, Inspector Joseph French takes charge of the investigation and applies his trademark methods to track down the kidnappers and thwart their intentions . . .

'*Freeman Wills Crofts is among the few muscular writers of detective fiction. He has never let me down.*'

DAILY EXPRESS